AGENT MOOSE
OPERATION OWL

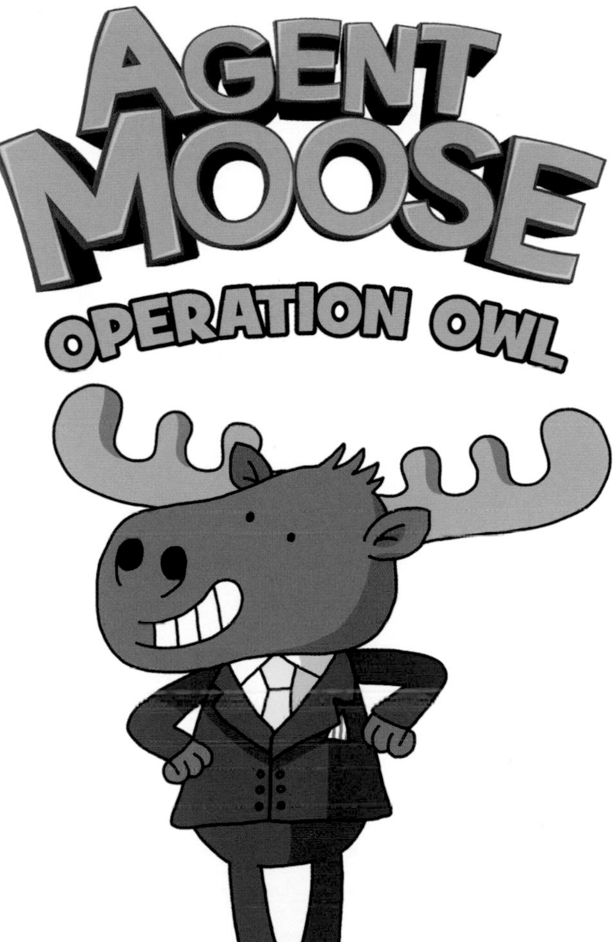

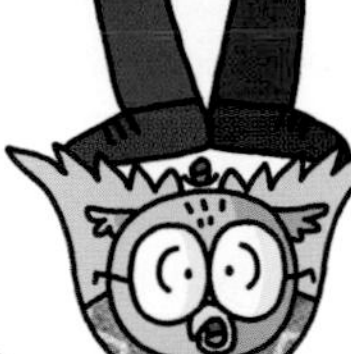

Mo O'Hara

WITH ART BY

Jess Bradley

Feiwel and Friends
New York

To my son, Dan, who always inspires me
—M. O.

For Mum, Dad, and Ben x
—J. B.

A Feiwel and Friends Book
An imprint of Macmillan Publishing Group, LLC
120 Broadway, New York, NY 10271
mackids.com

Our books may be purchased in bulk for promotional, educational, or business use. Please contact your local bookseller or the Macmillan Corporate and Premium Sales Department at (800) 221-7945 ext. 5442 or by email at MacmillanSpecialMarkets@macmillan.com.

Library of Congress Cataloging-in-Publication Data is available.

First edition, 2022
Book design by Liz Dresner • Color by John-Paul Bove • Lettering by Micah Meyer
Feiwel and Friends logo designed by Filomena Tuosto
Printed in China by RR Donnelley Asia Printing Solutions Ltd.,
Dongguan City, Guangdong Province.

ISBN 978-1-250-22225-1 (hardcover)
1 3 5 7 9 10 8 6 4 2

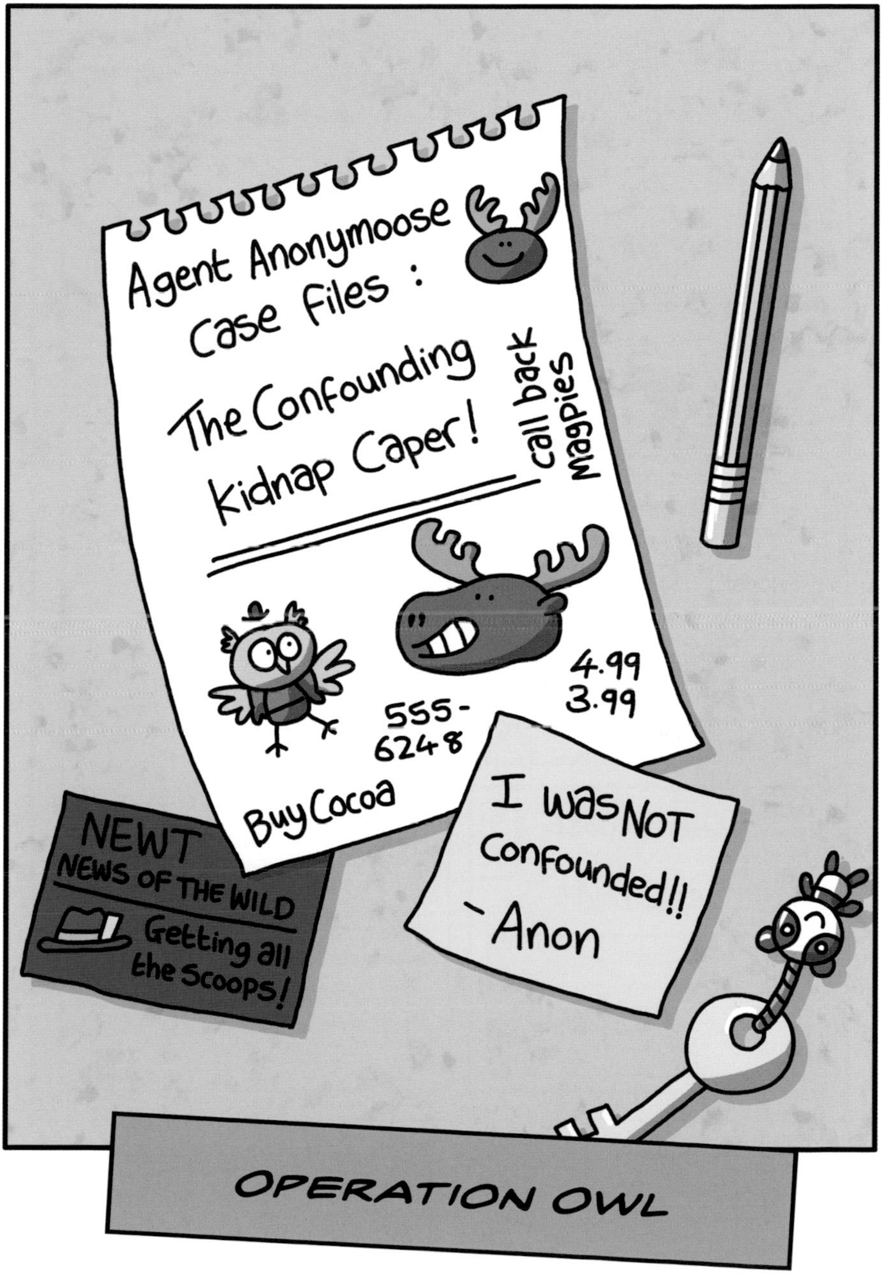
Agent Anonymoose
Case Files :
The Confounding
Kidnap Caper!
call back Magpies
555-
6248
4.99
3.99
Buy Cocoa
NEWT
NEWS OF THE WILD
Getting all the Scoops!
I was NOT Confounded!!
-Anon

OPERATION OWL

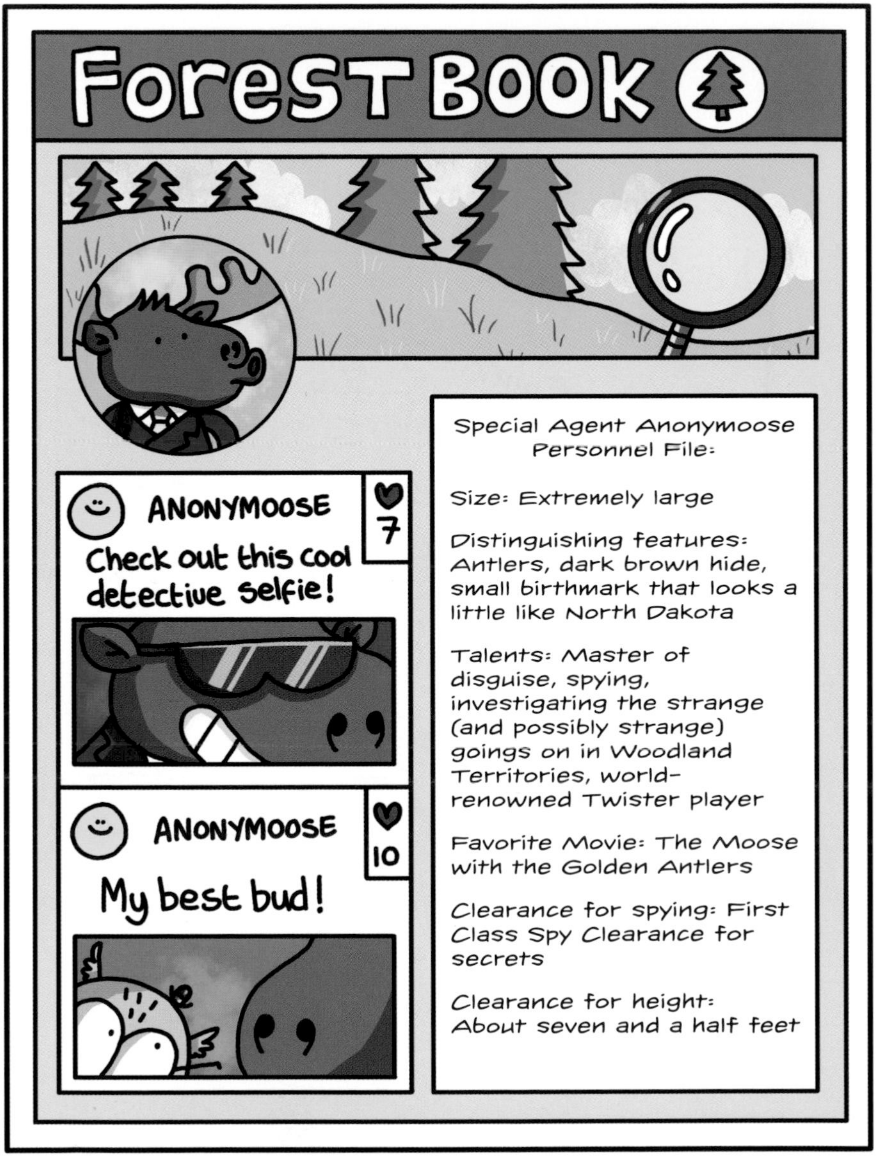
Forest Book
ANONYMOOSE
7
Check out this cool detective selfie!
ANONYMOOSE
10
My best bud!
Special Agent Anonymoose Personnel File:
Size: Extremely large
Distinguishing features: Antlers, dark brown hide, small birthmark that looks a little like North Dakota
Talents: Master of disguise, spying, investigating the strange (and possibly strange) goings on in Woodland Territories, world-renowned Twister player
Favorite Movie: The Moose with the Golden Antlers
Clearance for spying: First Class Spy Clearance for secrets
Clearance for height: About seven and a half feet

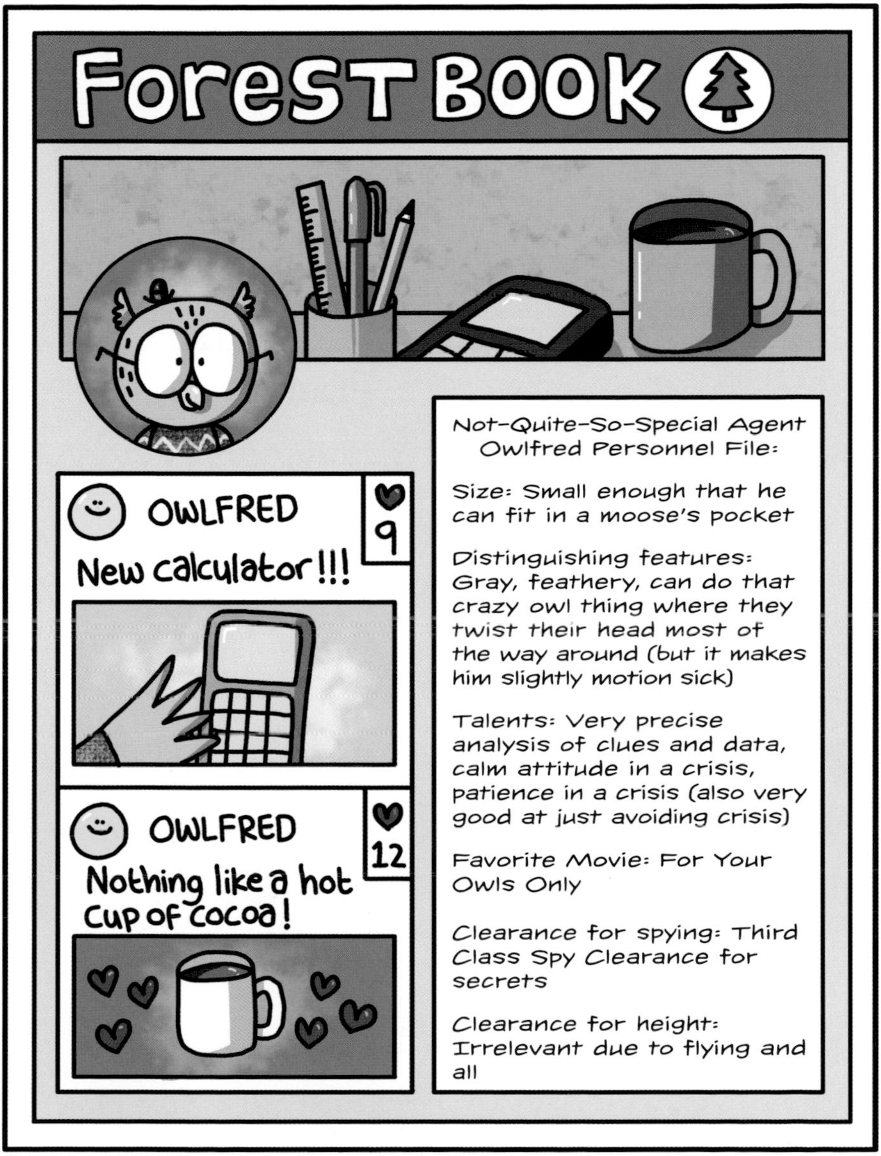

FOREST BOOK
OWLFRED
9
New calculator!!!
OWLFRED
12
Nothing like a hot cup of cocoa!
Not-Quite-So-Special Agent Owlfred Personnel File:
Size: Small enough that he can fit in a moose's pocket
Distinguishing features: Gray, feathery, can do that crazy owl thing where they twist their head most of the way around (but it makes him slightly motion sick)
Talents: Very precise analysis of clues and data, calm attitude in a crisis, patience in a crisis (also very good at just avoiding crisis)
Favorite Movie: For Your Owls Only
Clearance for spying: Third Class Spy Clearance for secrets
Clearance for height: Irrelevant due to flying and all

Chapter 1

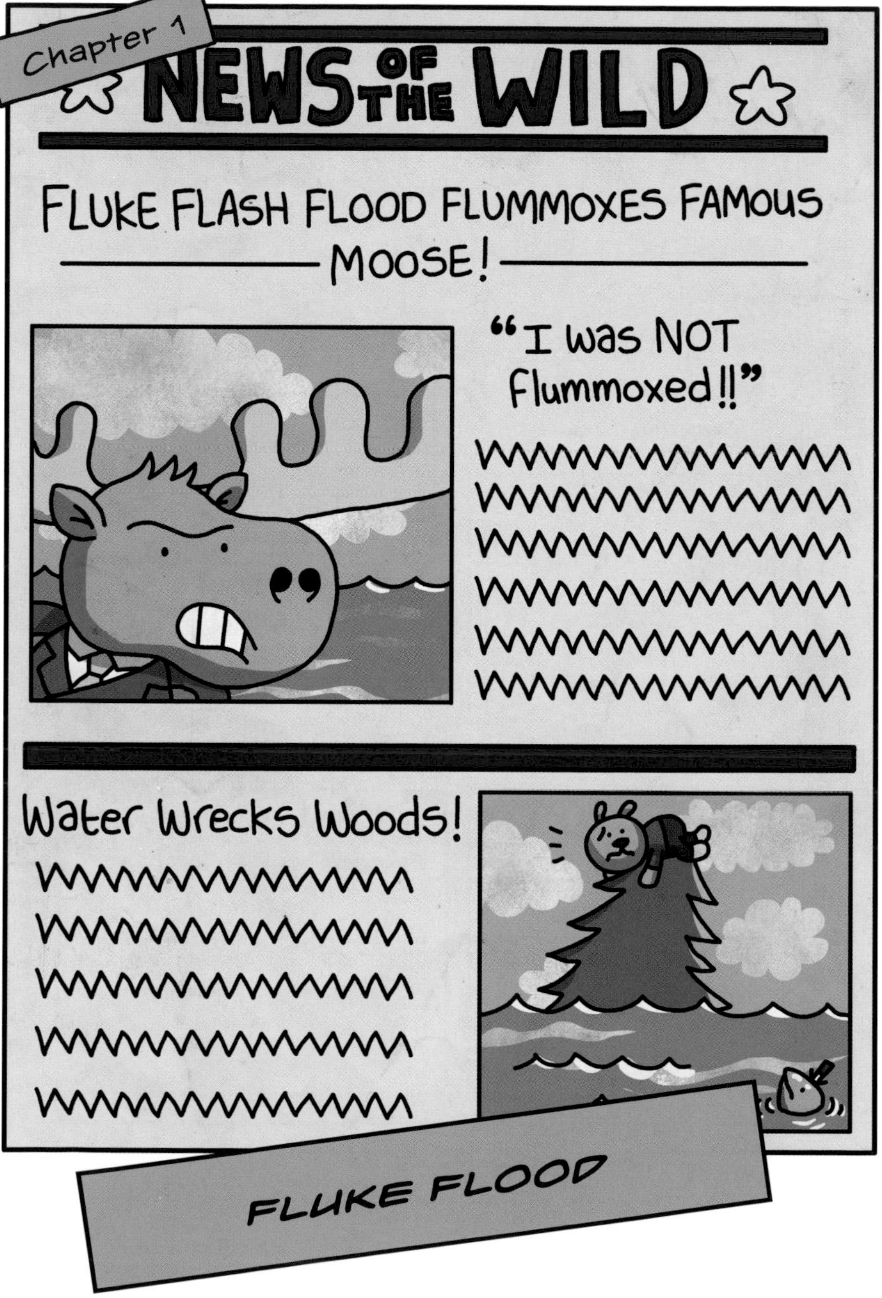
NEWS OF THE WILD
FLUKE FLASH FLOOD FLUMMOXES FAMOUS MOOSE!
"I was NOT Flummoxed!!"
Water Wrecks Woods!

FLUKE FLOOD

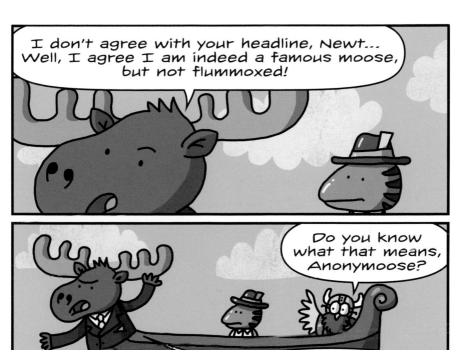

I don't agree with your headline, Newt... Well, I agree I am indeed a famous moose, but not flummoxed!

Do you know what that means, Anonymoose?

Yes...no... mostly. I don't think it sounds good.

It means you are bewildered... stumped by the cause of the flood.

I've never been stumped, just slightly annoyed.

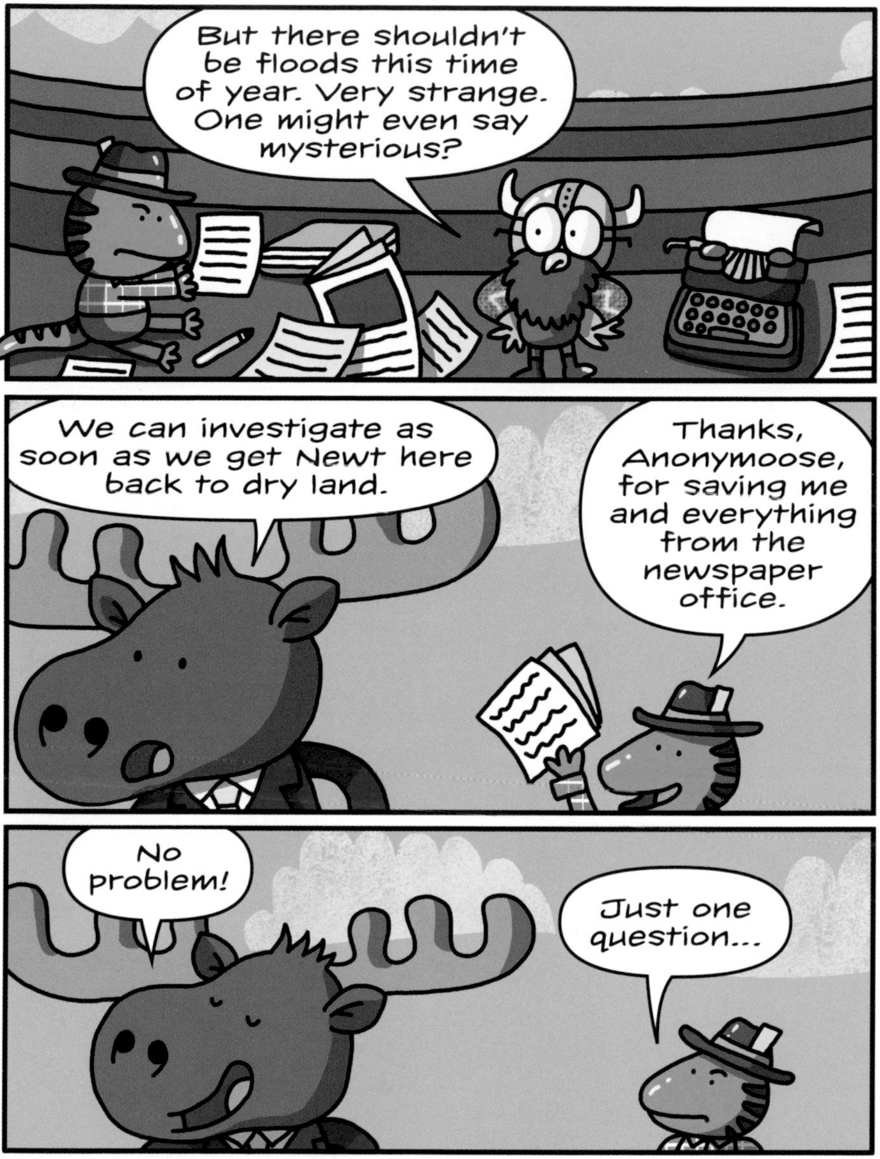
But there shouldn't be floods this time of year. Very strange. One might even say mysterious?
We can investigate as soon as we get Newt here back to dry land.
Thanks, Anonymoose, for saving me and everything from the newspaper office.
No problem!
Just one question...

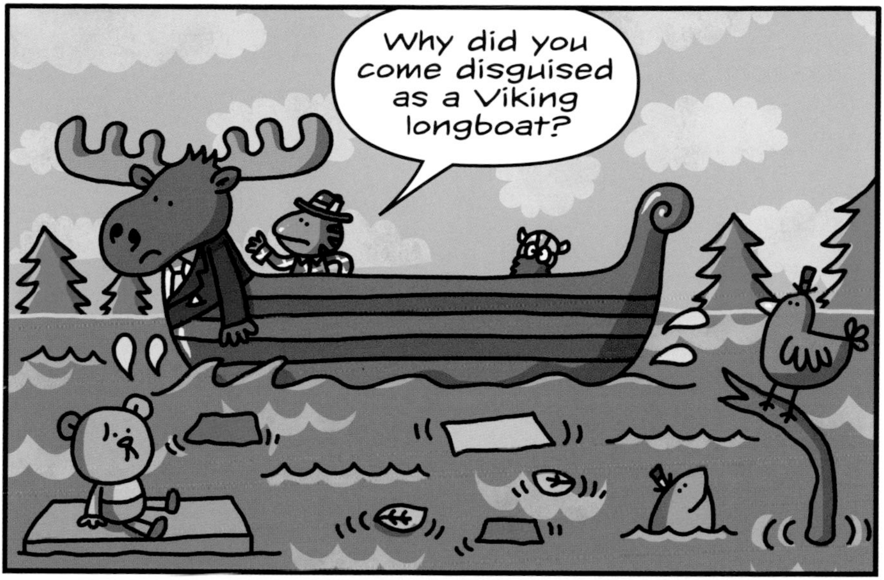
Why did you come disguised as a Viking longboat?

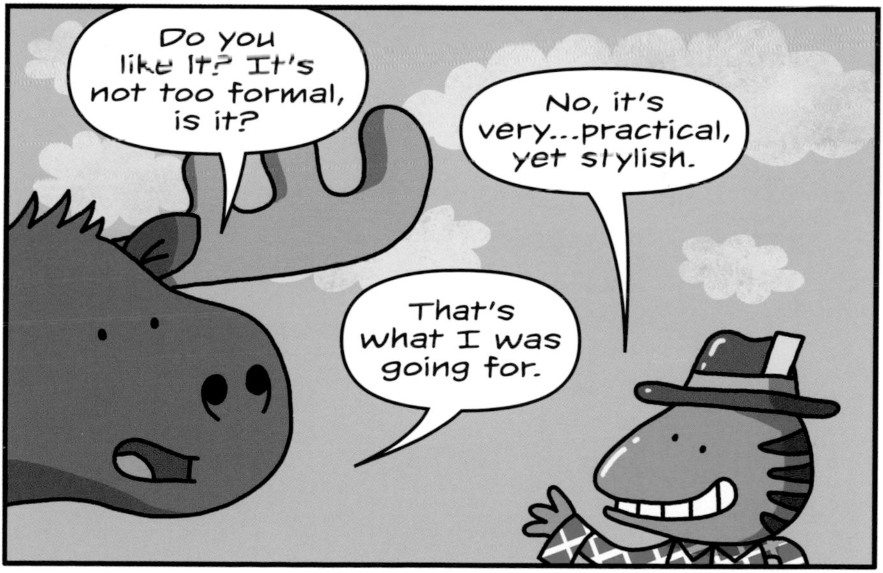
Do you like it? It's not too formal, is it?
No, it's very...practical, yet stylish.
That's what I was going for.

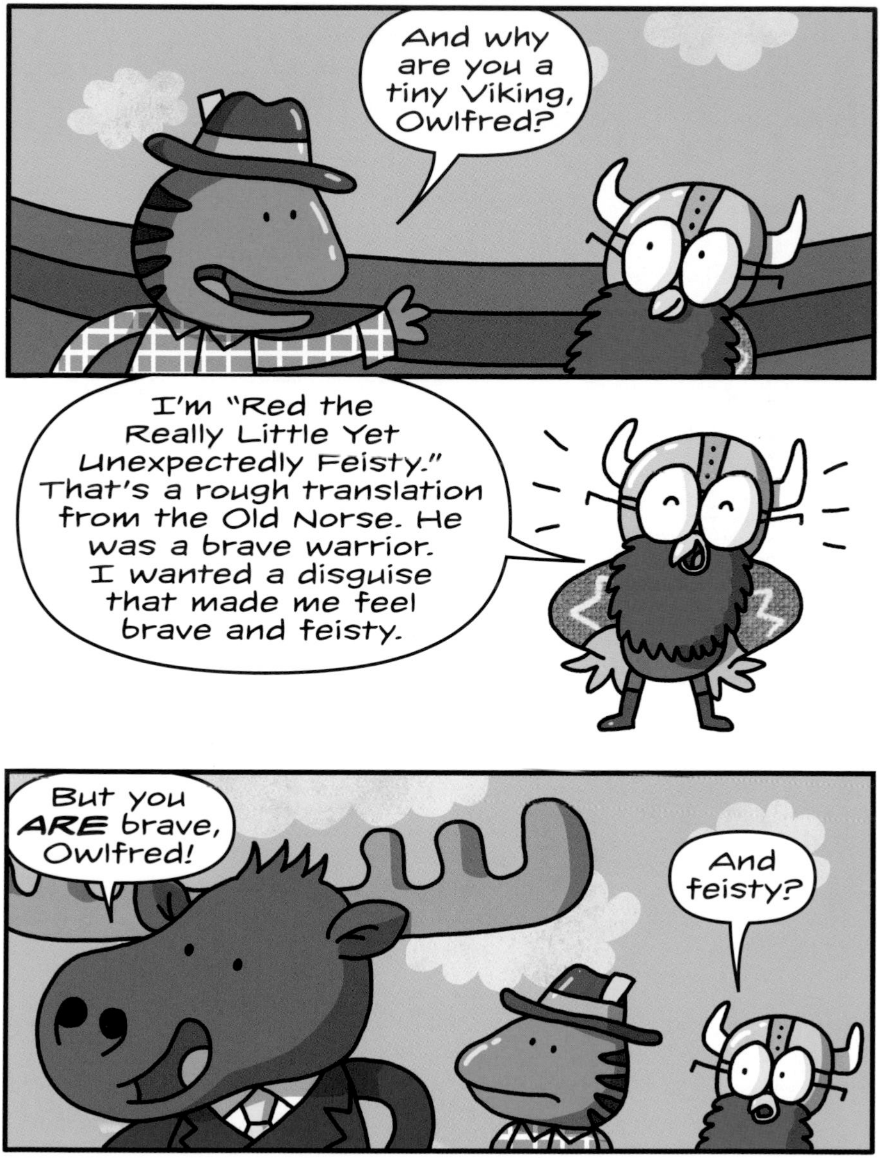
And why are you a tiny Viking, Owlfred?
I'm "Red the Really Little Yet Unexpectedly Feisty." That's a rough translation from the Old Norse. He was a brave warrior. I wanted a disguise that made me feel brave and feisty.
But you ***ARE*** brave, Owlfred!
And feisty?

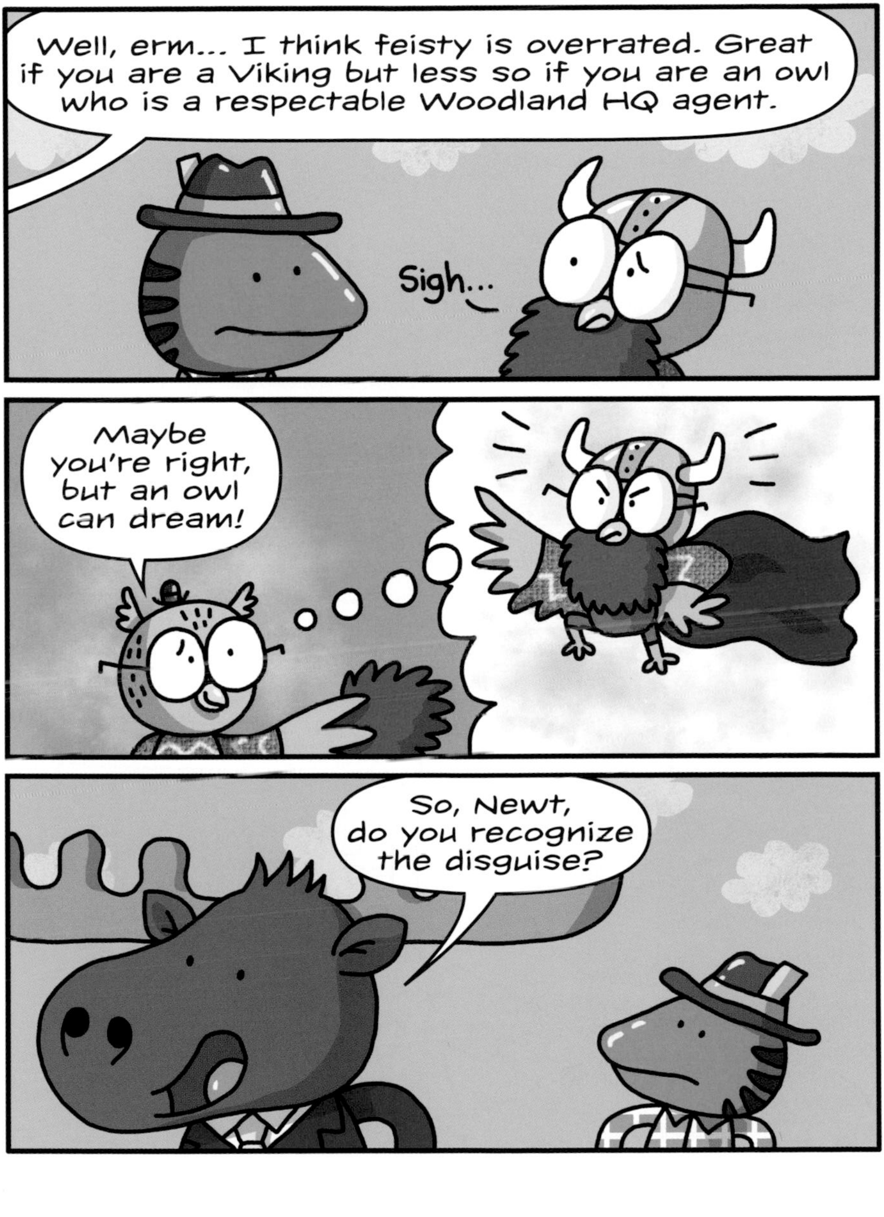
Well, erm... I think feisty is overrated. Great if you are a Viking but less so if you are an owl who is a respectable Woodland HQ agent.
Sigh...
Maybe you're right, but an owl can dream!
So, Newt, do you recognize the disguise?

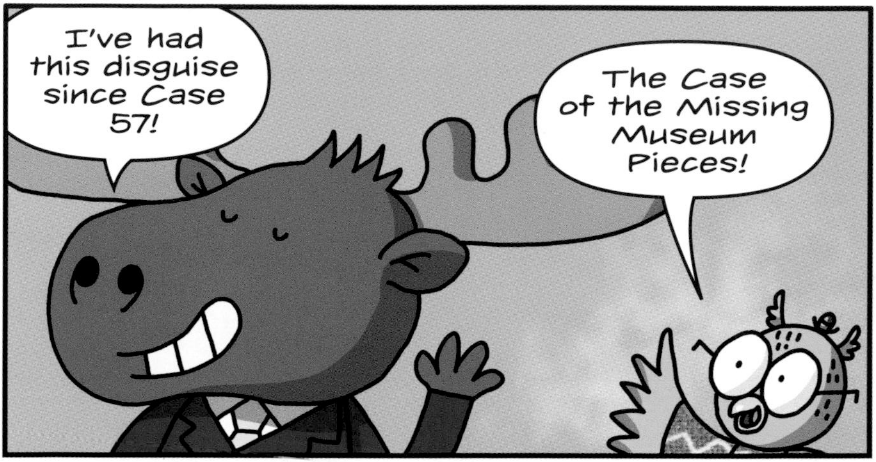
I've had this disguise since Case 57!
The Case of the Missing Museum Pieces!

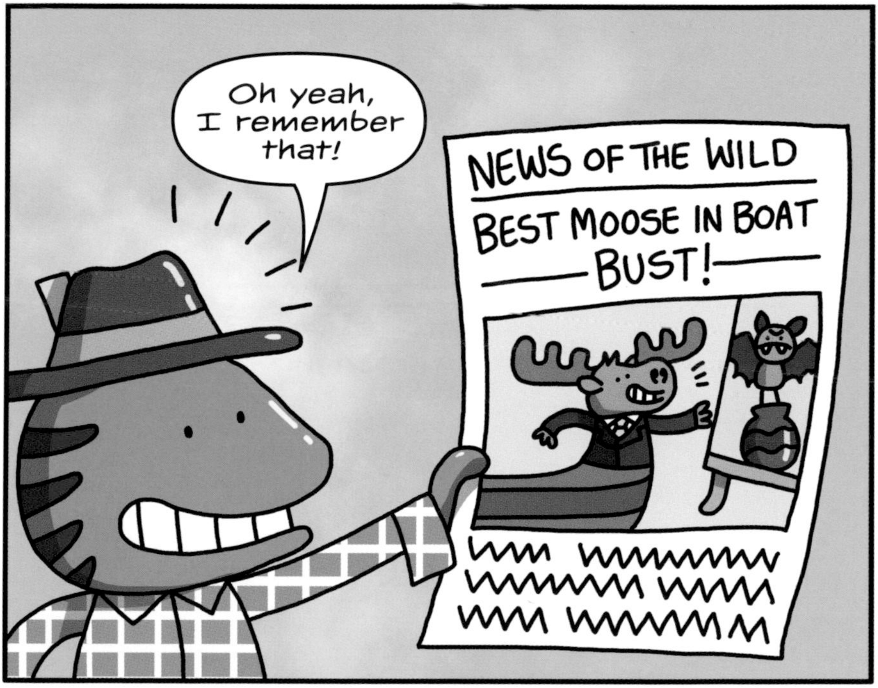
Oh yeah, I remember that!
NEWS OF THE WILD
BEST MOOSE IN BOAT BUST!

Fluke Flood

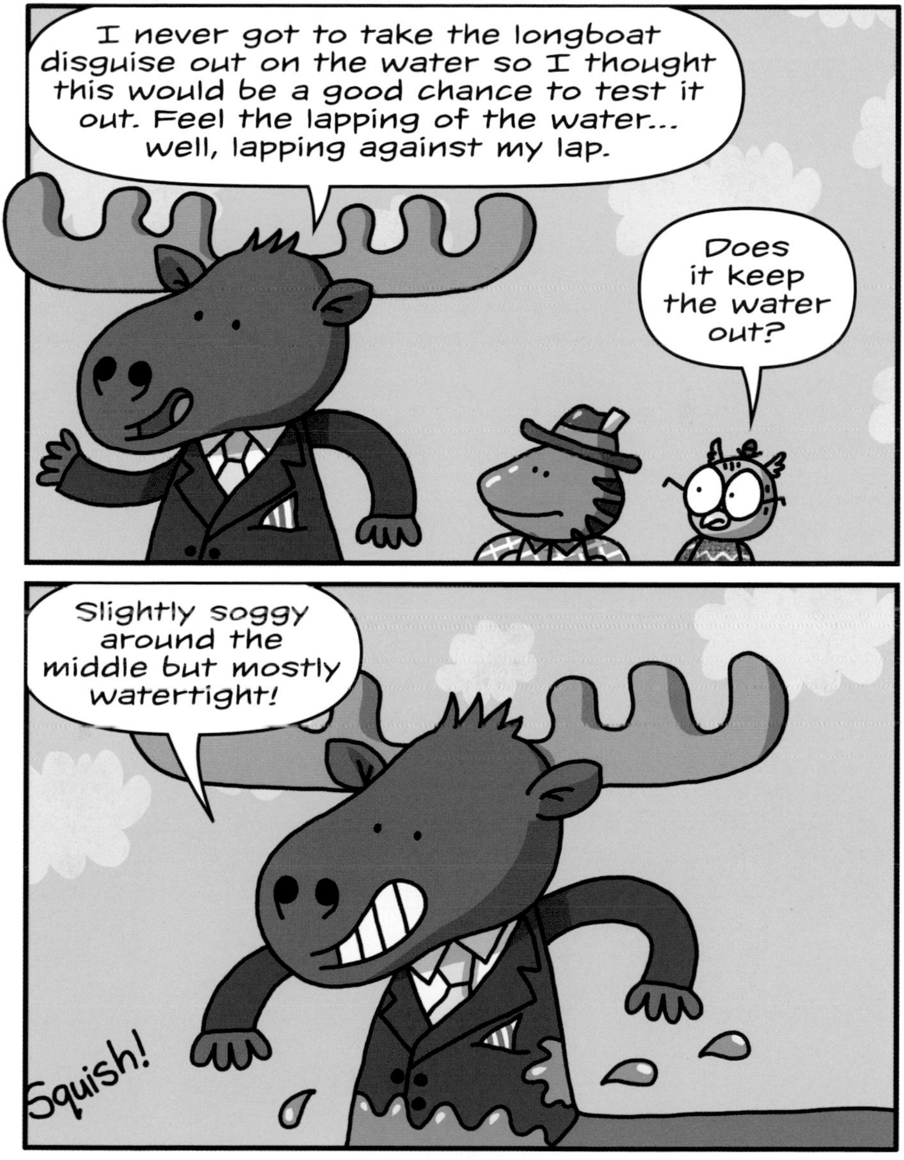
I never got to take the longboat disguise out on the water so I thought this would be a good chance to test it out. Feel the lapping of the water... well, lapping against my lap.
Does it keep the water out?
Slightly soggy around the middle but mostly watertight!
Squish!

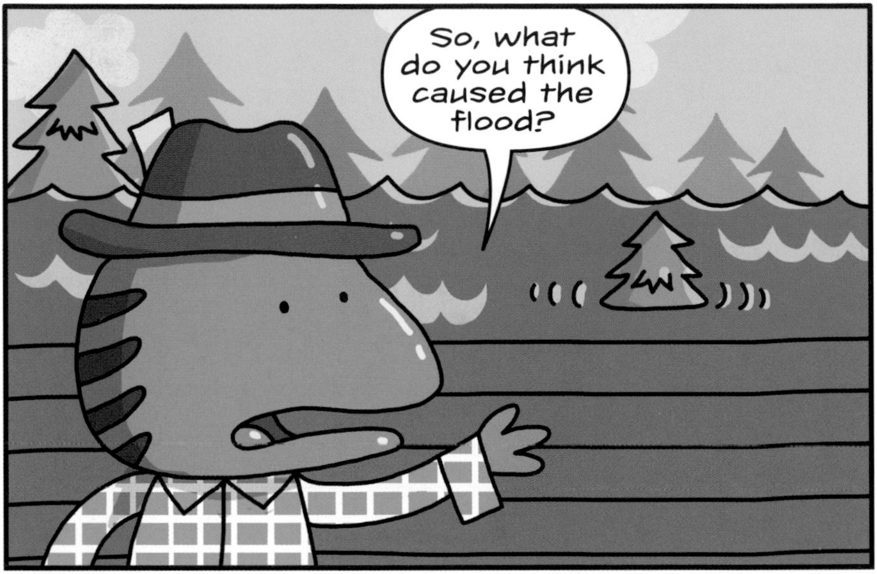
So, what do you think caused the flood?

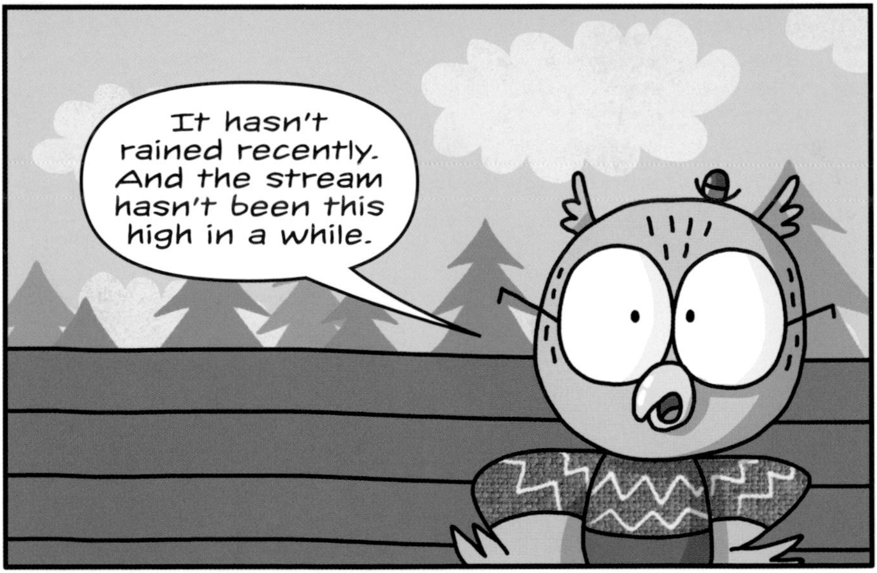
It hasn't rained recently. And the stream hasn't been this high in a while.

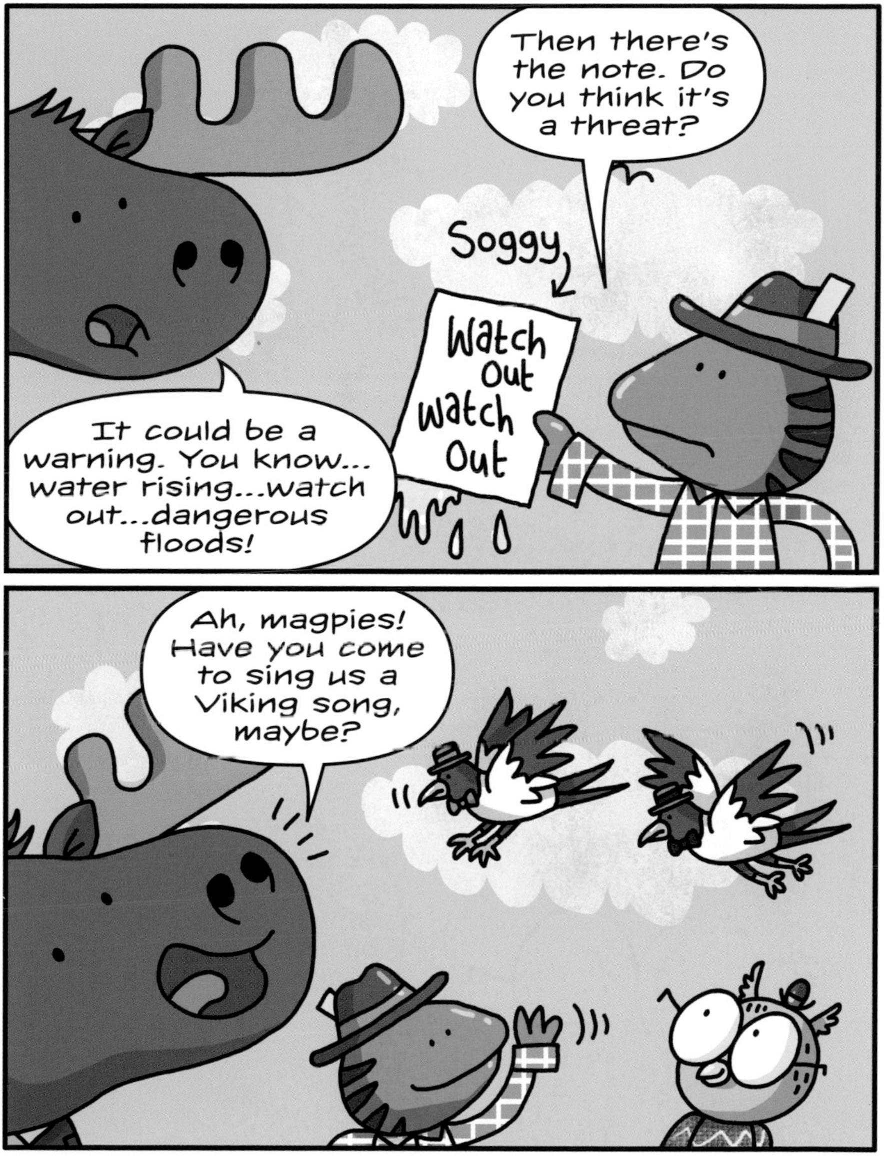
Then there's the note. Do you think it's a threat?
Soggy
Watch out watch out
It could be a warning. You know... water rising...watch out...dangerous floods!
Ah, magpies! Have you come to sing us a Viking song, maybe?

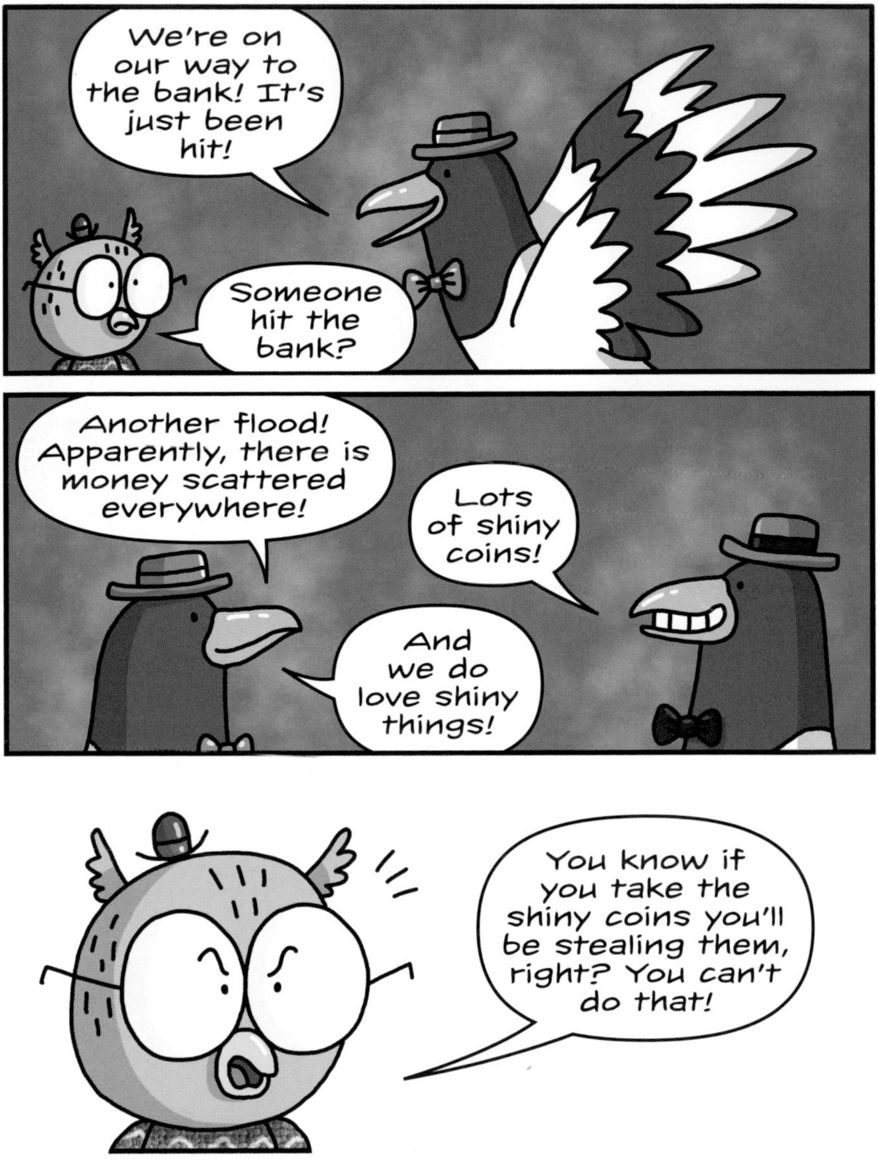
We're on our way to the bank! It's just been hit!
Someone hit the bank?
Another flood! Apparently, there is money scattered everywhere!
Lots of shiny coins!
And we do love shiny things!
You know if you take the shiny coins you'll be stealing them, right? You can't do that!

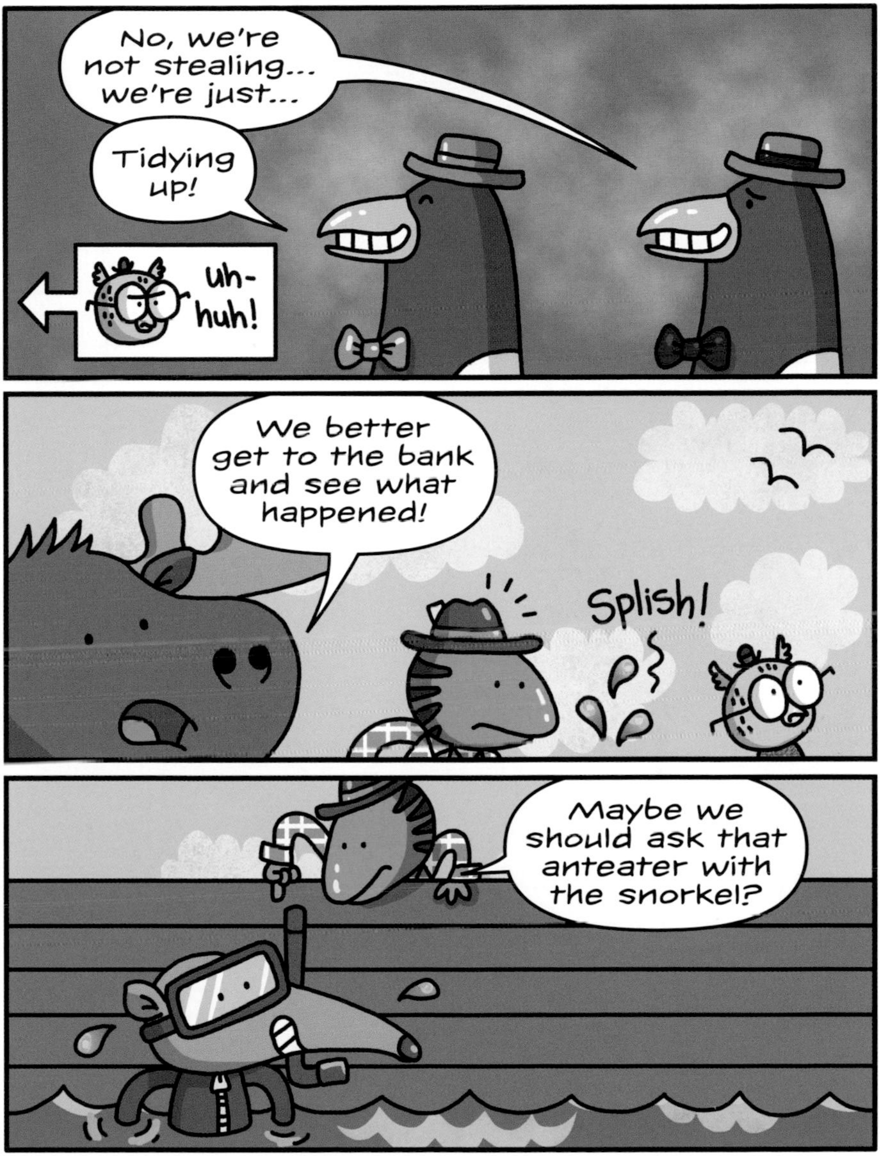
No, we're not stealing... we're just...
Tidying up!
uh-huh!
We better get to the bank and see what happened!
Splish!
Maybe we should ask that anteater with the snorkel?

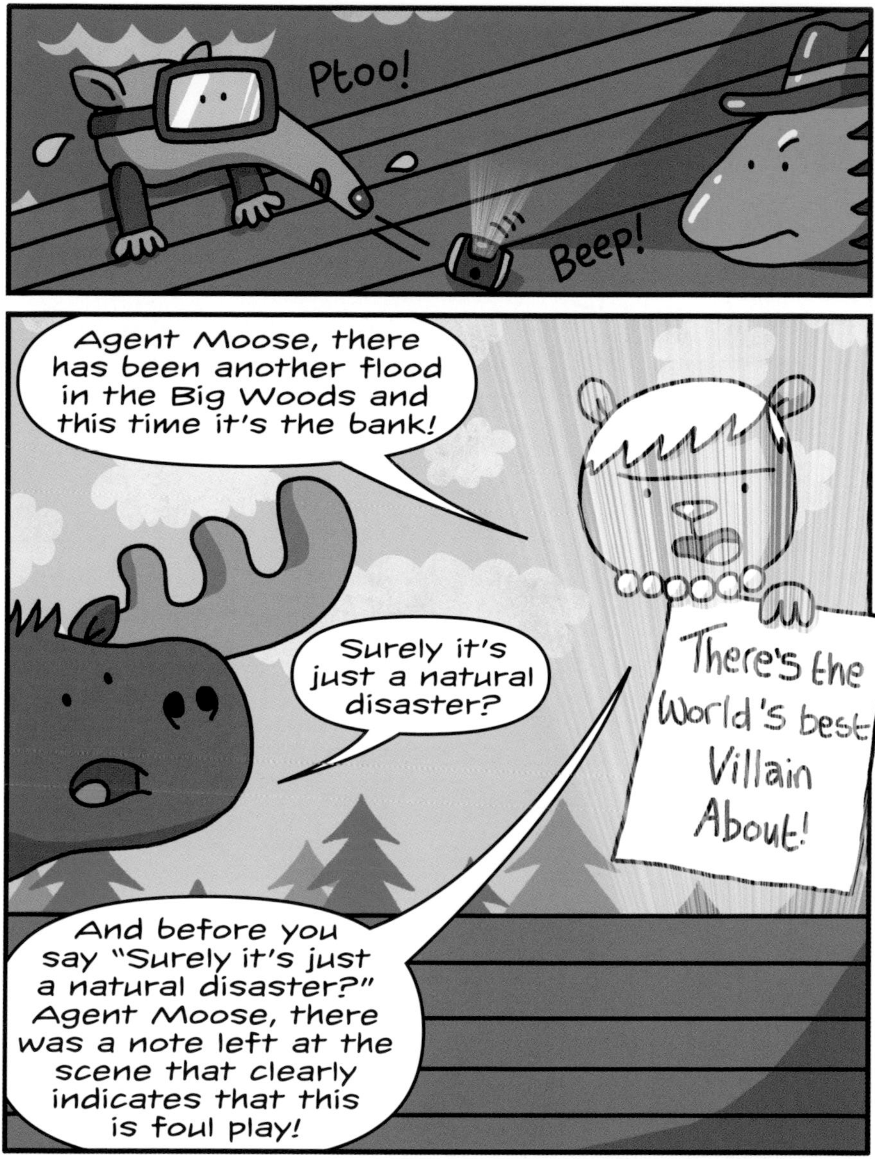
Ptoo!
Beep!
Agent Moose, there has been another flood in the Big Woods and this time it's the bank!
Surely it's just a natural disaster?
And before you say "Surely it's just a natural disaster?" Agent Moose, there was a note left at the scene that clearly indicates that this is foul play!
There's the World's best Villain About!

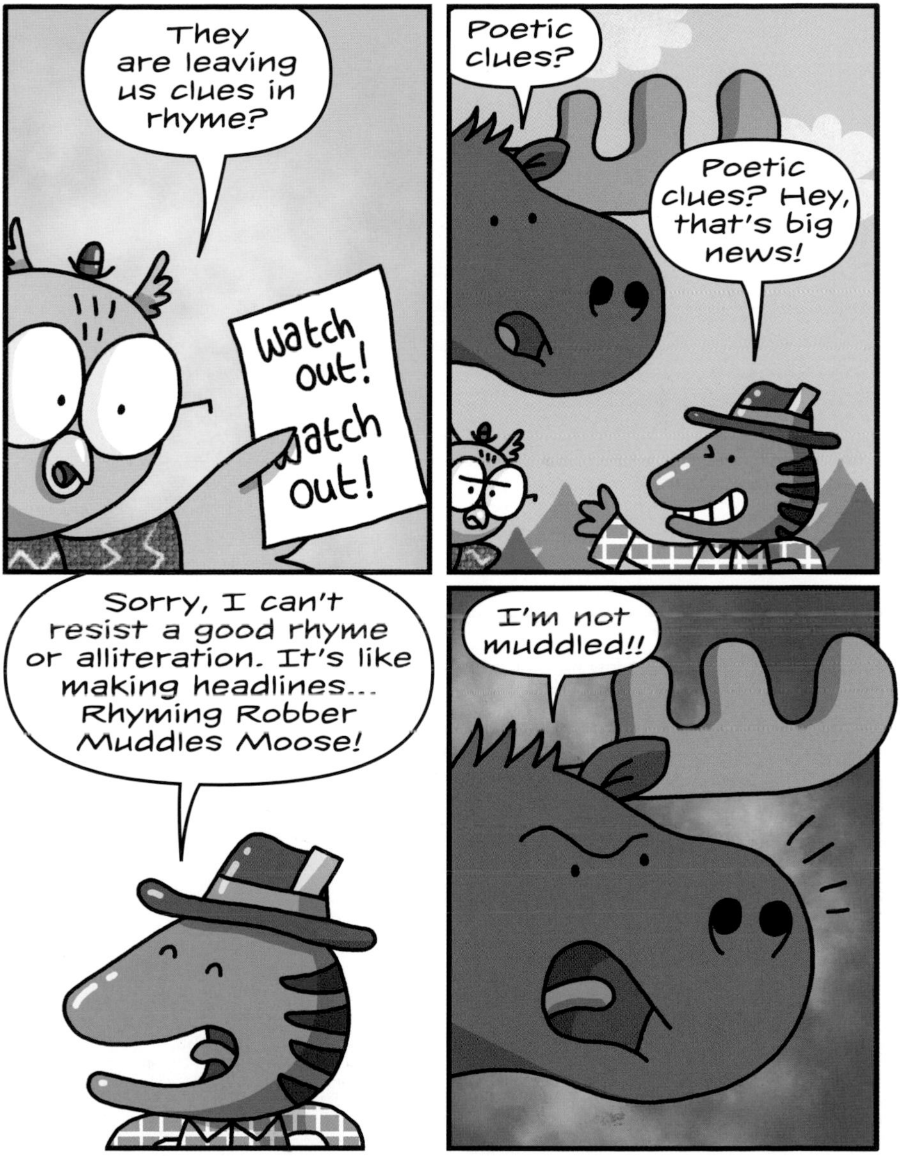
They are leaving us clues in rhyme?
Watch out! Watch out!
Poetic clues?
Poetic clues? Hey, that's big news!
Sorry, I can't resist a good rhyme or alliteration. It's like making headlines... Rhyming Robber Muddles Moose!
I'm not muddled!!

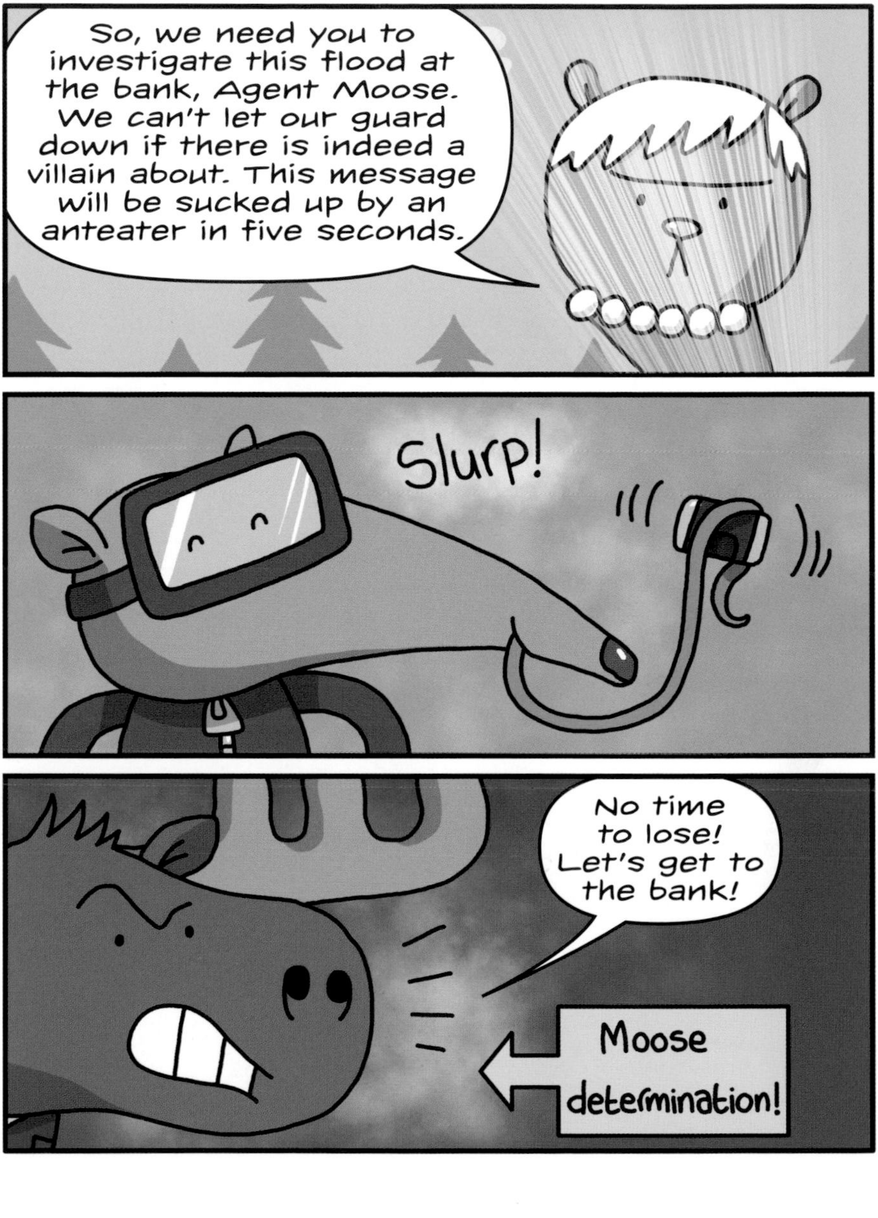
So, we need you to investigate this flood at the bank, Agent Moose. We can't let our guard down if there is indeed a villain about. This message will be sucked up by an anteater in five seconds.
Slurp!
No time to lose! Let's get to the bank!
Moose determination!

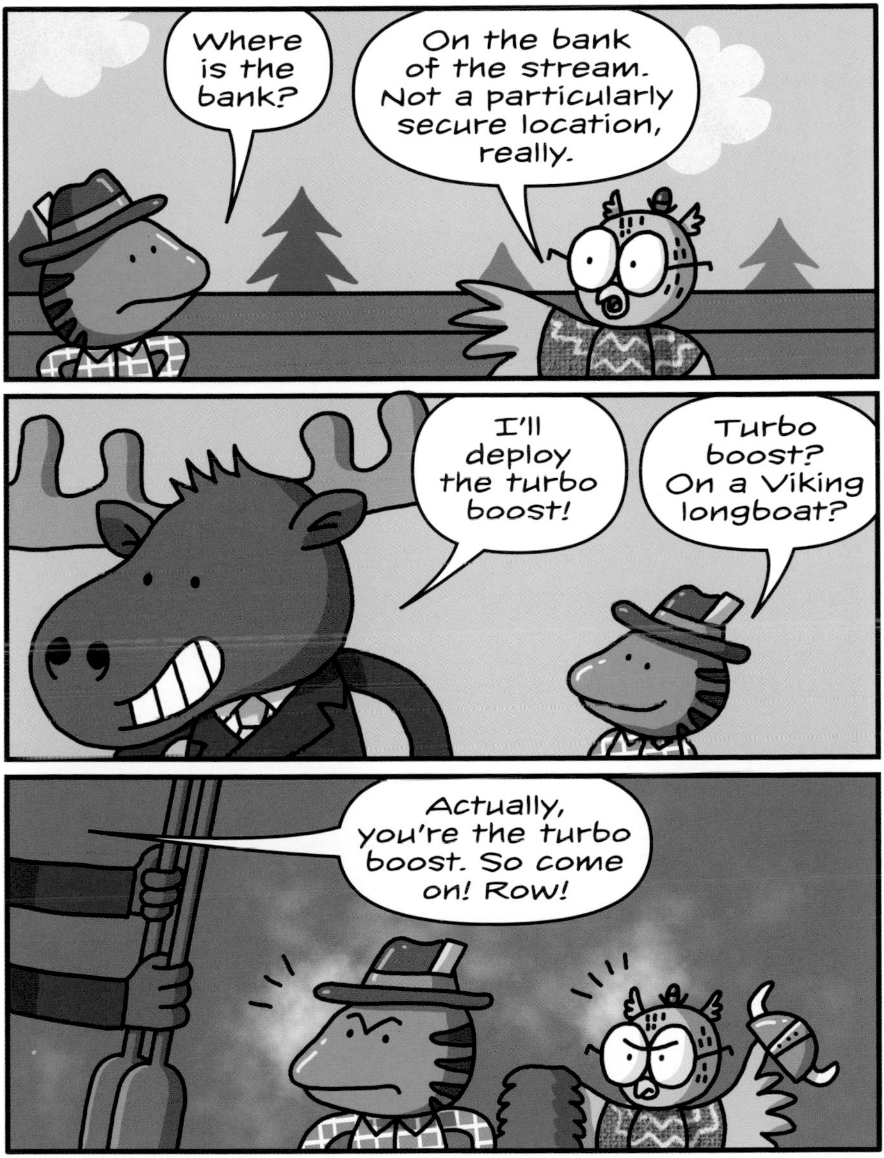
Where is the bank?
On the bank of the stream. Not a particularly secure location, really.
I'll deploy the turbo boost!
Turbo boost? On a Viking longboat?
Actually, you're the turbo boost. So come on! Row!

Chapter 2

BANK BREAK-IN

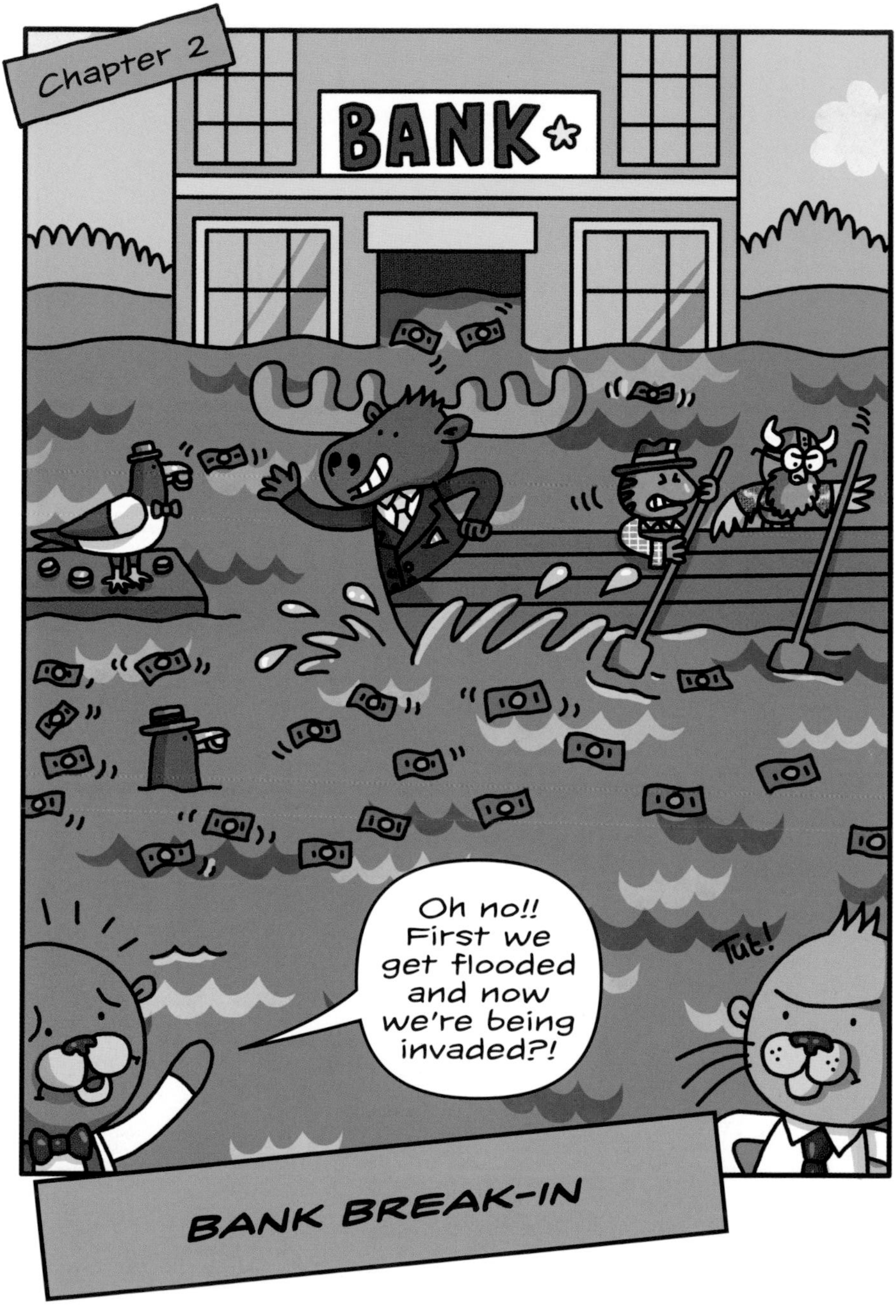
BANK
Oh no!! First we get flooded and now we're being invaded?!
Tut!

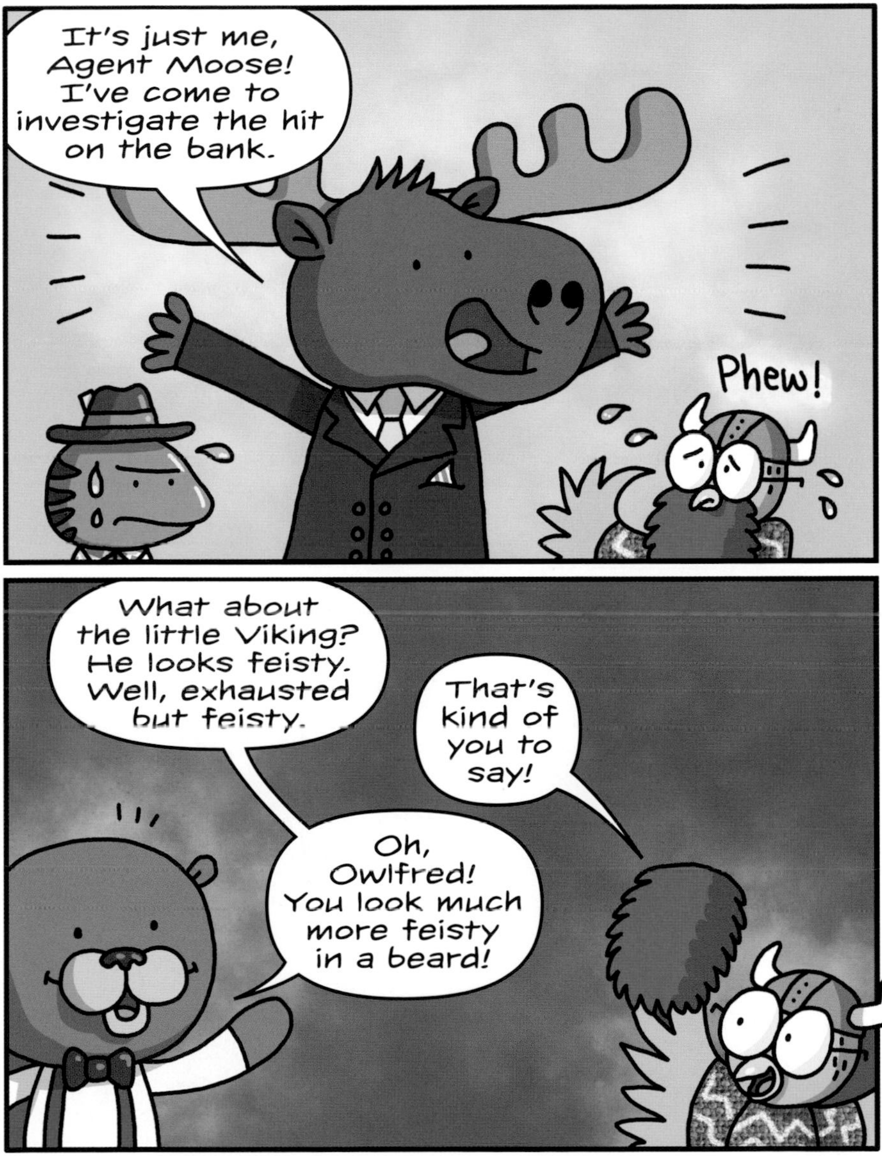
It's just me, Agent Moose! I've come to investigate the hit on the bank.
Phew!
What about the little Viking? He looks feisty. Well, exhausted but feisty.
Oh, Owlfred! You look much more feisty in a beard!
That's kind of you to say!

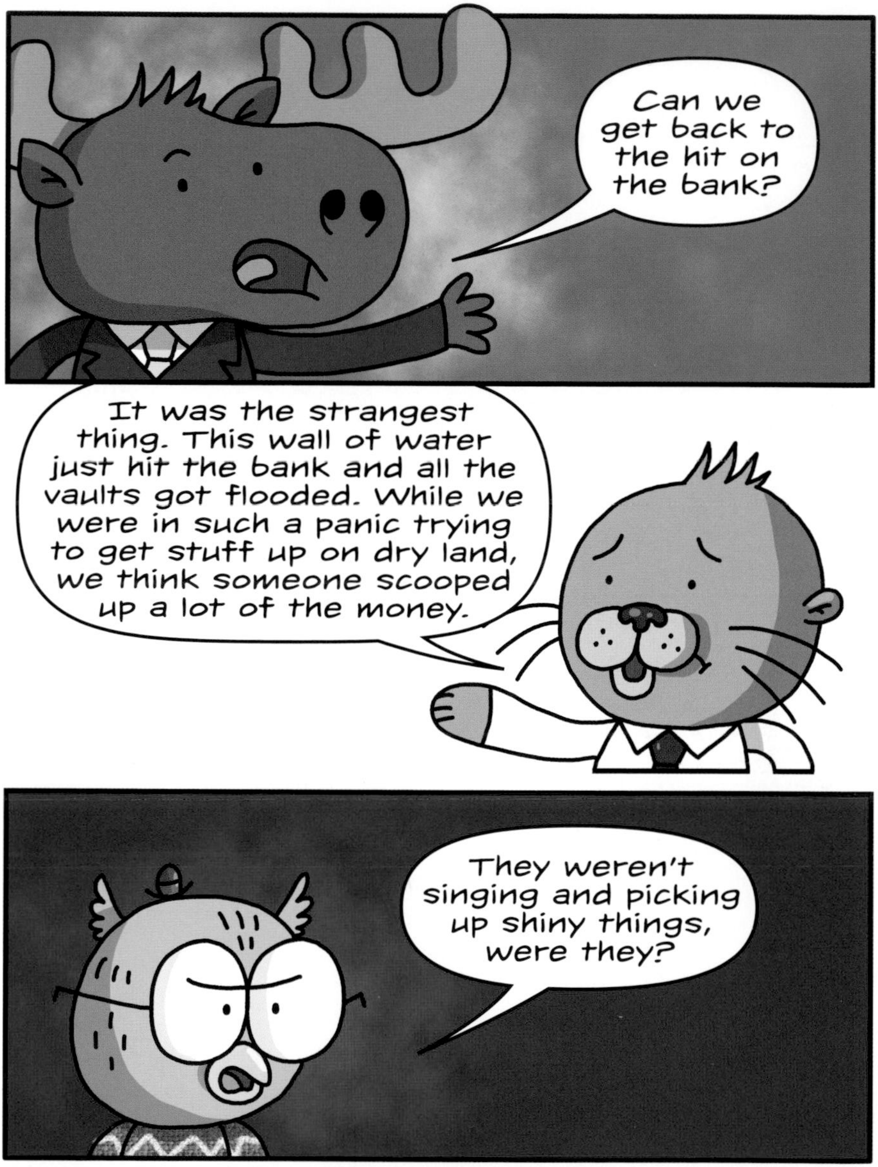
Can we get back to the hit on the bank?
It was the strangest thing. This wall of water just hit the bank and all the vaults got flooded. While we were in such a panic trying to get stuff up on dry land, we think someone scooped up a lot of the money.
They weren't singing and picking up shiny things, were they?

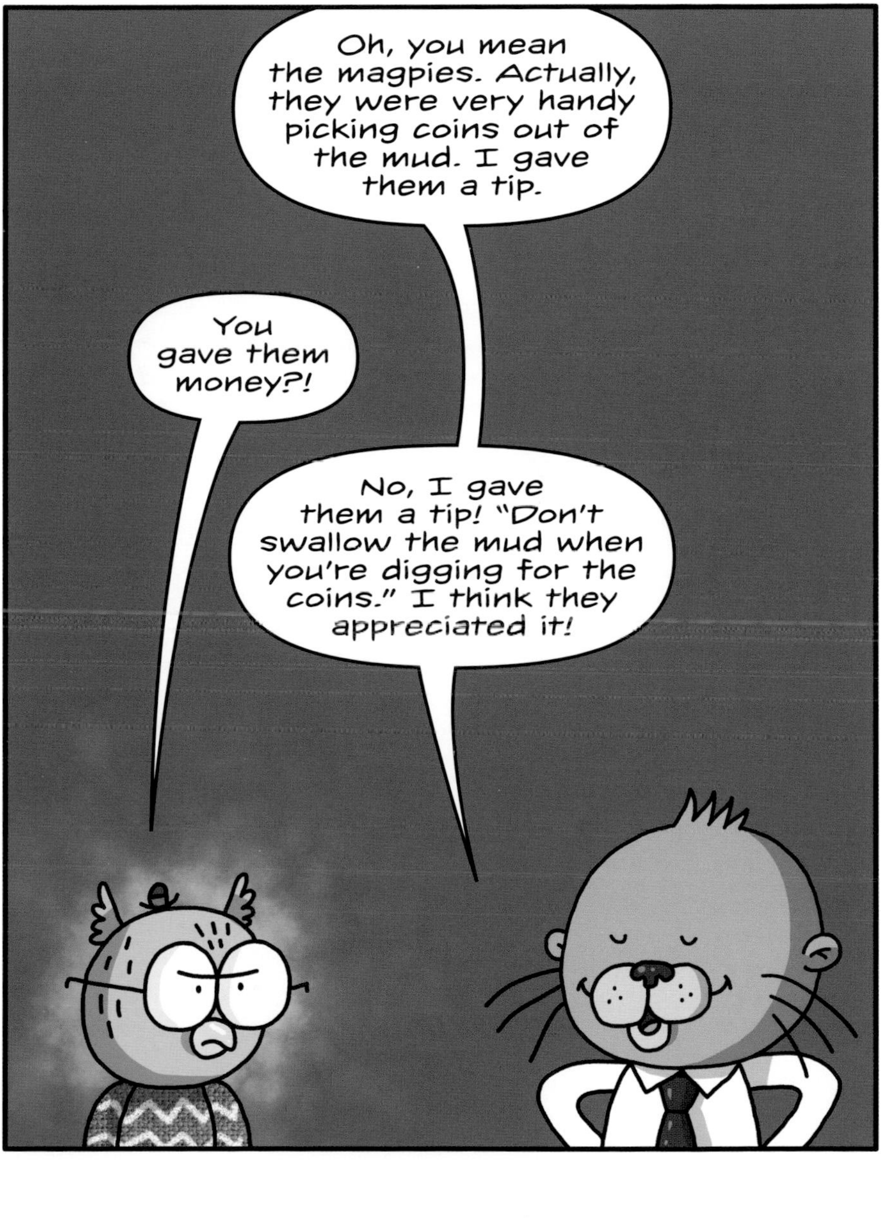
Oh, you mean the magpies. Actually, they were very handy picking coins out of the mud. I gave them a tip.
You gave them money?!
No, I gave them a tip! "Don't swallow the mud when you're digging for the coins." I think they appreciated it!

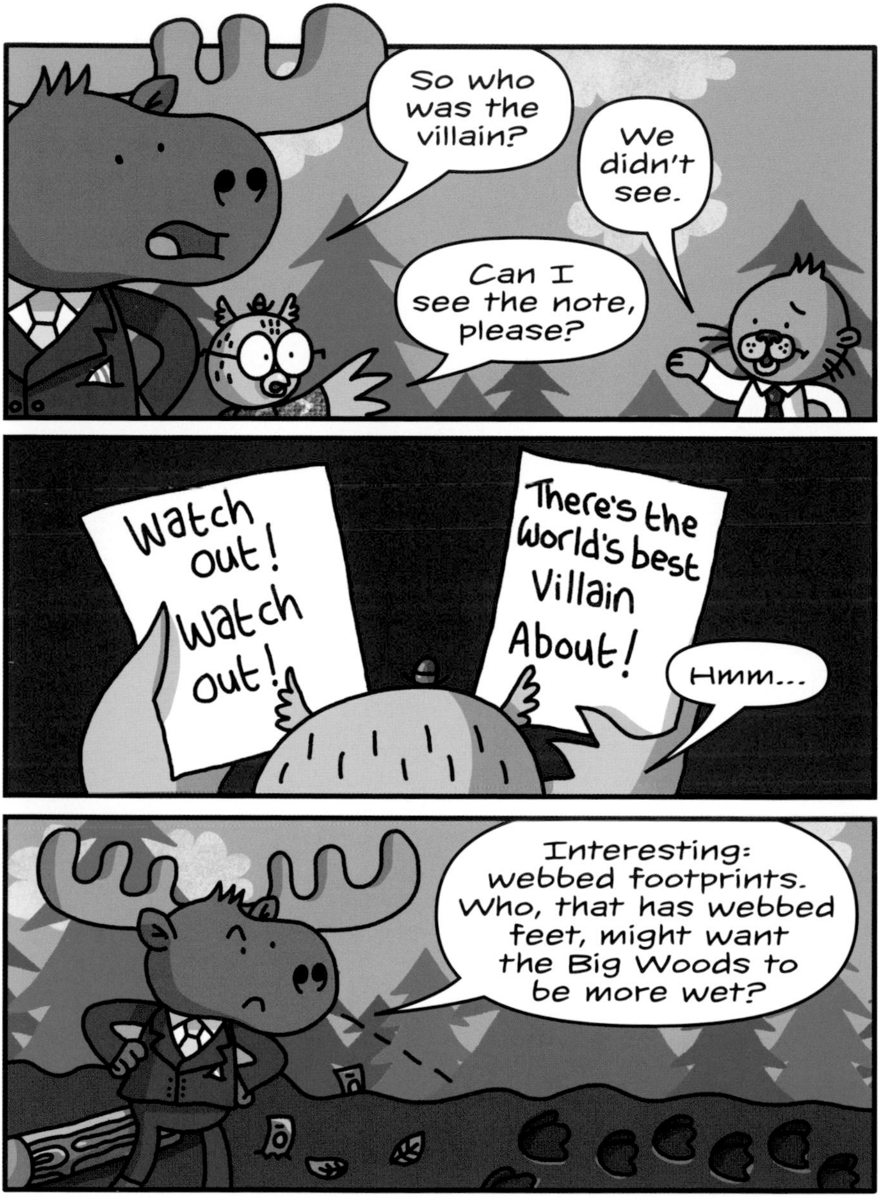
So who was the villain?
We didn't see.
Can I see the note, please?
Watch out! Watch out!
There's the World's best Villain About!
Hmm...
Interesting: webbed footprints. Who, that has webbed feet, might want the Big Woods to be more wet?

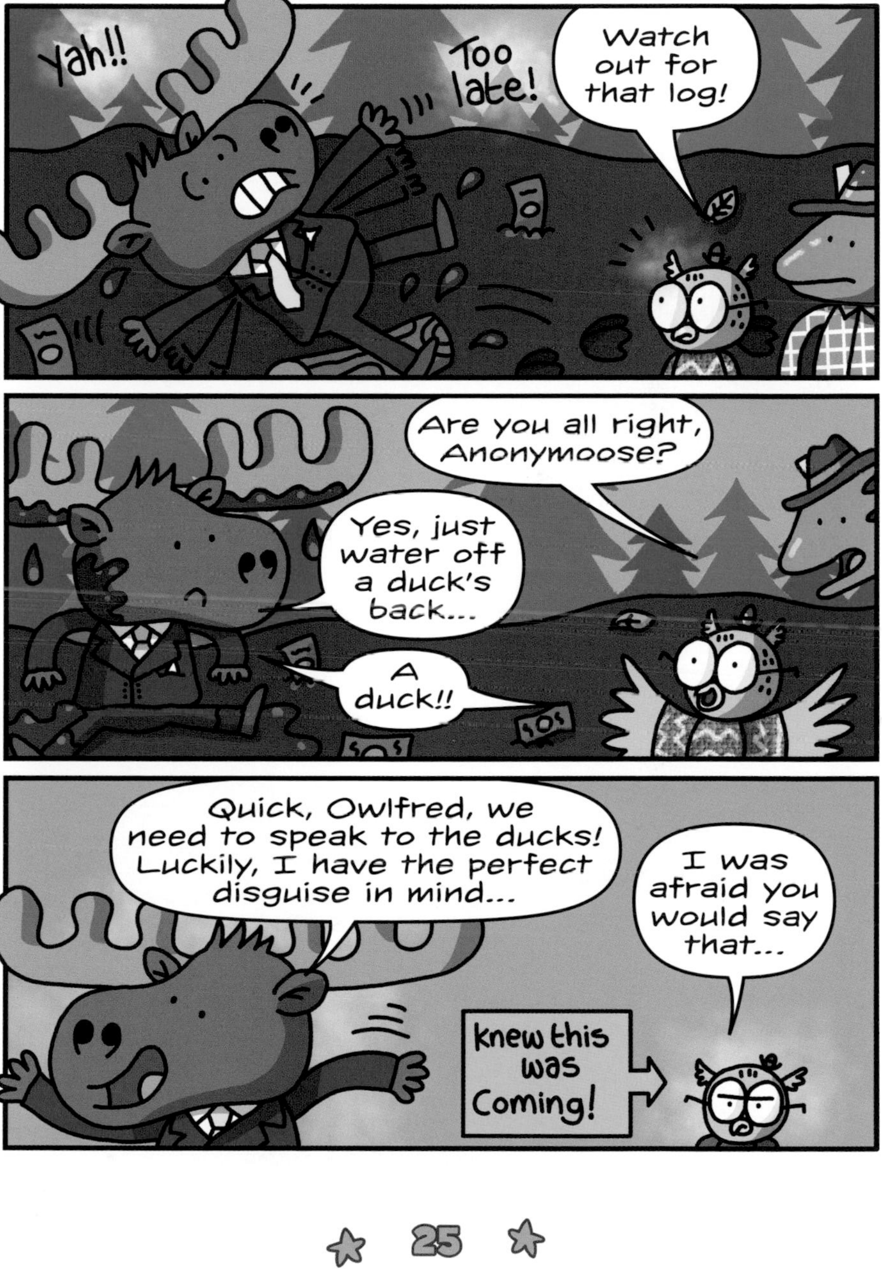
Yah!!
Too late!
Watch out for that log!
Are you all right, Anonymoose?
Yes, just water off a duck's back...
A duck!!
Quick, Owlfred, we need to speak to the ducks! Luckily, I have the perfect disguise in mind...
I was afraid you would say that...
knew this was Coming!

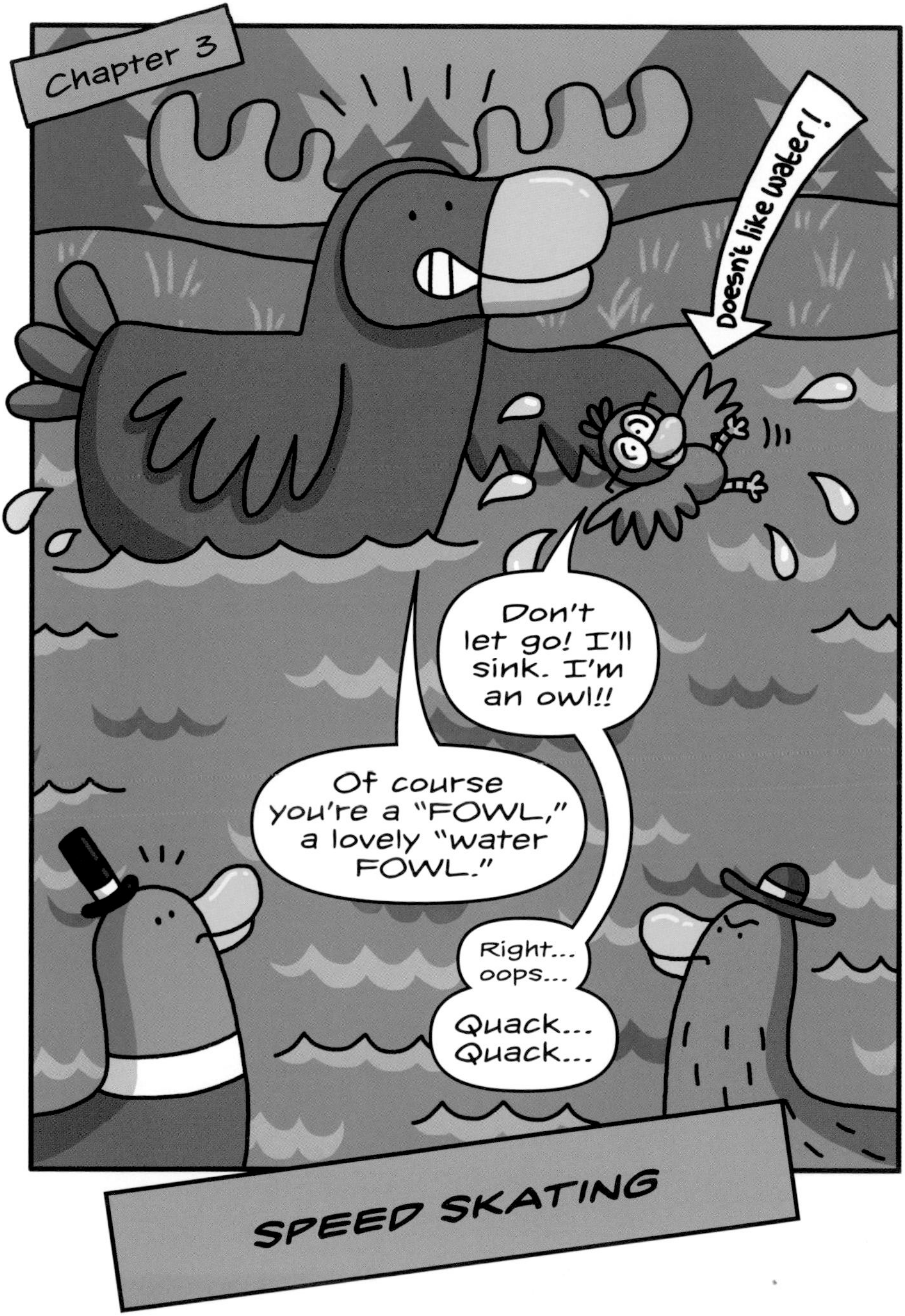
Chapter 3
Doesn't like water!
Don't let go! I'll sink. I'm an owl!!
Of course you're a "FOWL," a lovely "water FOWL."
Right... oops...
Quack... Quack...
SPEED SKATING

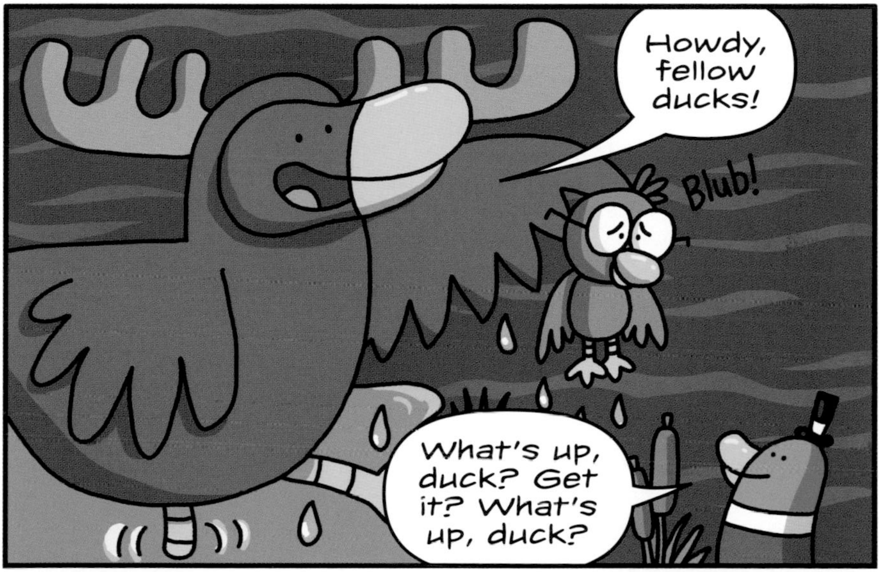
Howdy, fellow ducks!
Blub!
What's up, duck? Get it? What's up, duck?

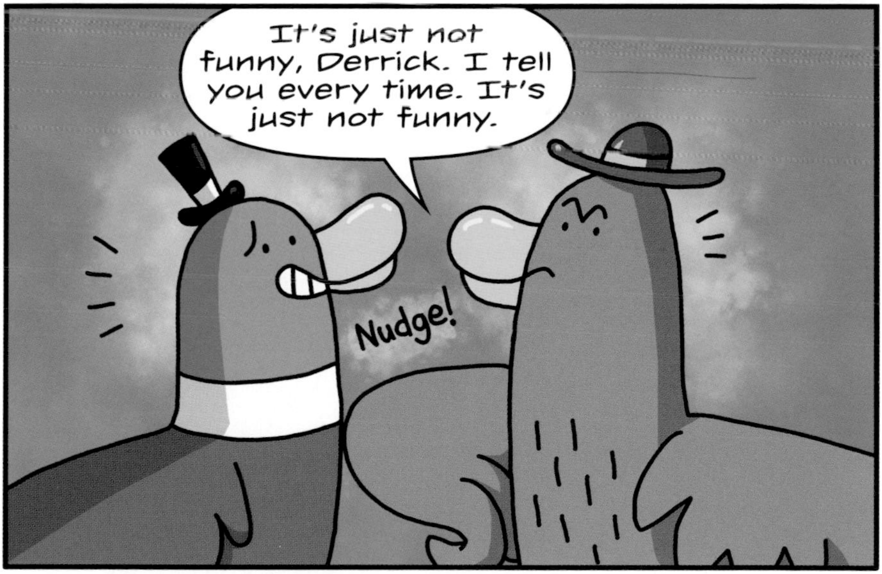
It's just not funny, Derrick. I tell you every time. It's just not funny.
Nudge!

Not much, we were... you know... just paddling along and we saw that something happened at the bank. You see anything?

Anything suspicious?

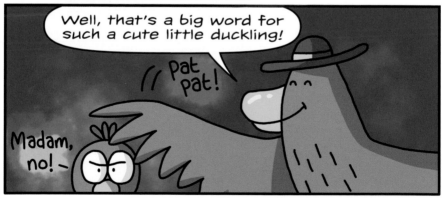

Well, that's a big word for such a cute little duckling!

Pat pat!

Madam, no!

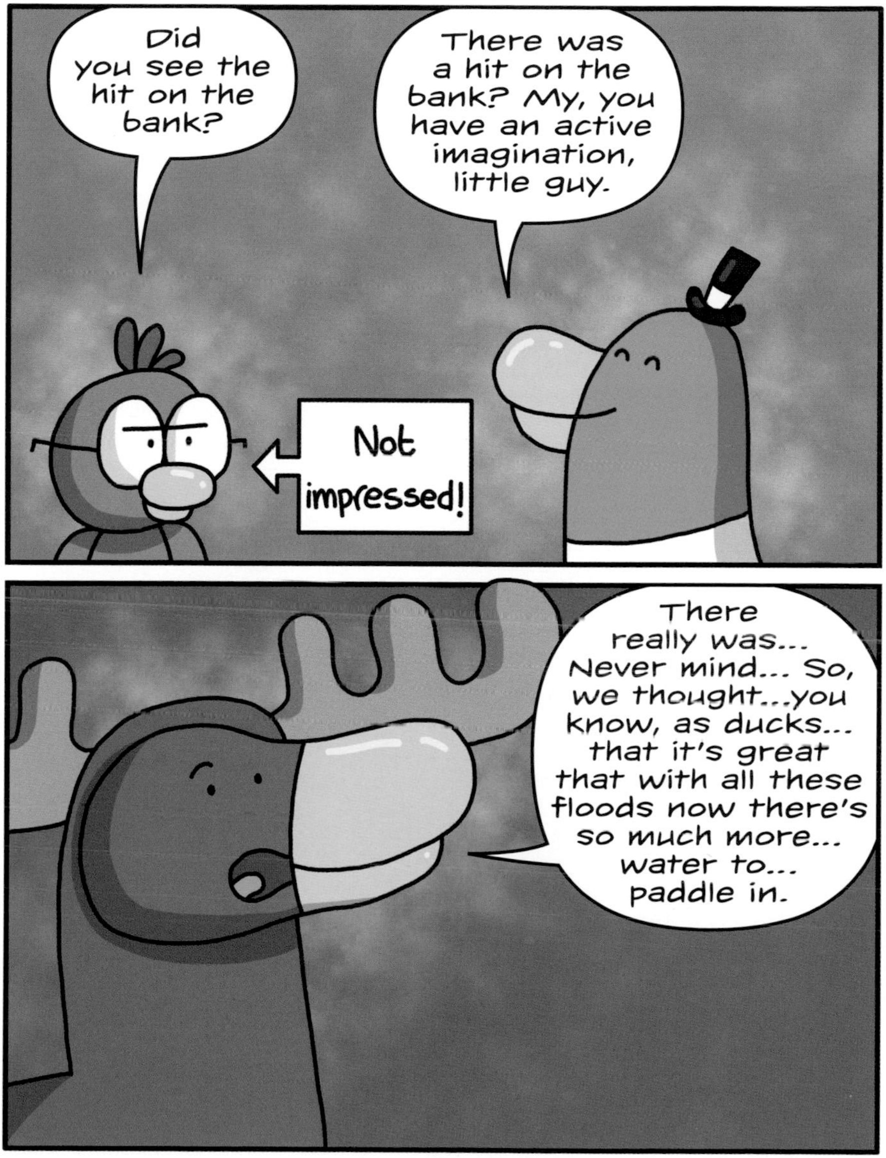
Did you see the hit on the bank?
There was a hit on the bank? My, you have an active imagination, little guy.
Not impressed!
There really was... Never mind... So, we thought...you know, as ducks... that it's great that with all these floods now there's so much more... water to... paddle in.

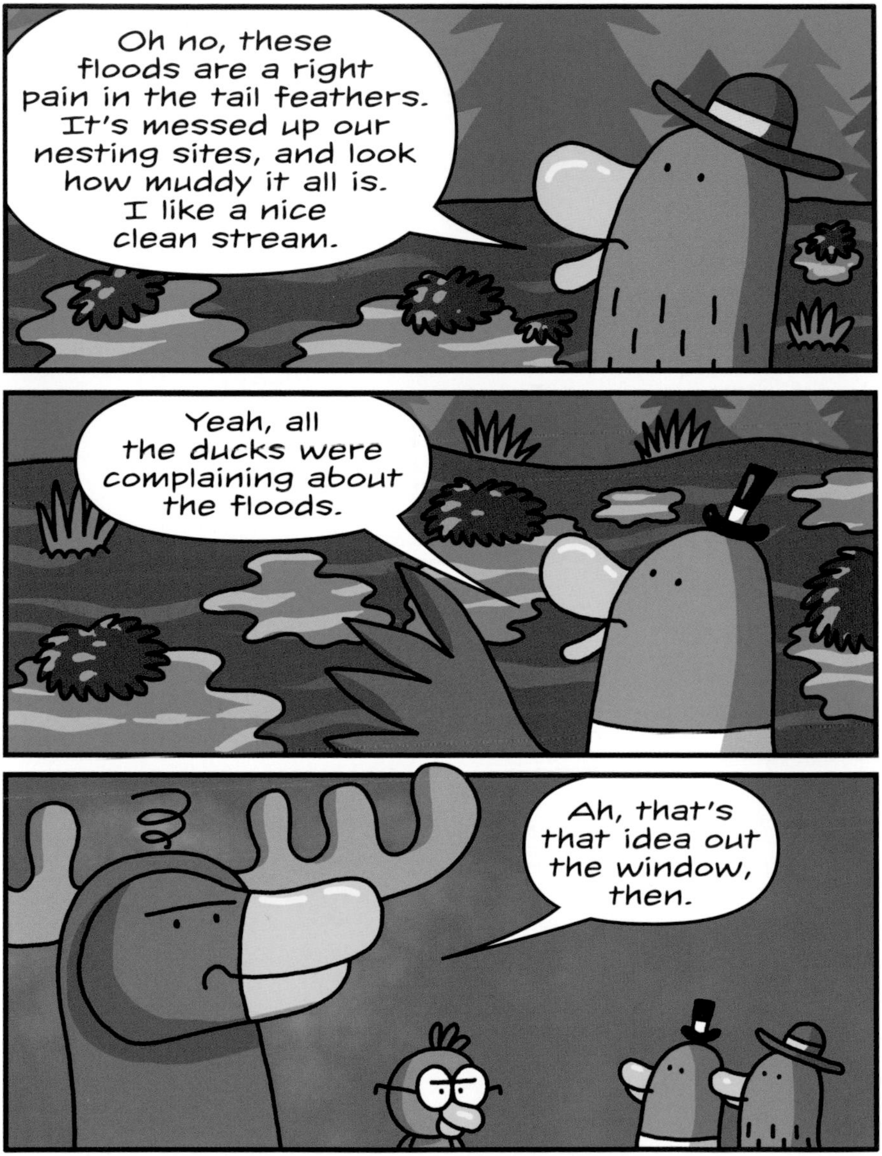
Oh no, these floods are a right pain in the tail feathers. It's messed up our nesting sites, and look how muddy it all is. I like a nice clean stream.
Yeah, all the ducks were complaining about the floods.
Ah, that's that idea out the window, then.

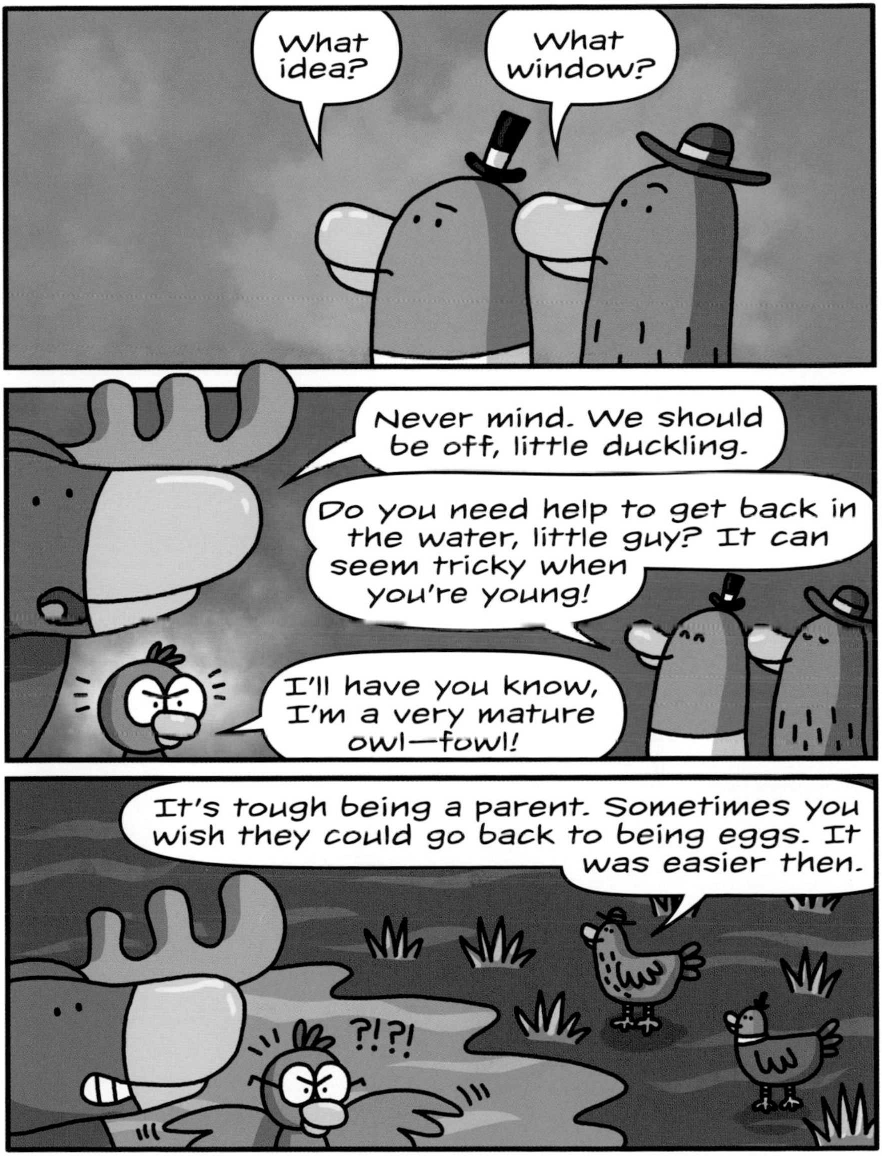
What idea?
What window?
Never mind. We should be off, little duckling.
Do you need help to get back in the water, little guy? It can seem tricky when you're young!
I'll have you know, I'm a very mature owl—fowl!
It's tough being a parent. Sometimes you wish they could go back to being eggs. It was easier then.
?!?!

AGENT MOOSE

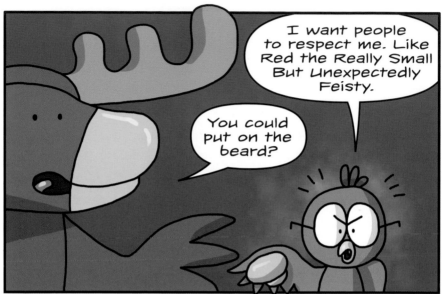

I want people to respect me. Like Red the Really Small But Unexpectedly Feisty.

You could put on the beard?

I want respect WITHOUT the beard!! I am a feisty yet professional agent!

Yes, feisty, professional, and... sinking.

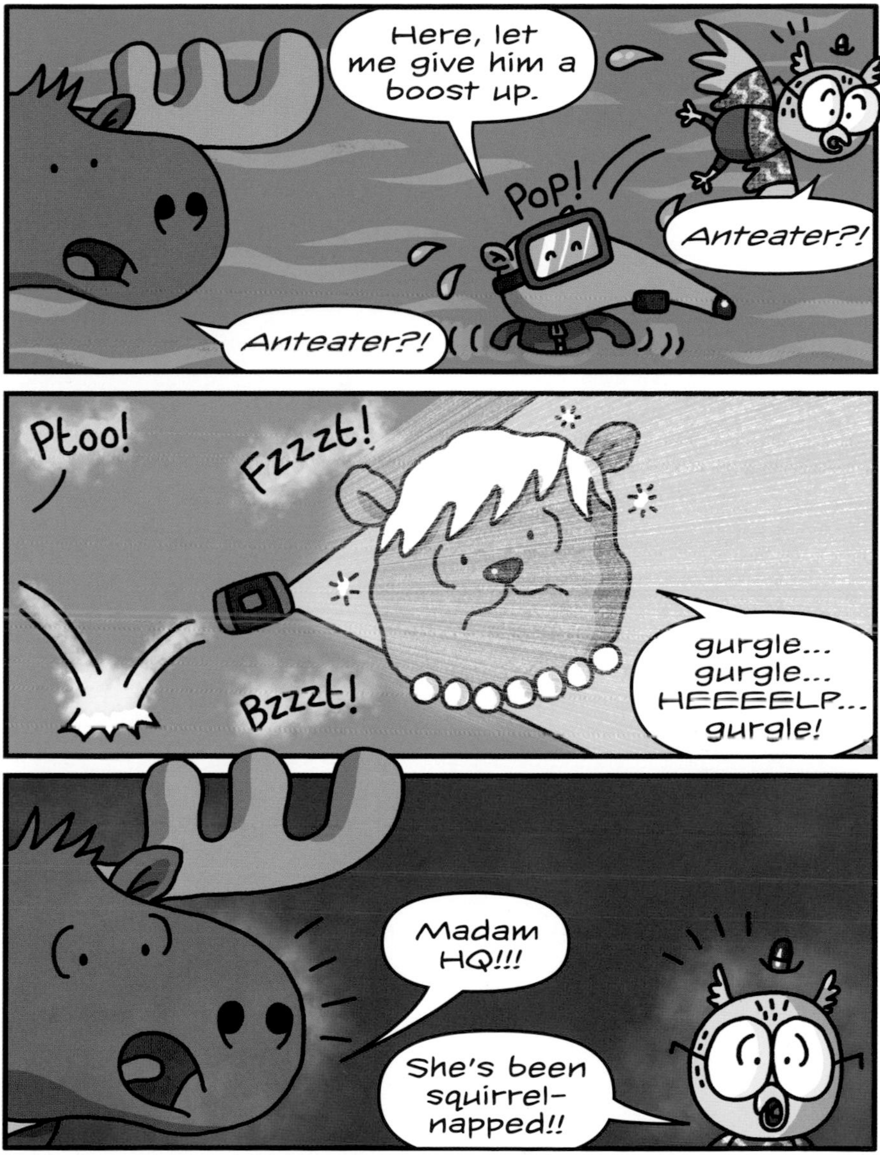
Here, let me give him a boost up.
POP!
Anteater?!
Anteater?!
Ptoo!
Fzzzt!
Bzzzt!
gurgle... gurgle... HEEEELP... gurgle!
Madam HQ!!!
She's been squirrel-napped!!

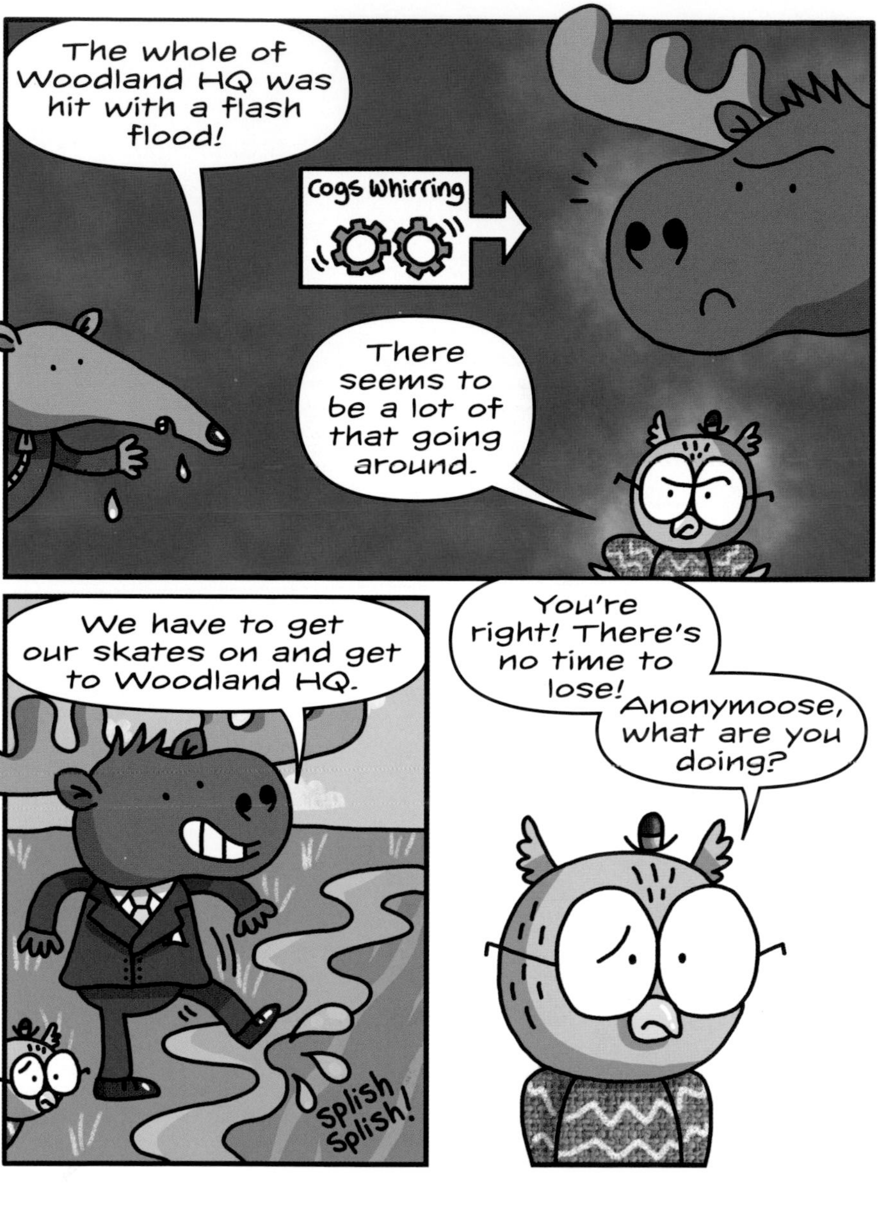
The whole of Woodland HQ was hit with a flash flood!
Cogs Whirring
There seems to be a lot of that going around.
We have to get our skates on and get to Woodland HQ.
Splish Splish!
You're right! There's no time to lose!
Anonymoose, what are you doing?

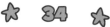

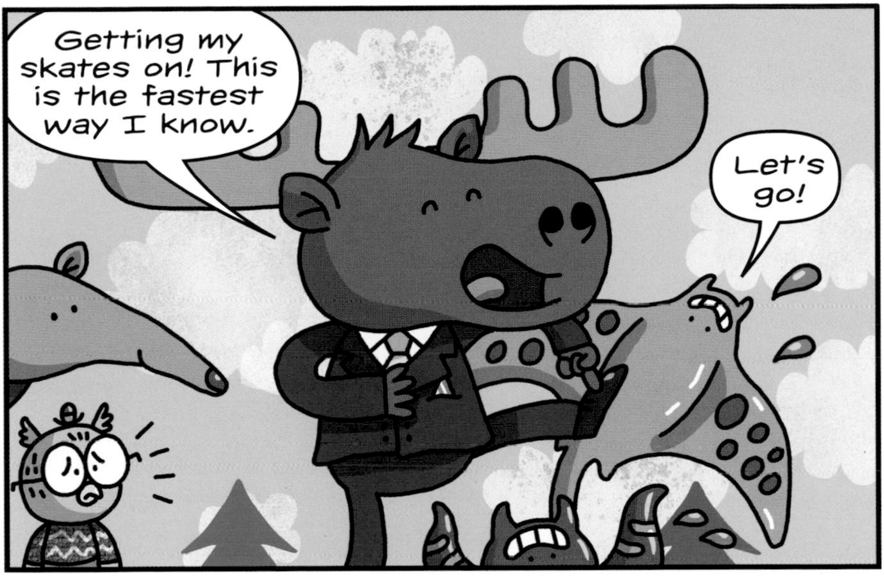
Getting my skates on! This is the fastest way I know.
Let's go!

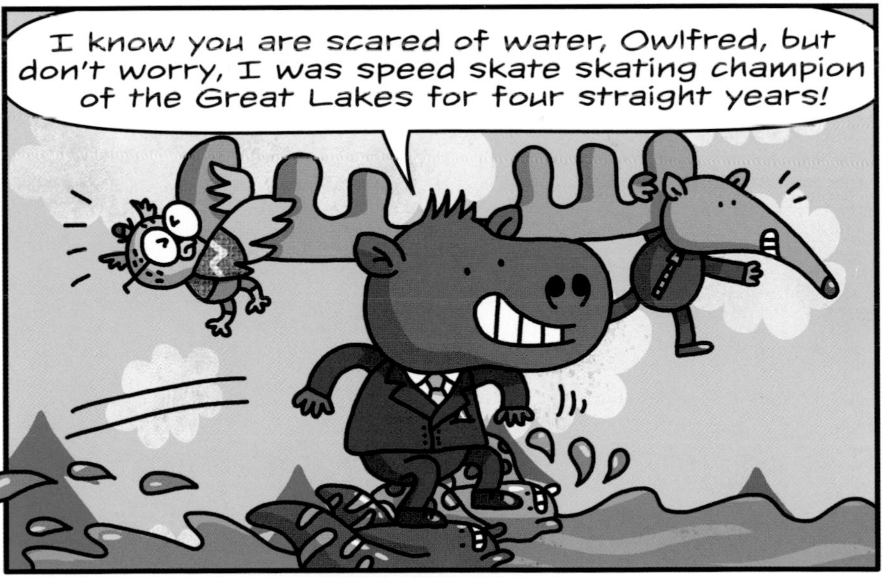
I know you are scared of water, Owlfred, but don't worry, I was speed skate skating champion of the Great Lakes for four straight years!

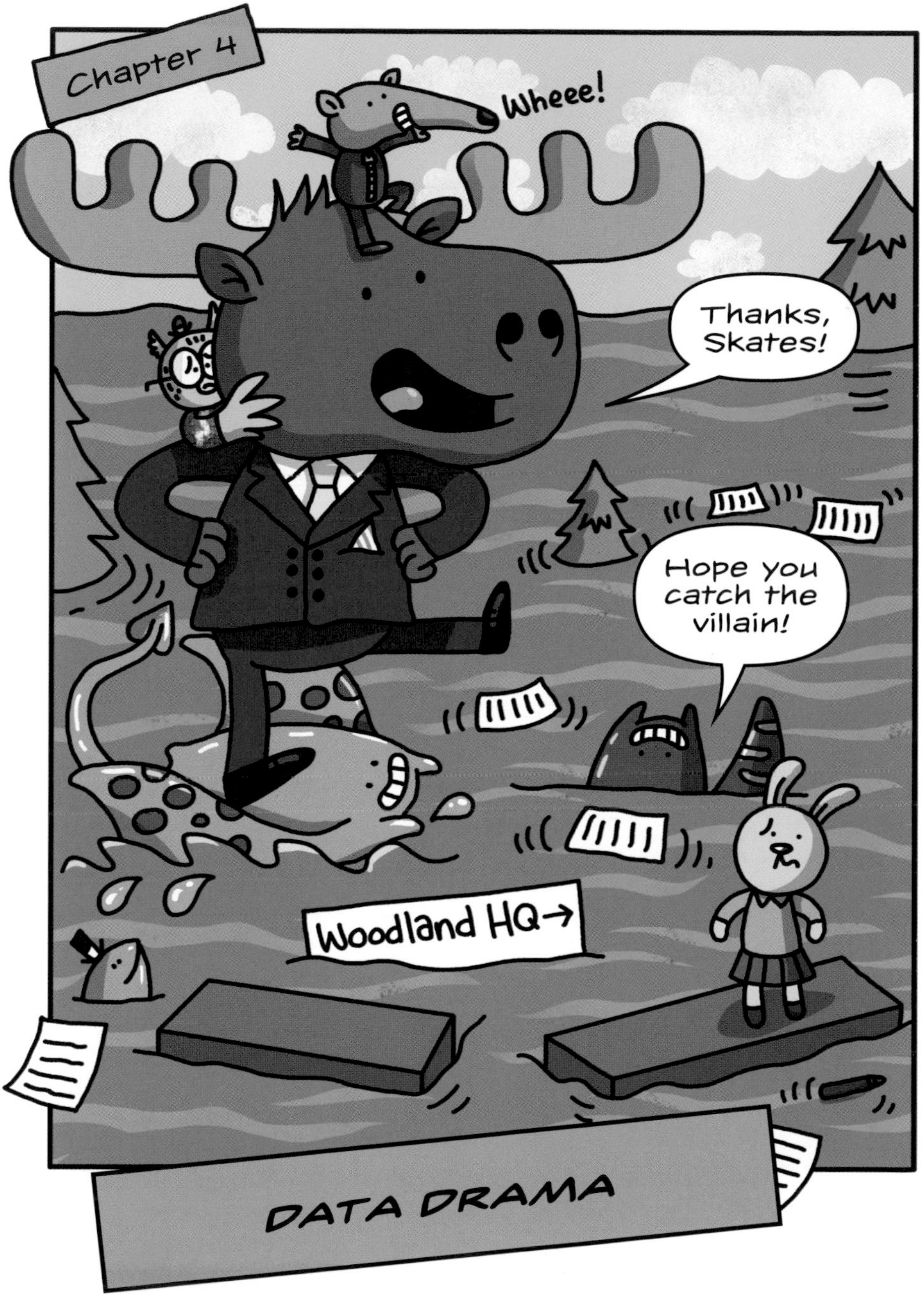
Chapter 4
Wheee!
Thanks, Skates!
Hope you catch the villain!
Woodland HQ→
DATA DRAMA

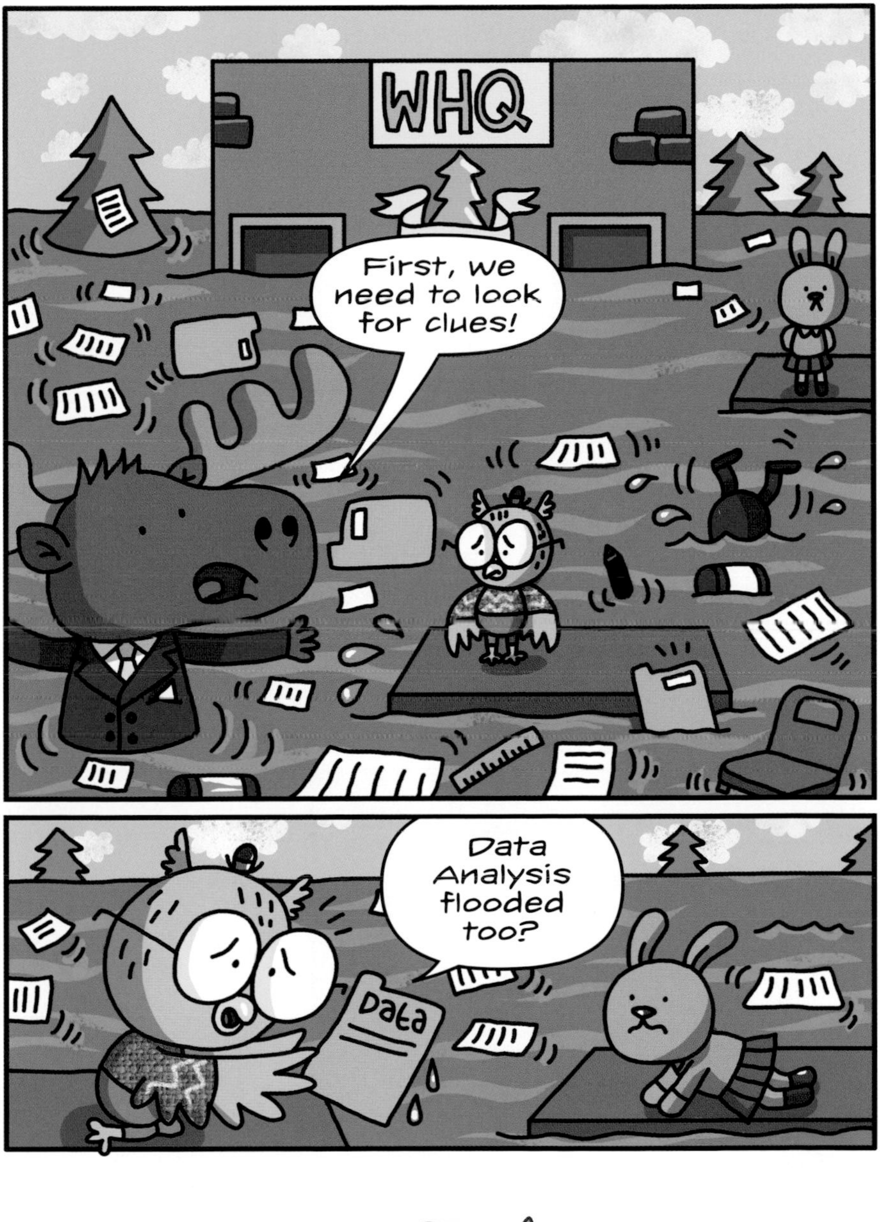
WHQ
First, we need to look for clues!
Data Analysis flooded too?
Data

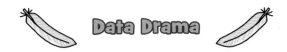

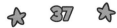

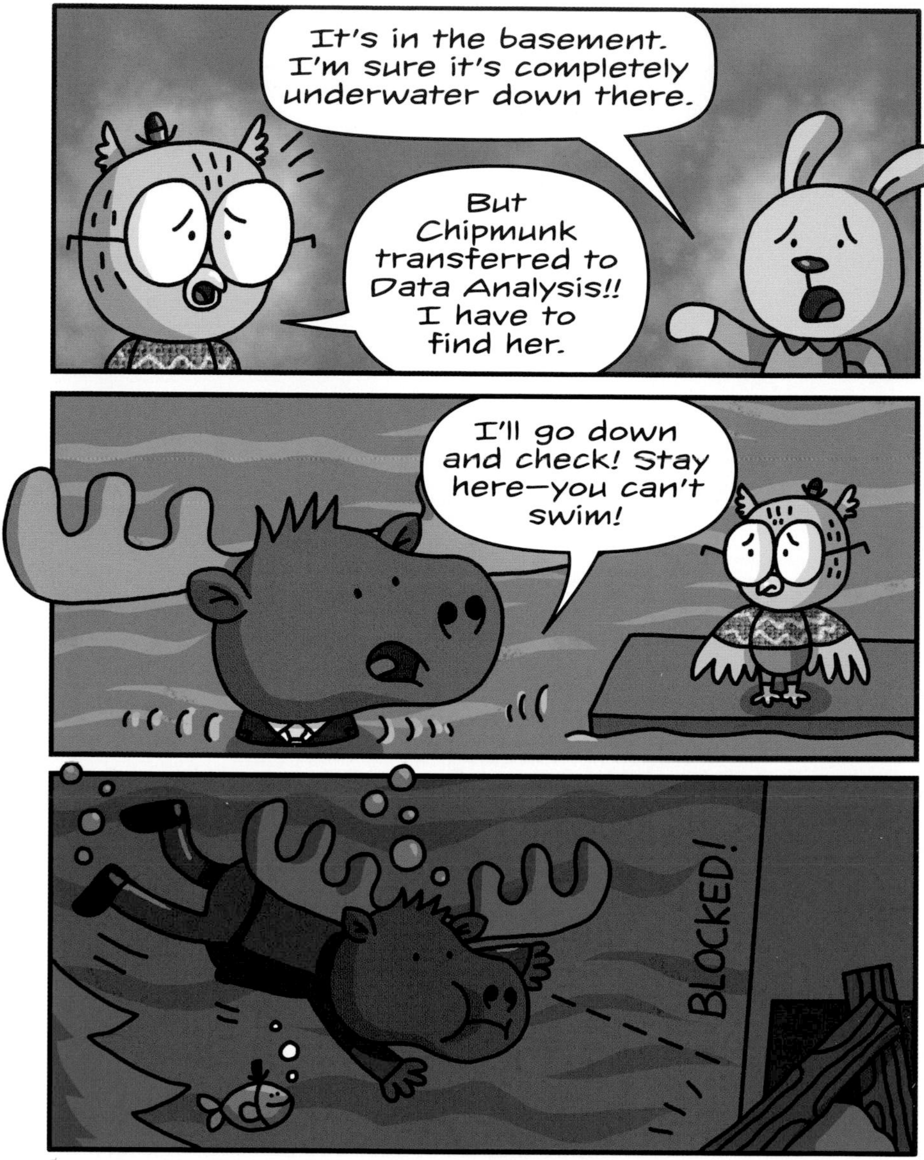
It's in the basement. I'm sure it's completely underwater down there.
But Chipmunk transferred to Data Analysis!! I have to find her.
I'll go down and check! Stay here—you can't swim!
BLOCKED!

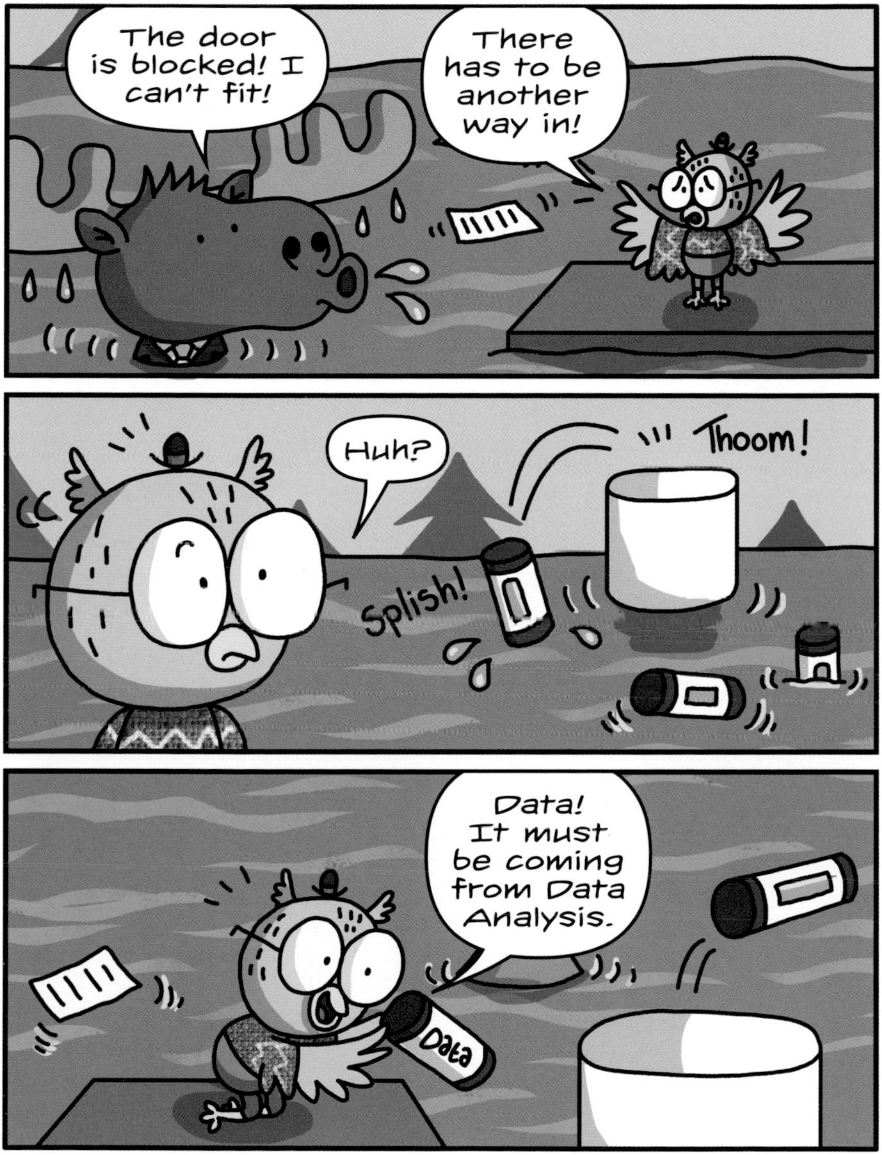
The door is blocked! I can't fit!
There has to be another way in!
Huh?
Thoom!
Splish!
Data! It must be coming from Data Analysis.
Data

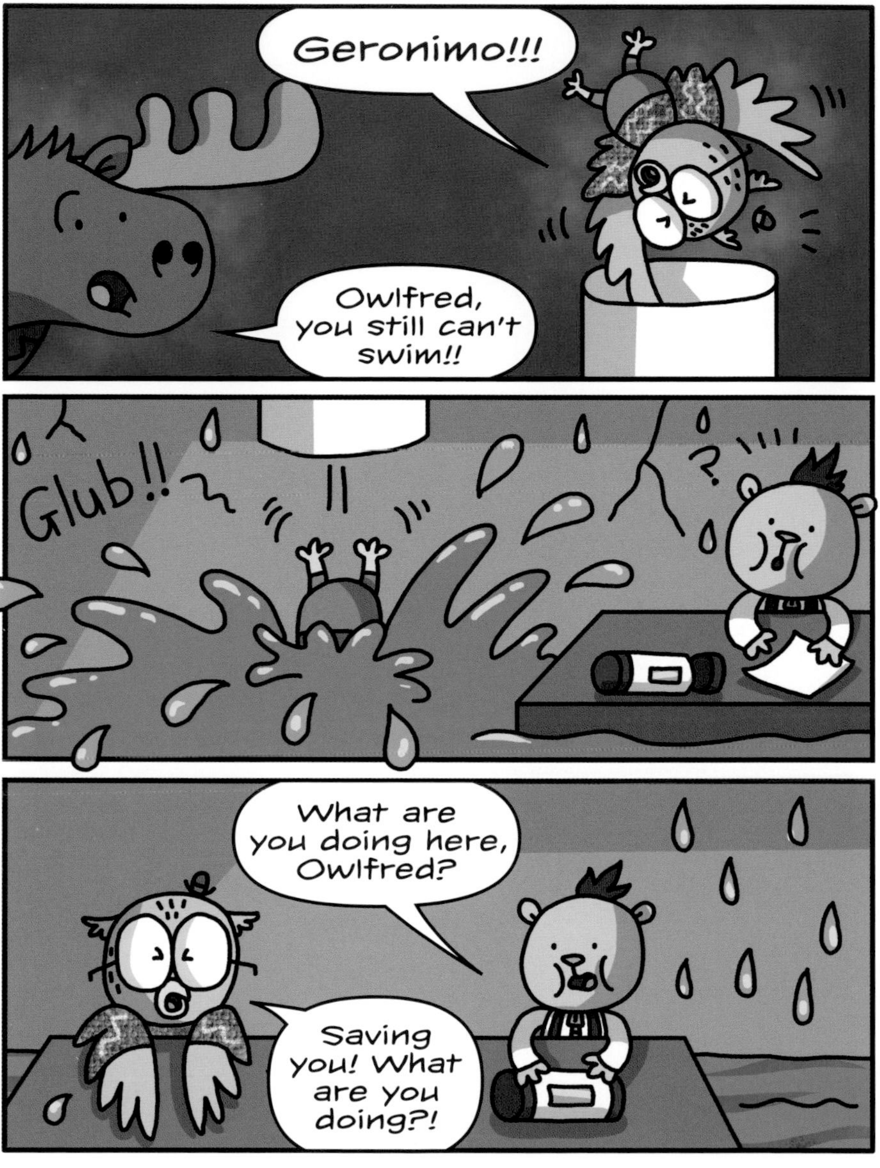
Geronimo!!!
Owlfred, you still can't swim!!
Glub!!
?
What are you doing here, Owlfred?
Saving you! What are you doing?!

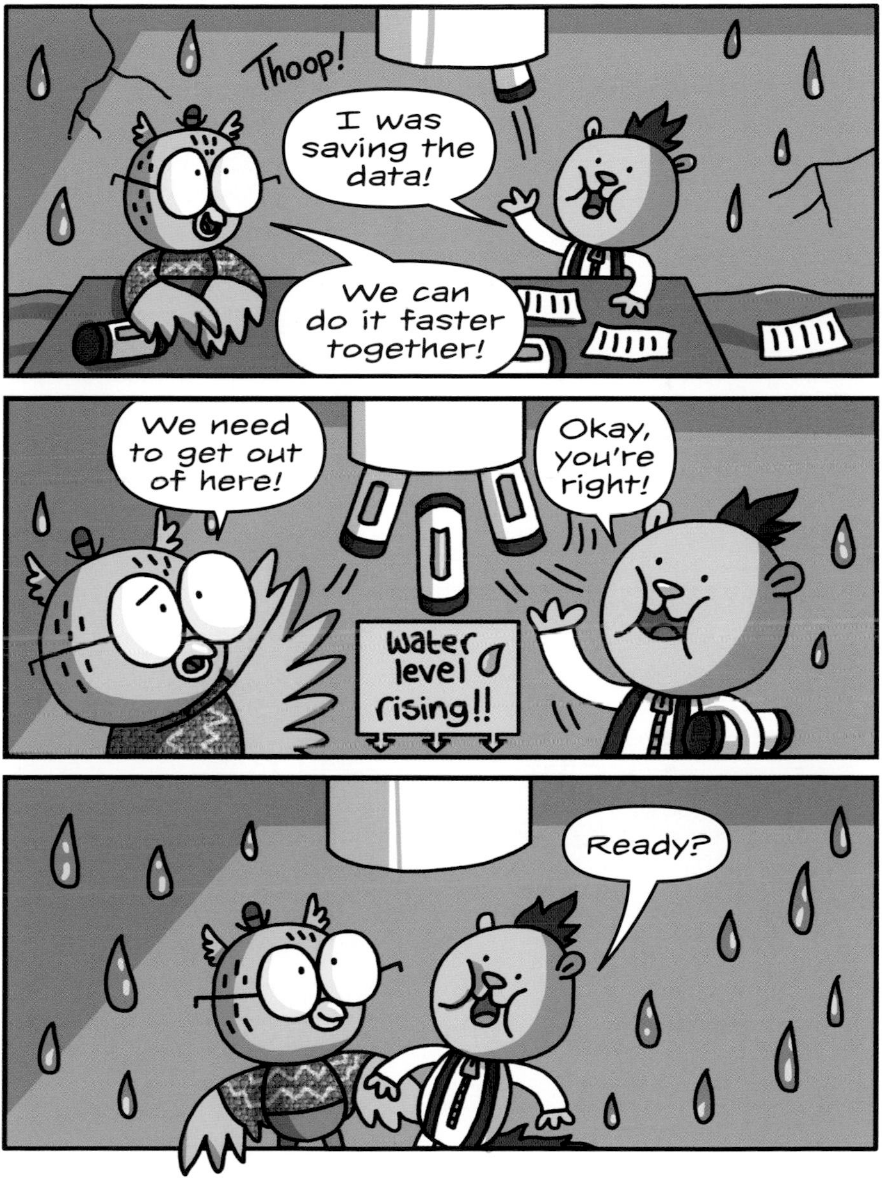
Thoop!
I was saving the data!
We can do it faster together!
We need to get out of here!
Okay, you're right!
water level rising!!
Ready?

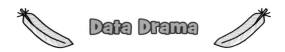

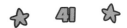

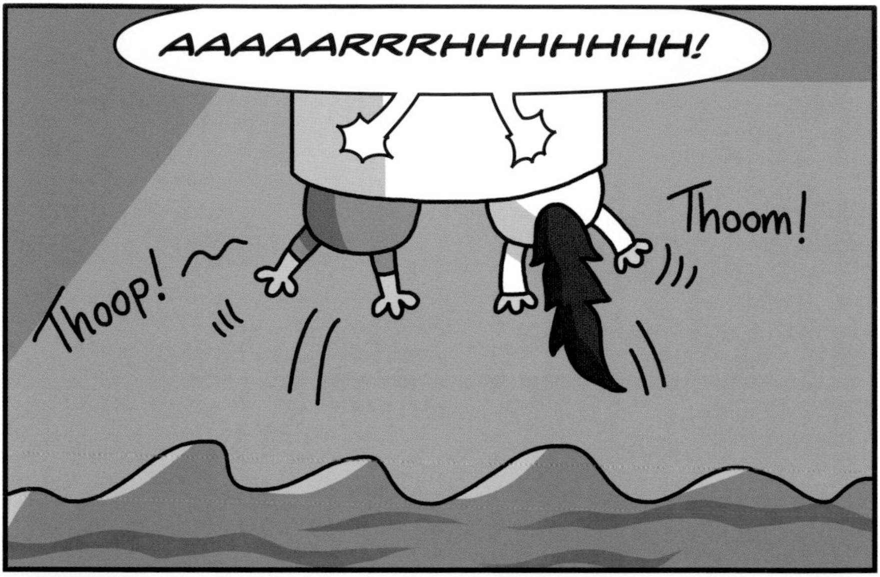
AAAAARRRHHHHHHH!
Thoop!
Thoom!

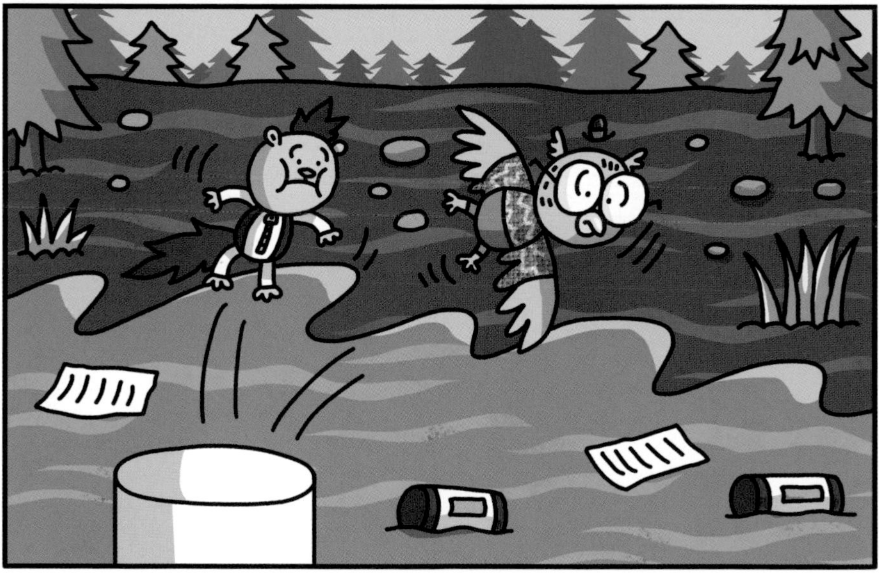

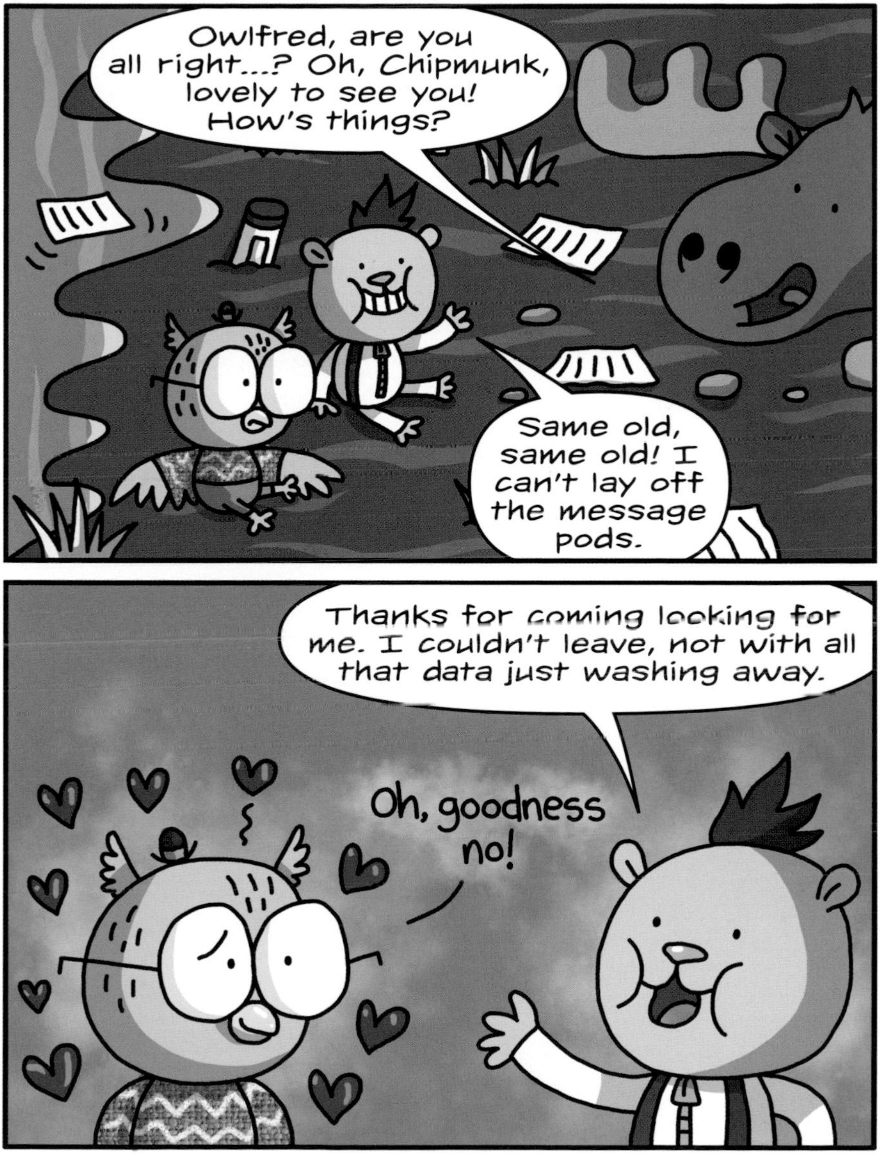
Owlfred, are you all right...? Oh, Chipmunk, lovely to see you! How's things?
Same old, same old! I can't lay off the message pods.
Thanks for coming looking for me. I couldn't leave, not with all that data just washing away.
Oh, goodness no!

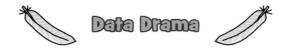

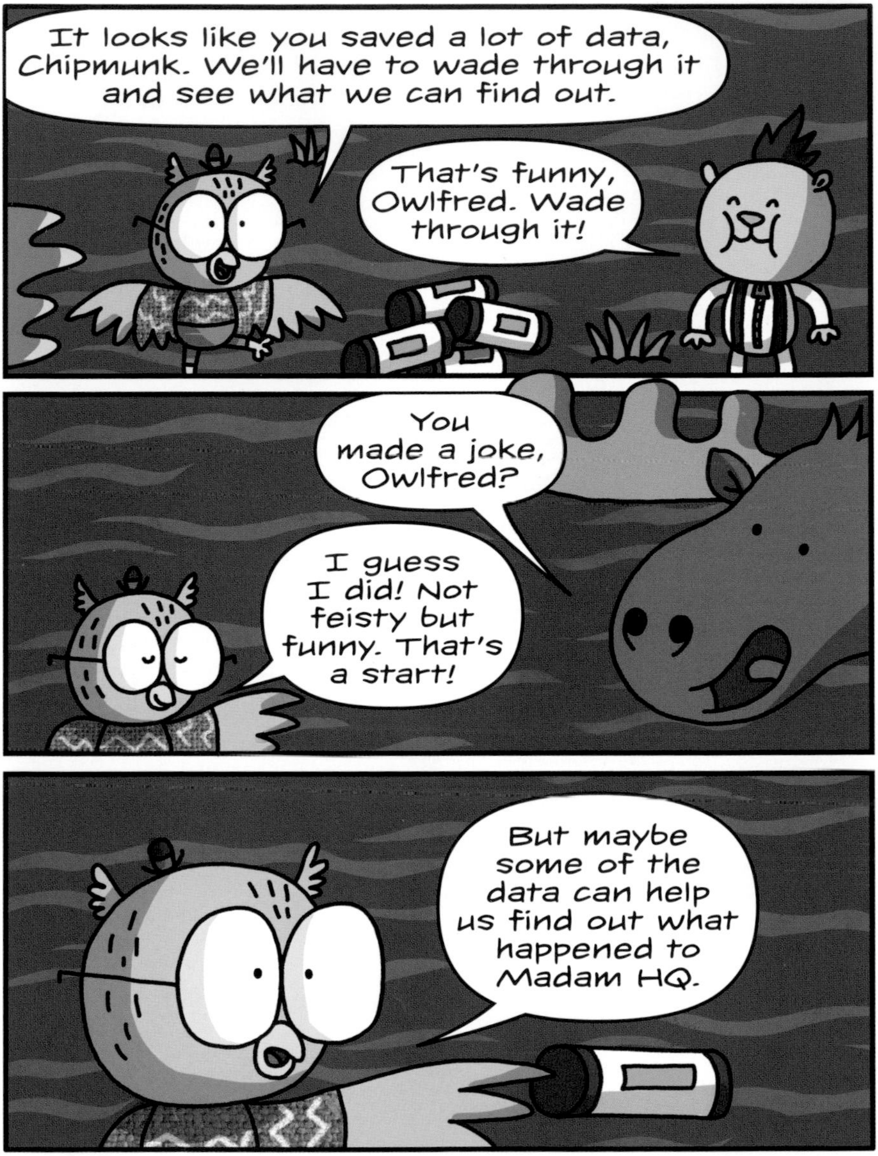
It looks like you saved a lot of data, Chipmunk. We'll have to wade through it and see what we can find out.
That's funny, Owlfred. Wade through it!
You made a joke, Owlfred?
I guess I did! Not feisty but funny. That's a start!
But maybe some of the data can help us find out what happened to Madam HQ.

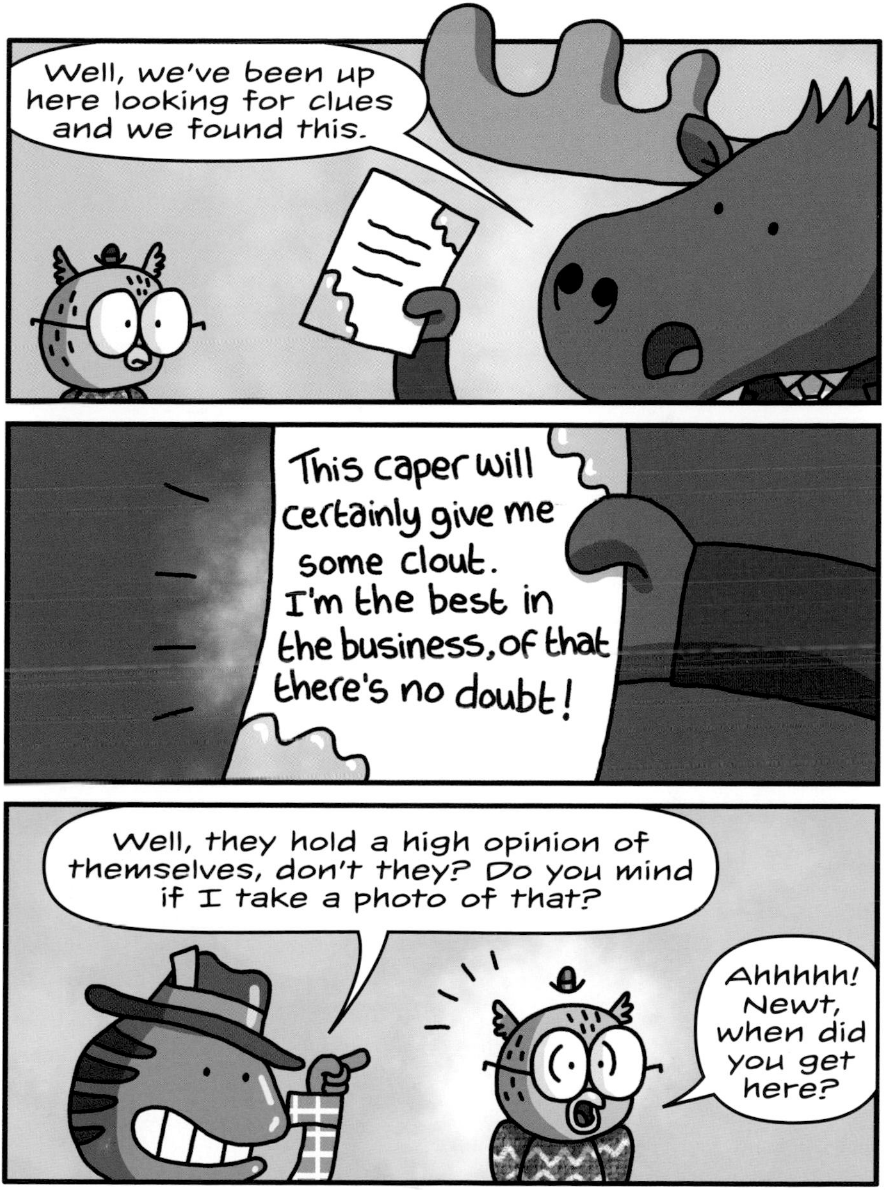
Well, we've been up here looking for clues and we found this.
This caper will certainly give me some clout. I'm the best in the business, of that there's no doubt!
Well, they hold a high opinion of themselves, don't they? Do you mind if I take a photo of that?
Ahhhhh! Newt, when did you get here?

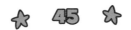

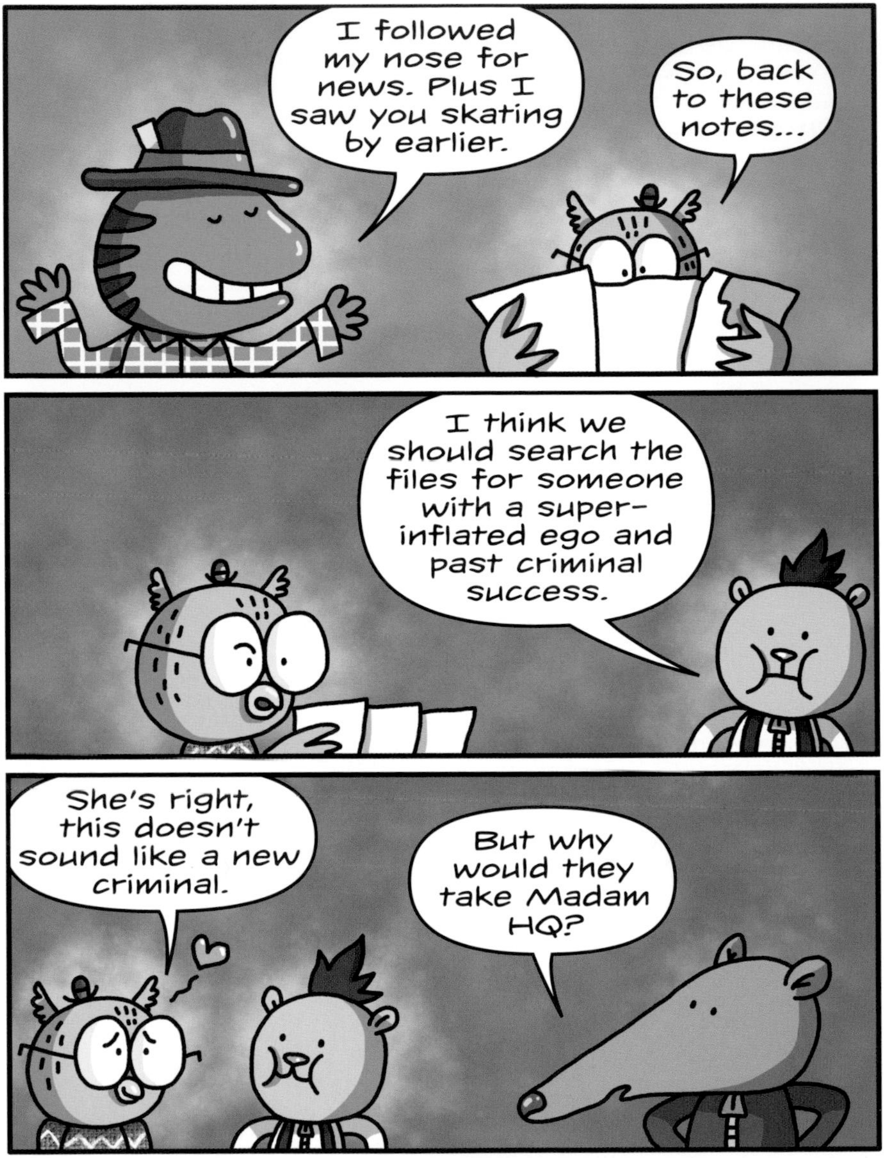
I followed my nose for news. Plus I saw you skating by earlier.
So, back to these notes...
I think we should search the files for someone with a super-inflated ego and past criminal success.
She's right, this doesn't sound like a new criminal.
But why would they take Madam HQ?

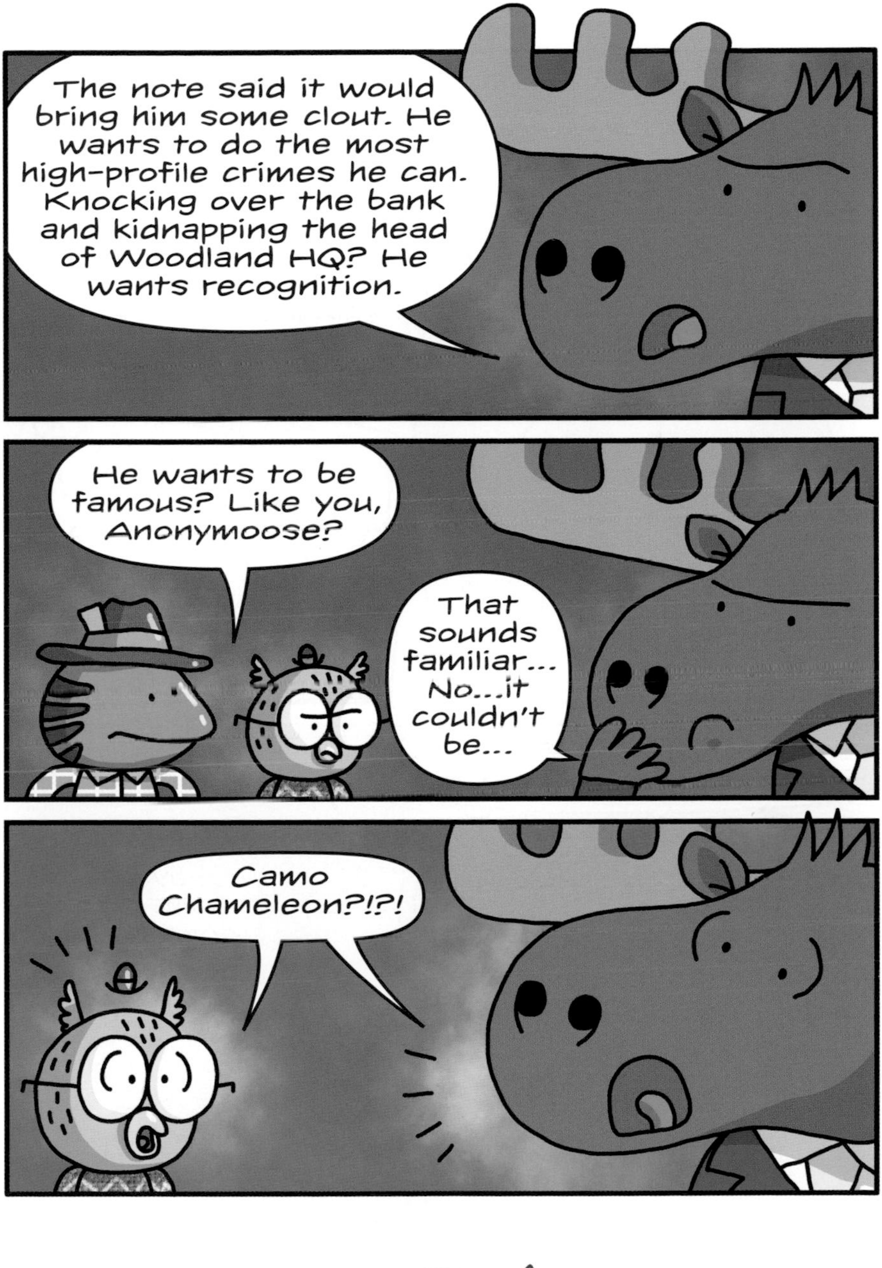
The note said it would bring him some clout. He wants to do the most high-profile crimes he can. Knocking over the bank and kidnapping the head of Woodland HQ? He wants recognition.
He wants to be famous? Like you, Anonymoose?
That sounds familiar... No...it couldn't be...
Camo Chameleon?!?!

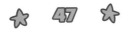

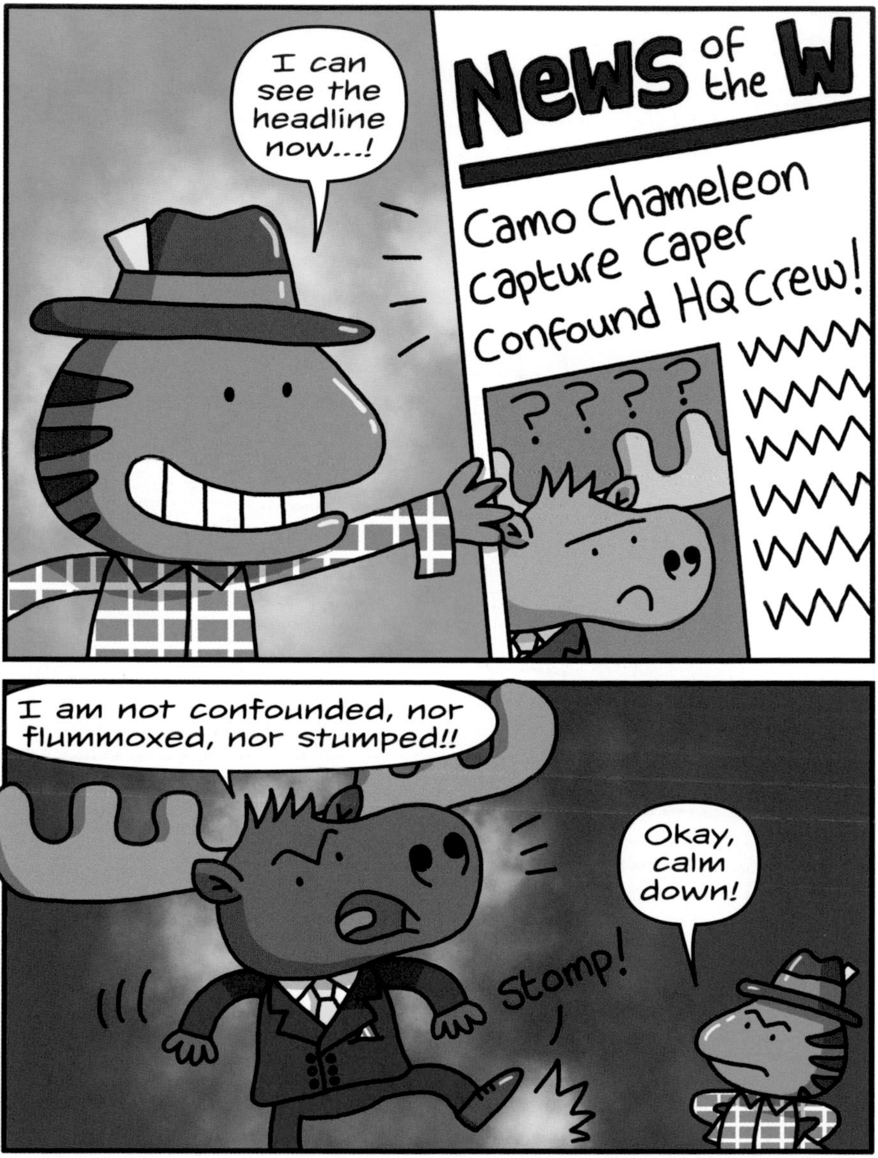
I can see the headline now...!
News of the W
Camo chameleon capture caper confound HQ crew!
????
I am not confounded, nor flummoxed, nor stumped!!
Okay, calm down!
Stomp!

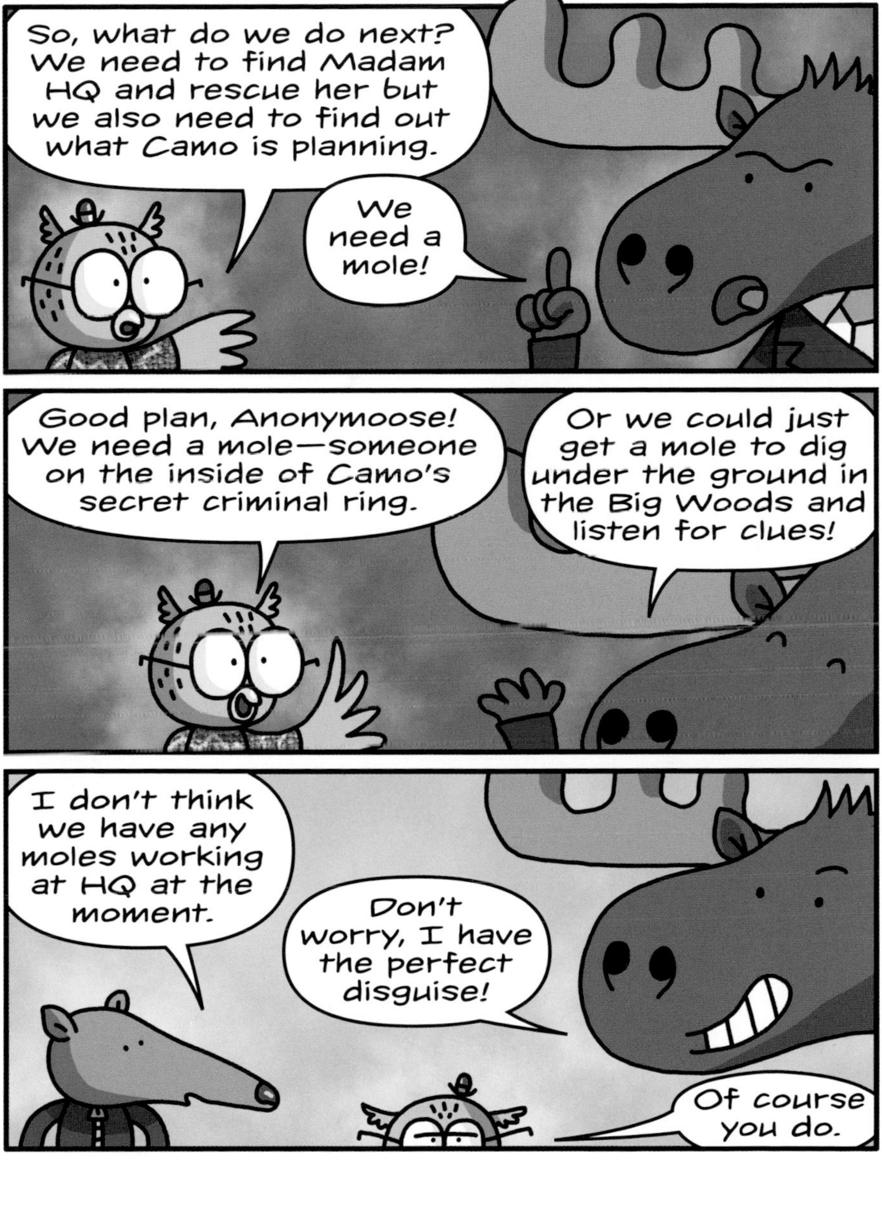
So, what do we do next? We need to find Madam HQ and rescue her but we also need to find out what Camo is planning.
We need a mole!
Good plan, Anonymoose! We need a mole—someone on the inside of Camo's secret criminal ring.
Or we could just get a mole to dig under the ground in the Big Woods and listen for clues!
I don't think we have any moles working at HQ at the moment.
Don't worry, I have the perfect disguise!
Of course you do.

Chapter 5

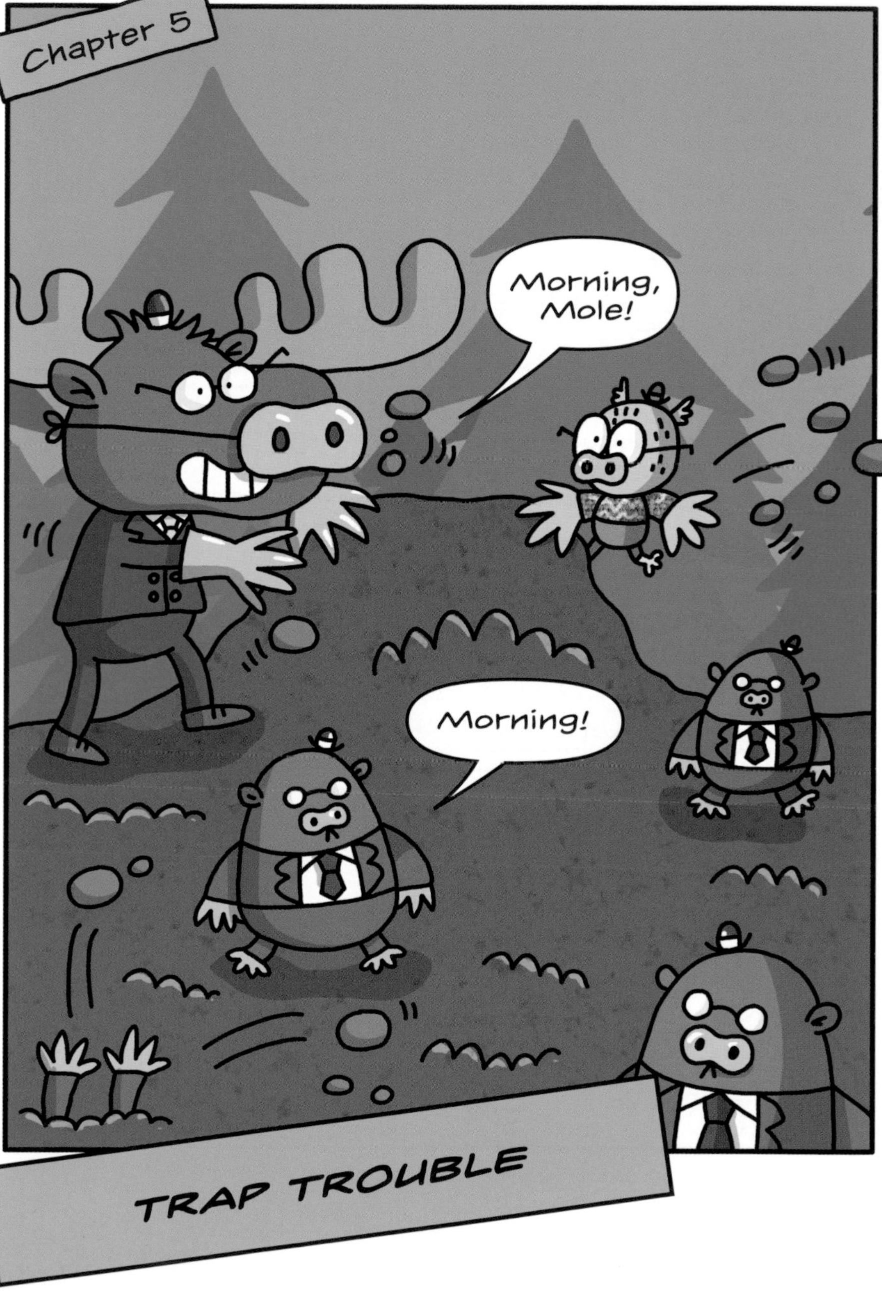
Morning, Mole!
Morning!

TRAP TROUBLE

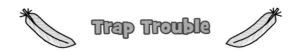

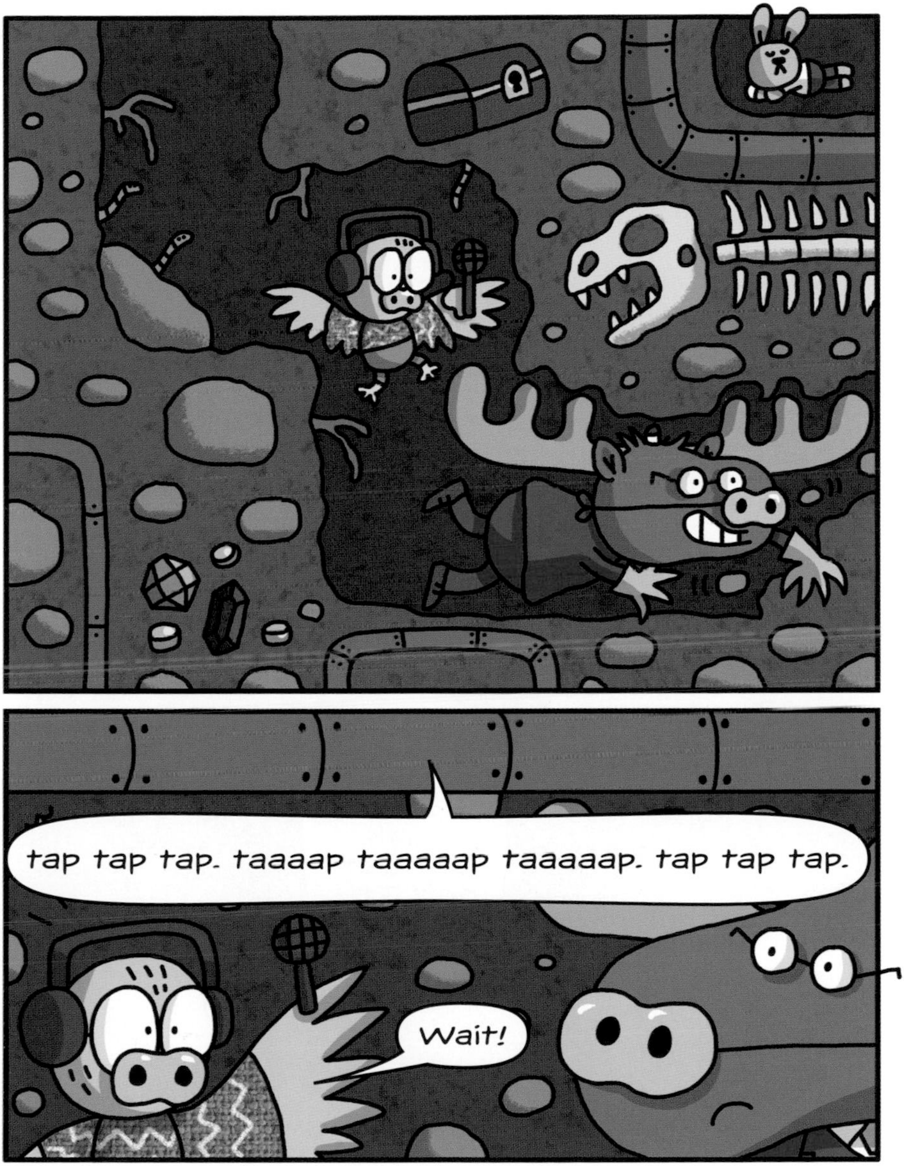
tap tap tap. taaaap taaaaap taaaaap. tap tap tap.
Wait!

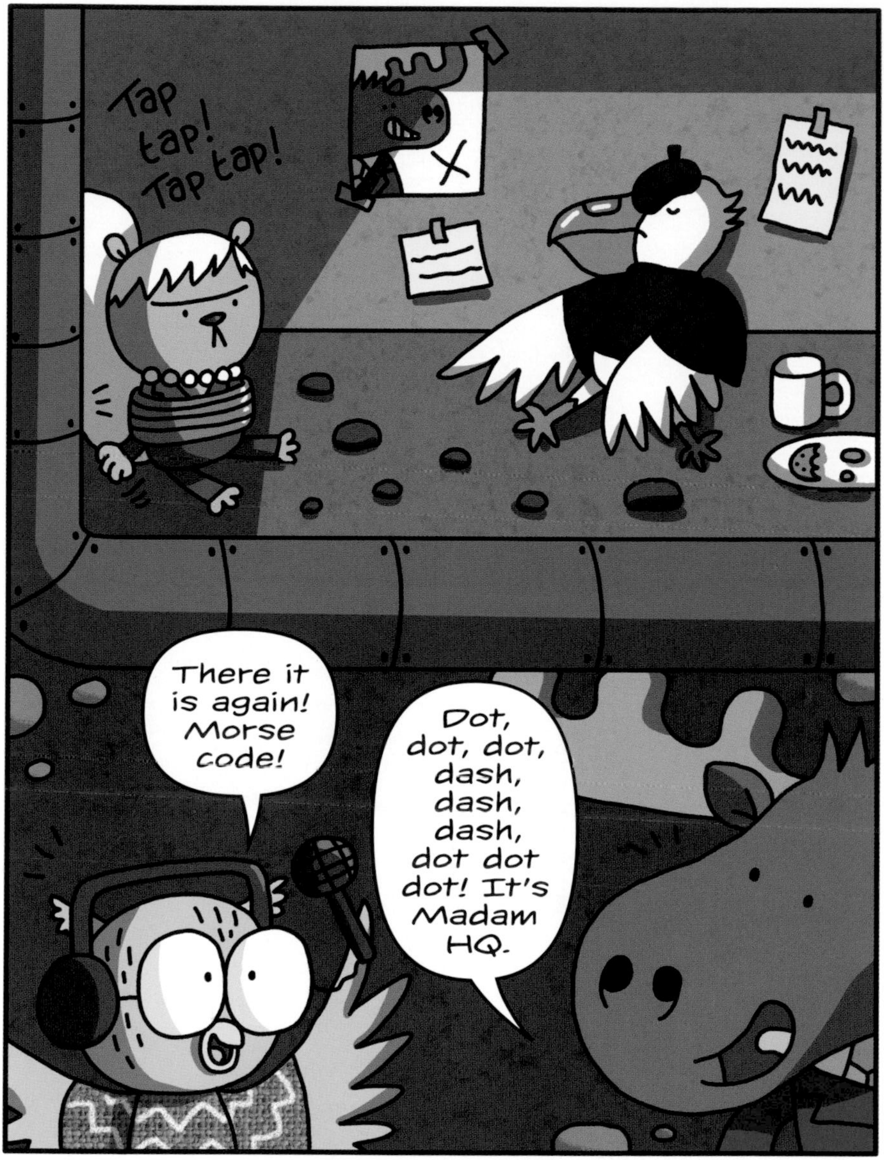
Tap tap! Tap tap!
There it is again! Morse code!
Dot, dot, dot, dash, dash, dash, dot dot dot! It's Madam HQ.

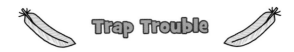

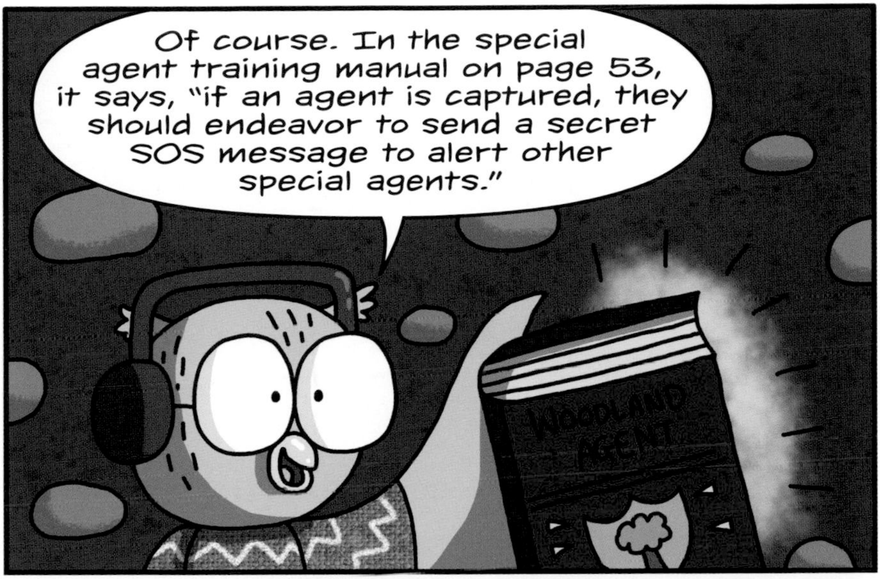
Of course. In the special agent training manual on page 53, it says, "if an agent is captured, they should endeavor to send a secret SOS message to alert other special agents."
WOODLAND AGENT

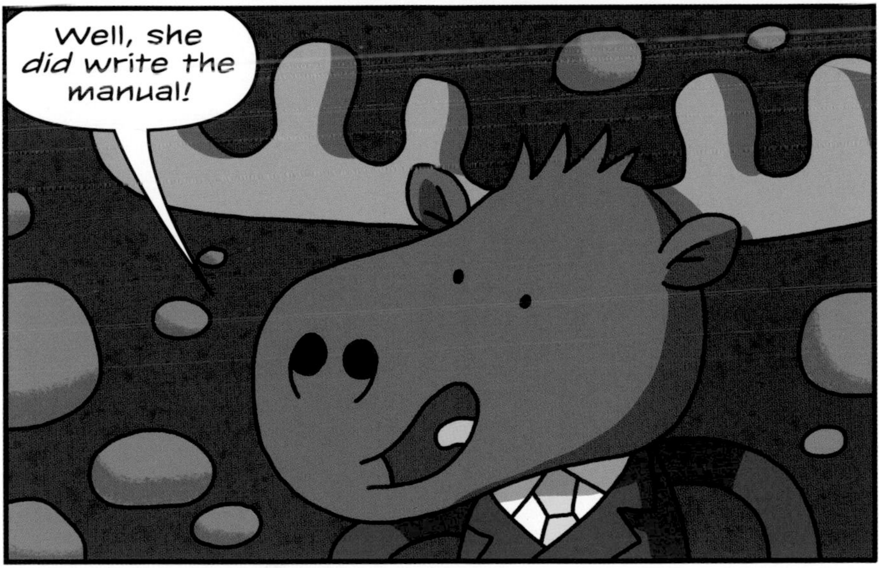
Well, she *did* write the manual!

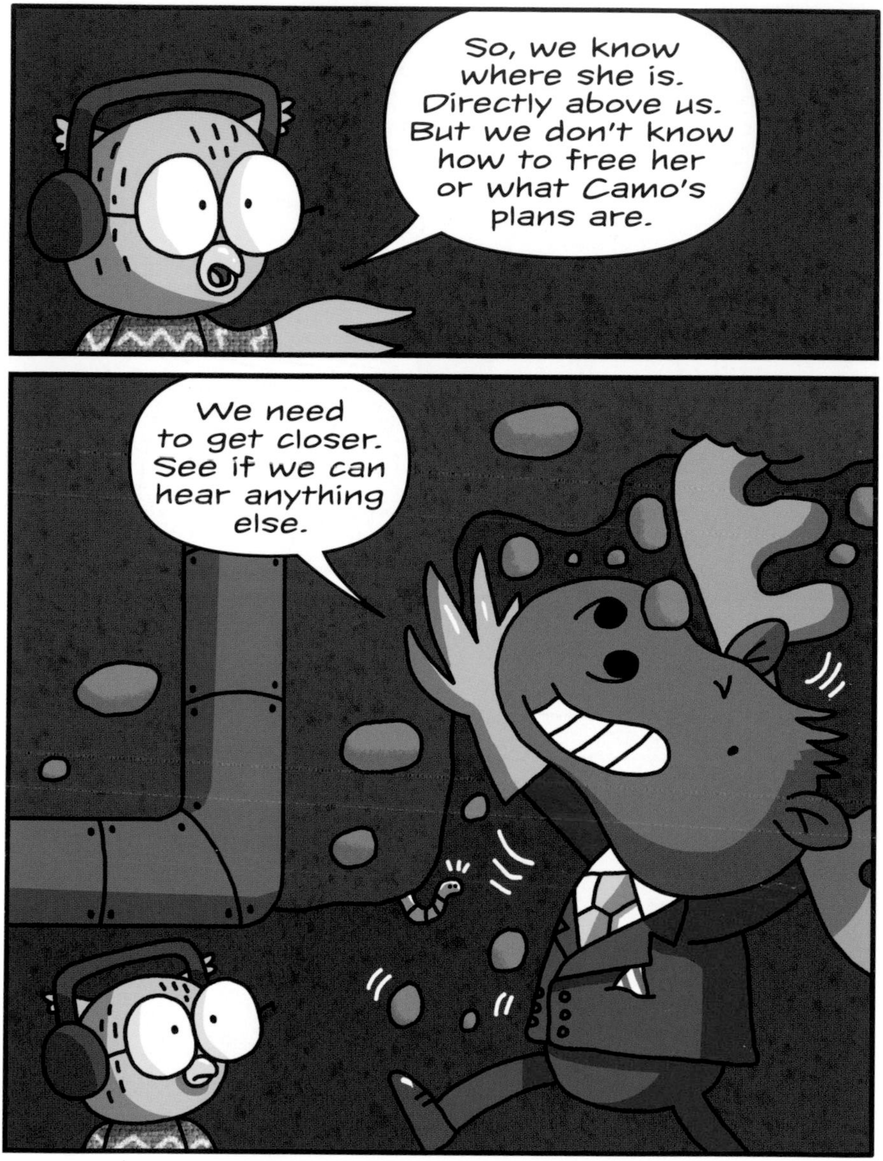
So, we know where she is. Directly above us. But we don't know how to free her or what Camo's plans are.
We need to get closer. See if we can hear anything else.

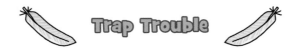

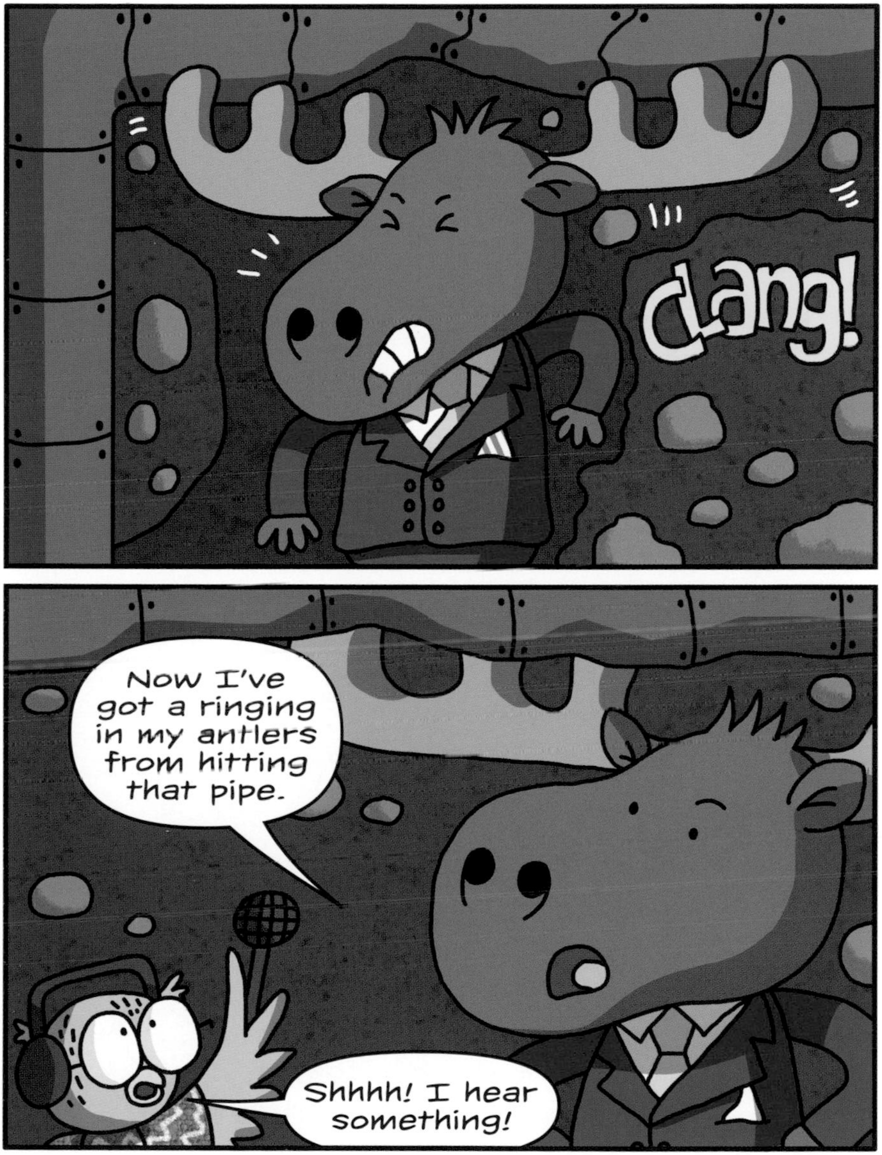
Clang!
Now I've got a ringing in my antlers from hitting that pipe.
Shhhh! I hear something!

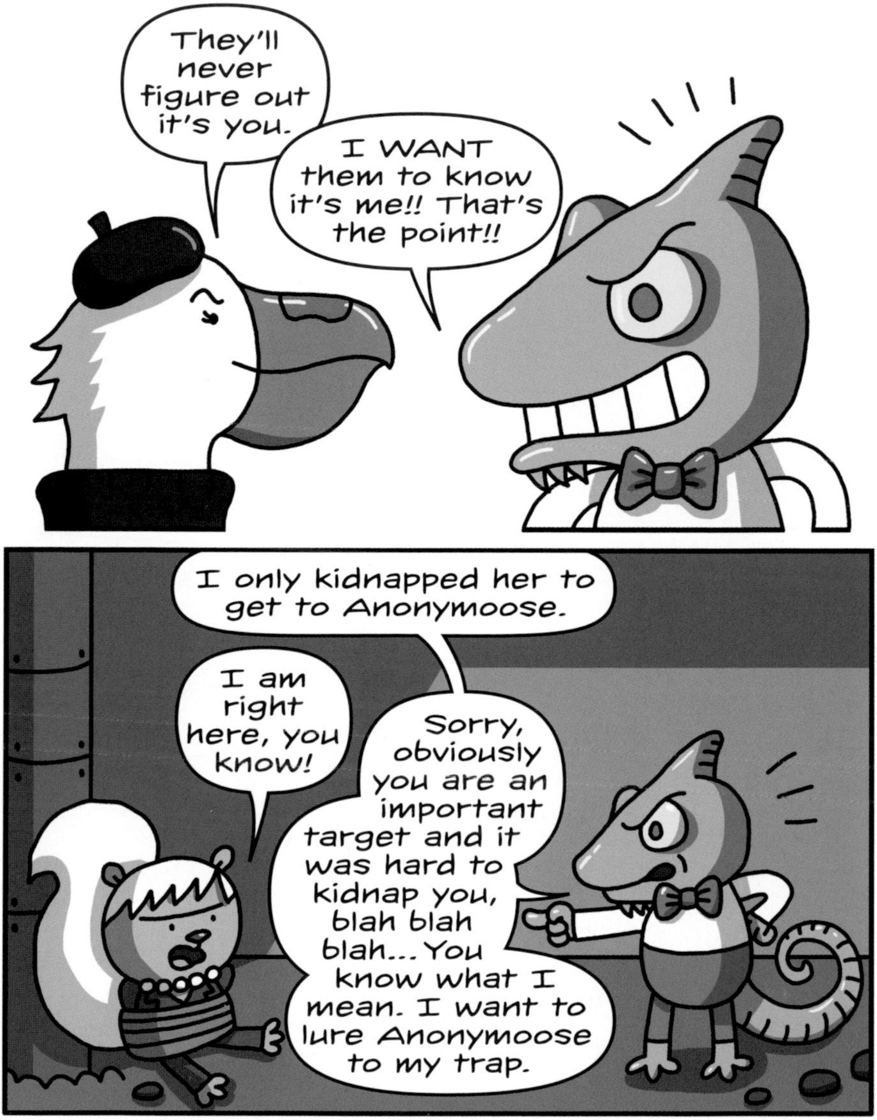
They'll never figure out it's you.
I WANT them to know it's me!! That's the point!!
I only kidnapped her to get to Anonymoose.
I am right here, you know!
Sorry, obviously you are an important target and it was hard to kidnap you, blah blah blah... You know what I mean. I want to lure Anonymoose to my trap.

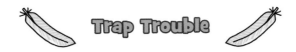

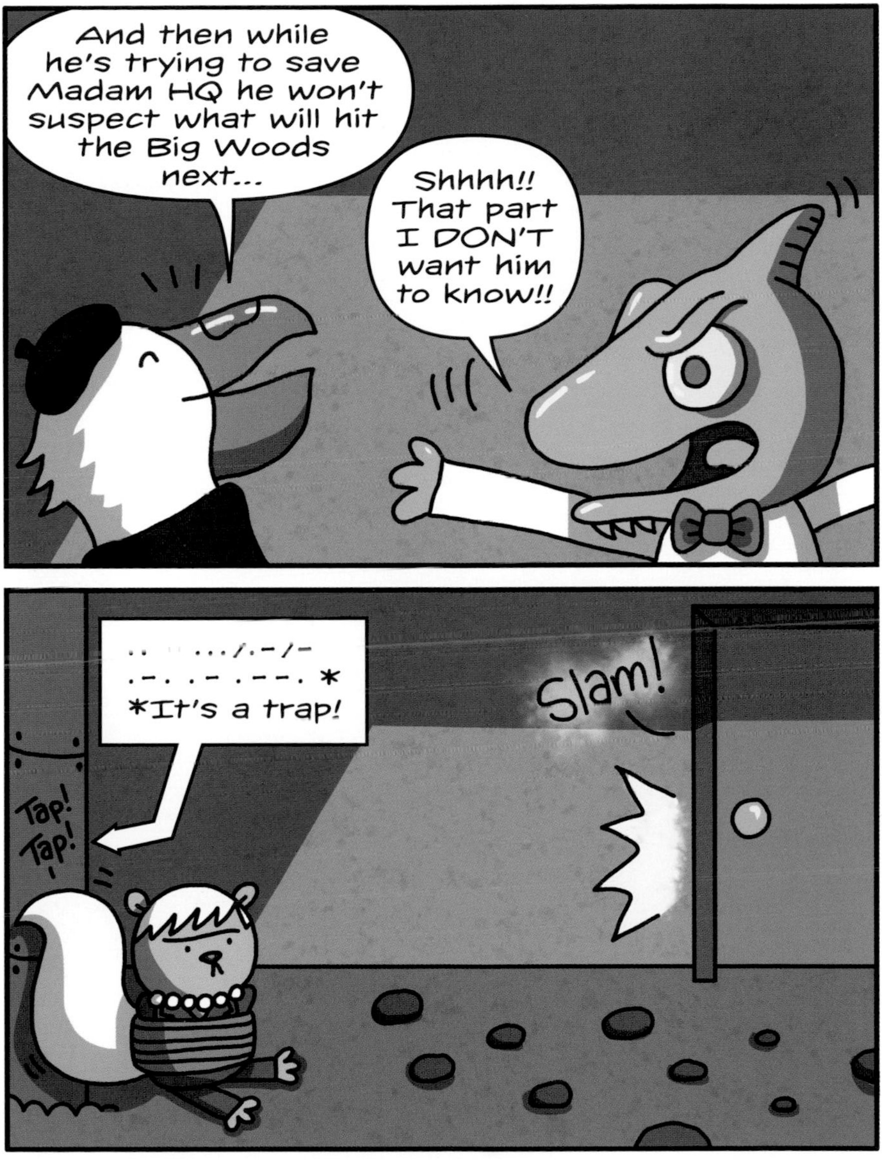
And then while he's trying to save Madam HQ he won't suspect what will hit the Big Woods next...
Shhhh!! That part I DON'T want him to know!!
.. - .../.-/-
.-. .- .--. *
*It's a trap!
Slam!
Tap! Tap!

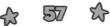

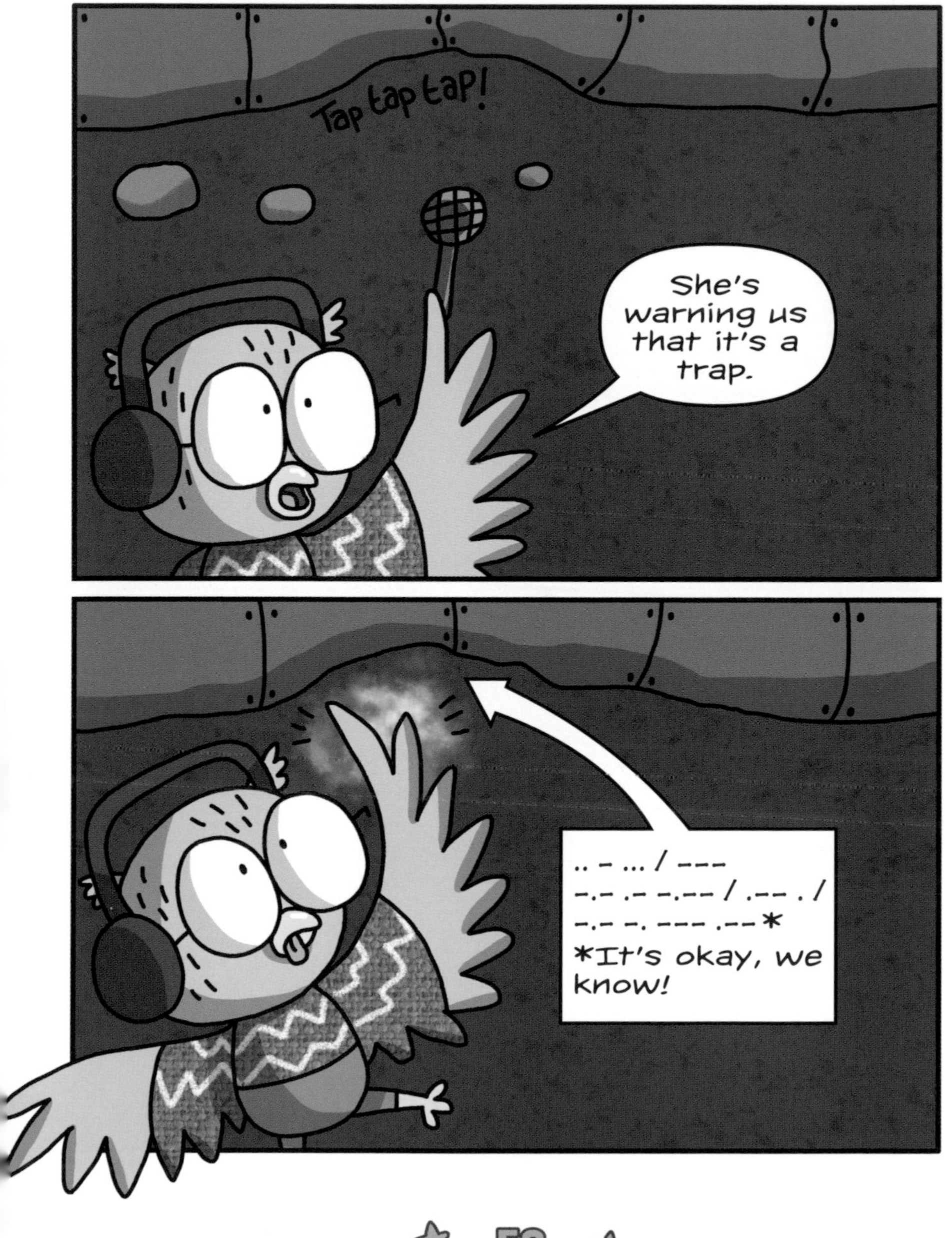
Tap tap tap!
She's warning us that it's a trap.
.. - ... / ---
-.- .- -.-- / .-- . /
-.- -. --- .--*
*It's okay, we know!

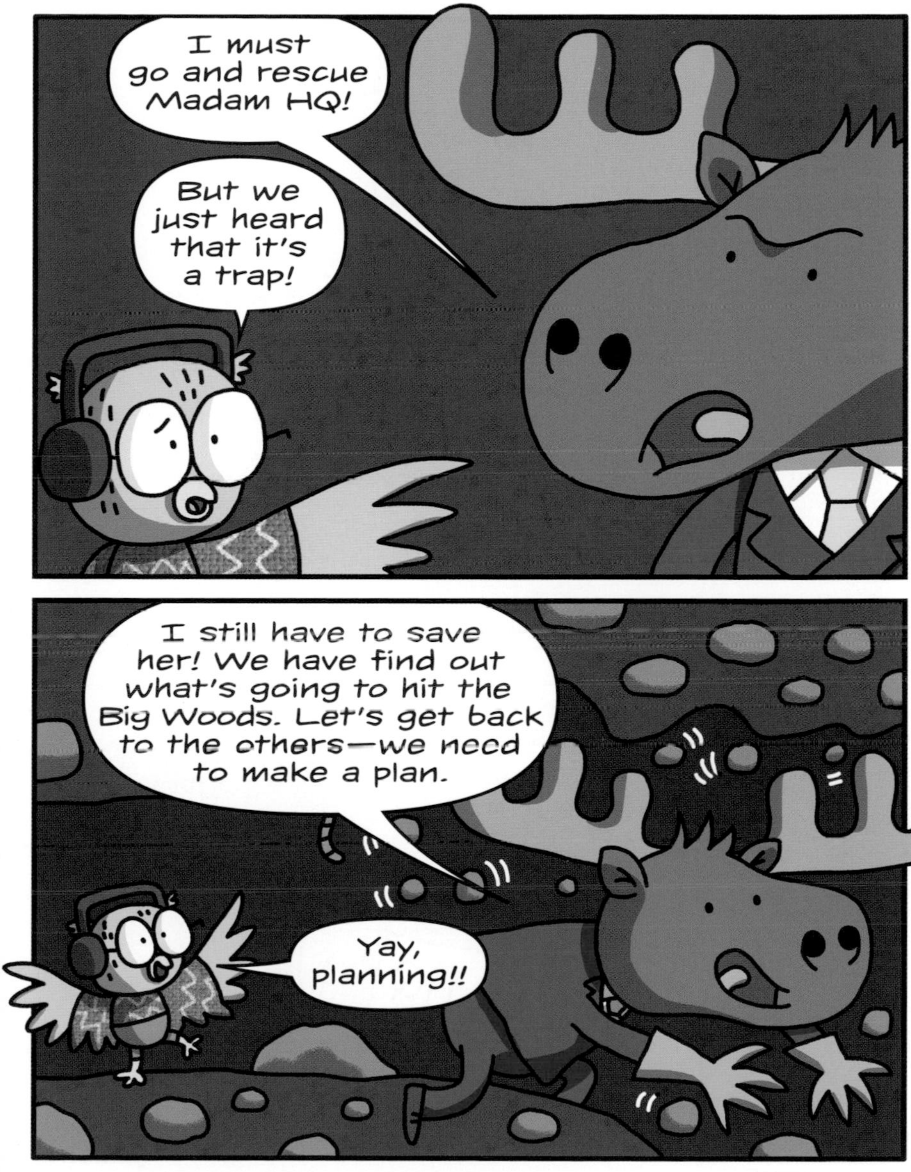
I must go and rescue Madam HQ!
But we just heard that it's a trap!
I still have to save her! We have find out what's going to hit the Big Woods. Let's get back to the others—we need to make a plan.
Yay, planning!!

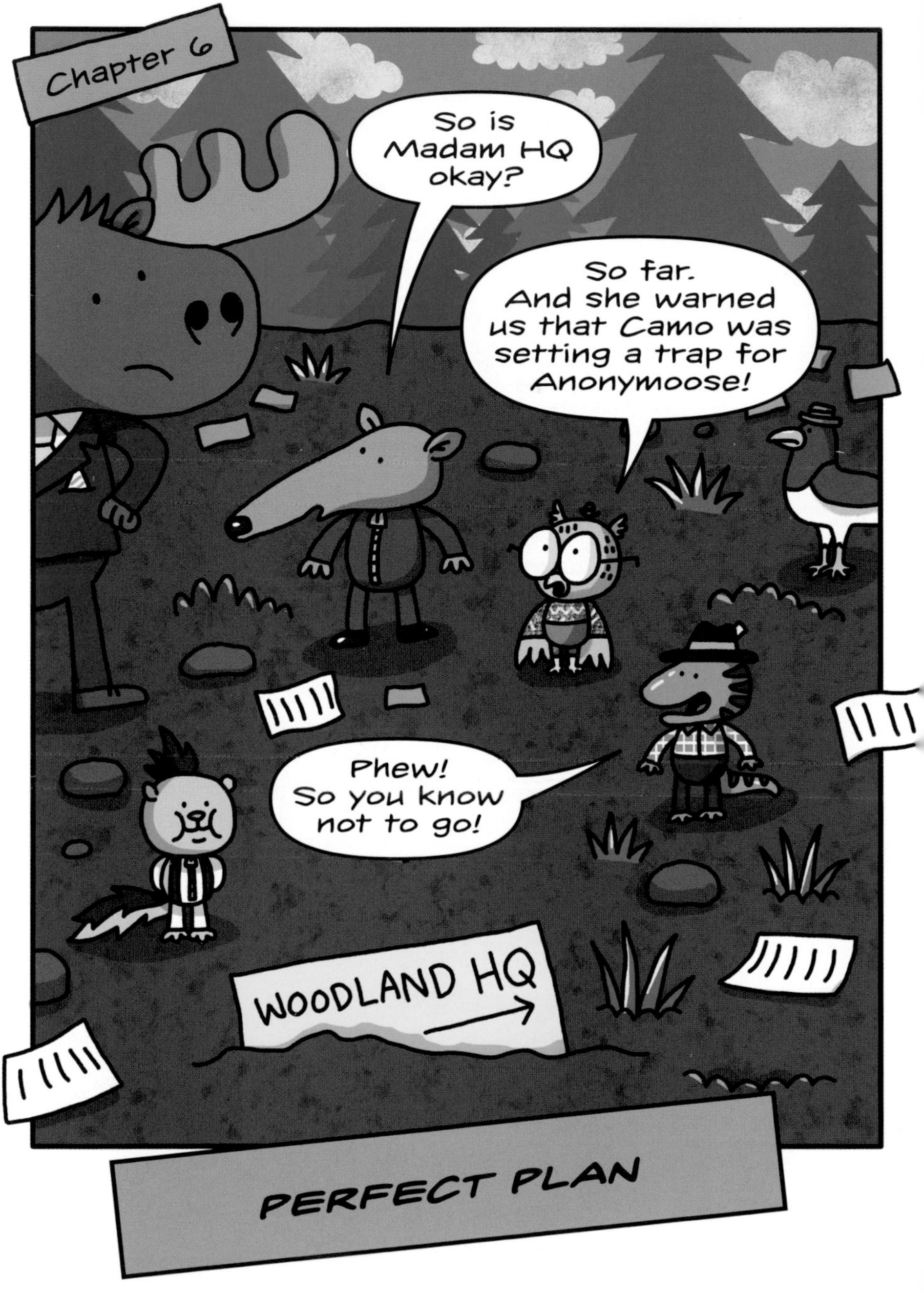
Chapter 6
So is Madam HQ okay?
So far. And she warned us that Camo was setting a trap for Anonymoose!
Phew! So you know not to go!
WOODLAND HQ
PERFECT PLAN

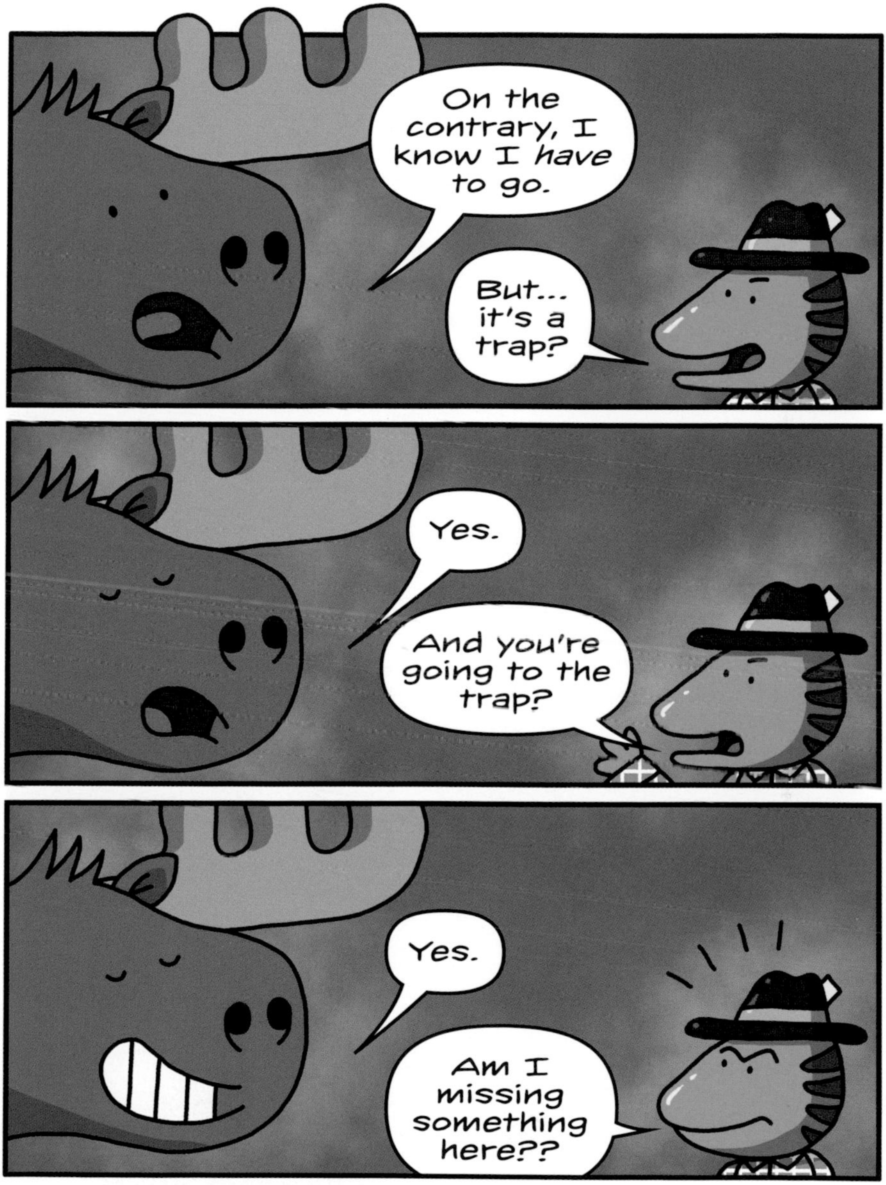
On the contrary, I know I *have* to go.
But... it's a trap?
Yes.
And you're going to the trap?
Yes.
Am I missing something here??

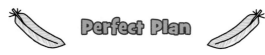

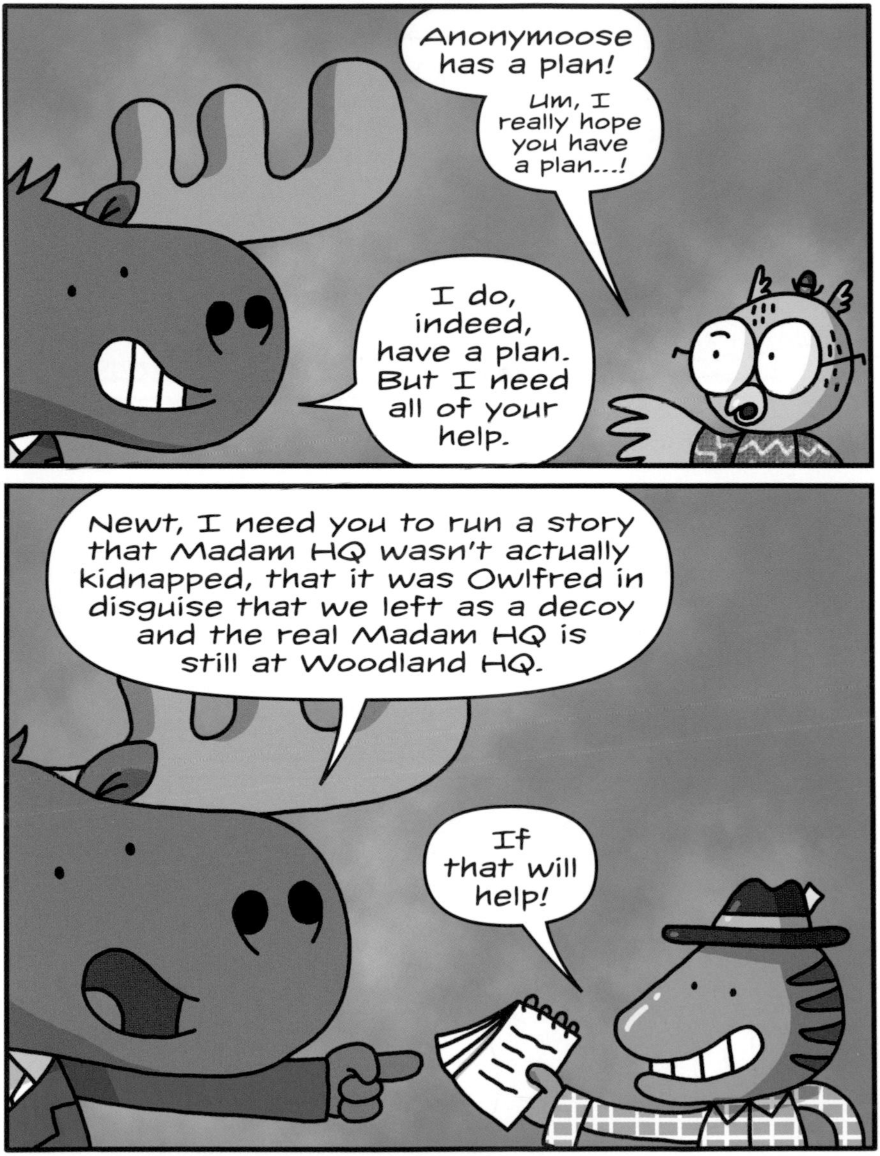
Anonymoose has a plan!
Um, I really hope you have a plan...!
I do, indeed, have a plan. But I need all of your help.
Newt, I need you to run a story that Madam HQ wasn't actually kidnapped, that it was Owlfred in disguise that we left as a decoy and the real Madam HQ is still at Woodland HQ.
If that will help!

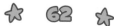

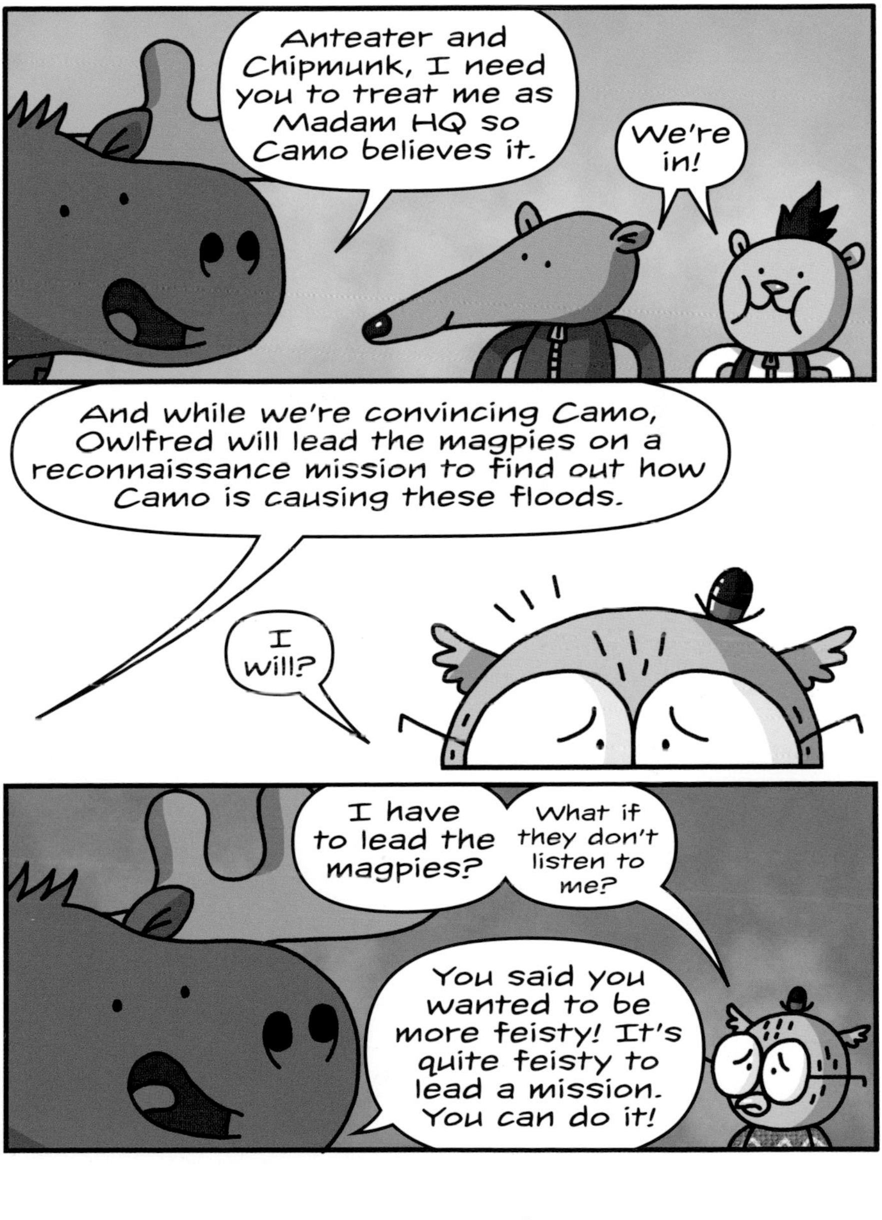
Anteater and Chipmunk, I need you to treat me as Madam HQ so Camo believes it.
We're in!
And while we're convincing Camo, Owlfred will lead the magpies on a reconnaissance mission to find out how Camo is causing these floods.
I will?
I have to lead the magpies?
What if they don't listen to me?
You said you wanted to be more feisty! It's quite feisty to lead a mission. You can do it!

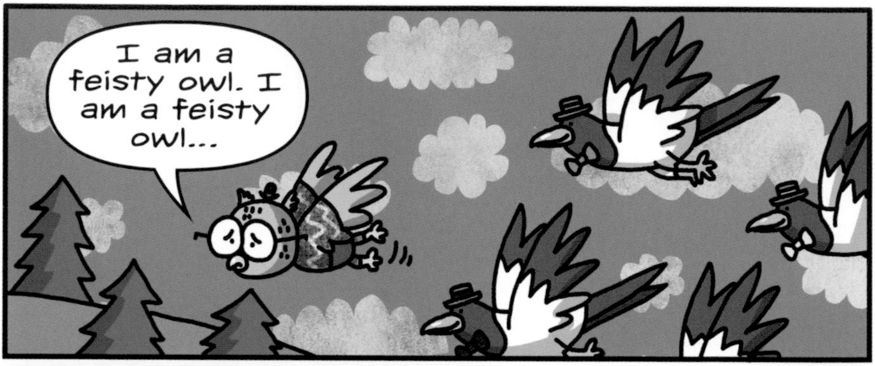
I am a feisty owl. I am a feisty owl...

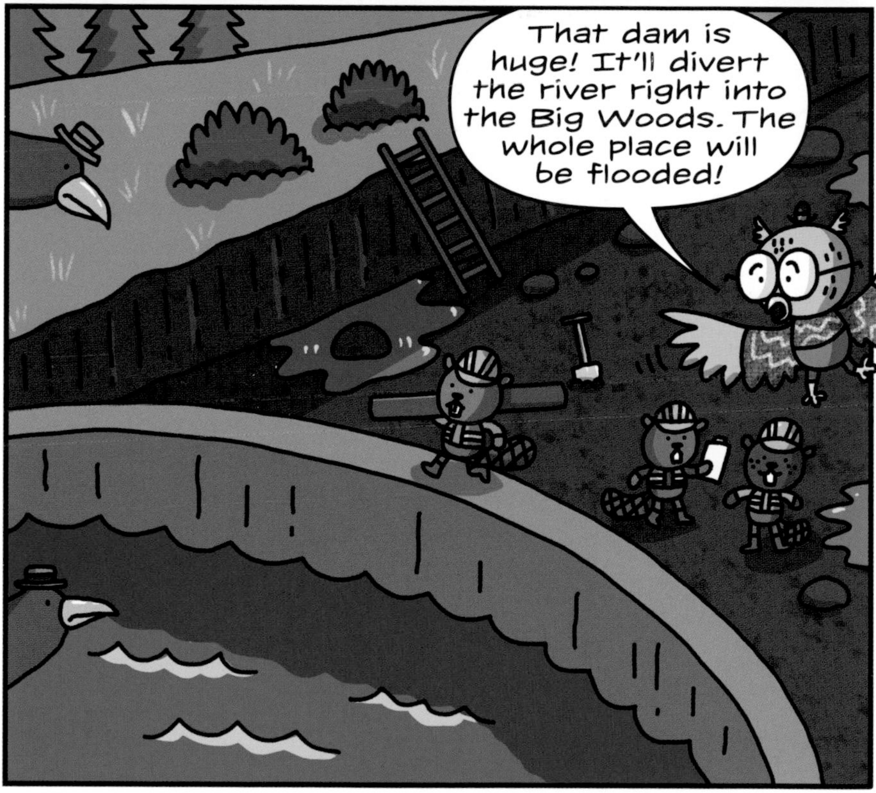
That dam is huge! It'll divert the river right into the Big Woods. The whole place will be flooded!

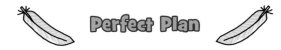

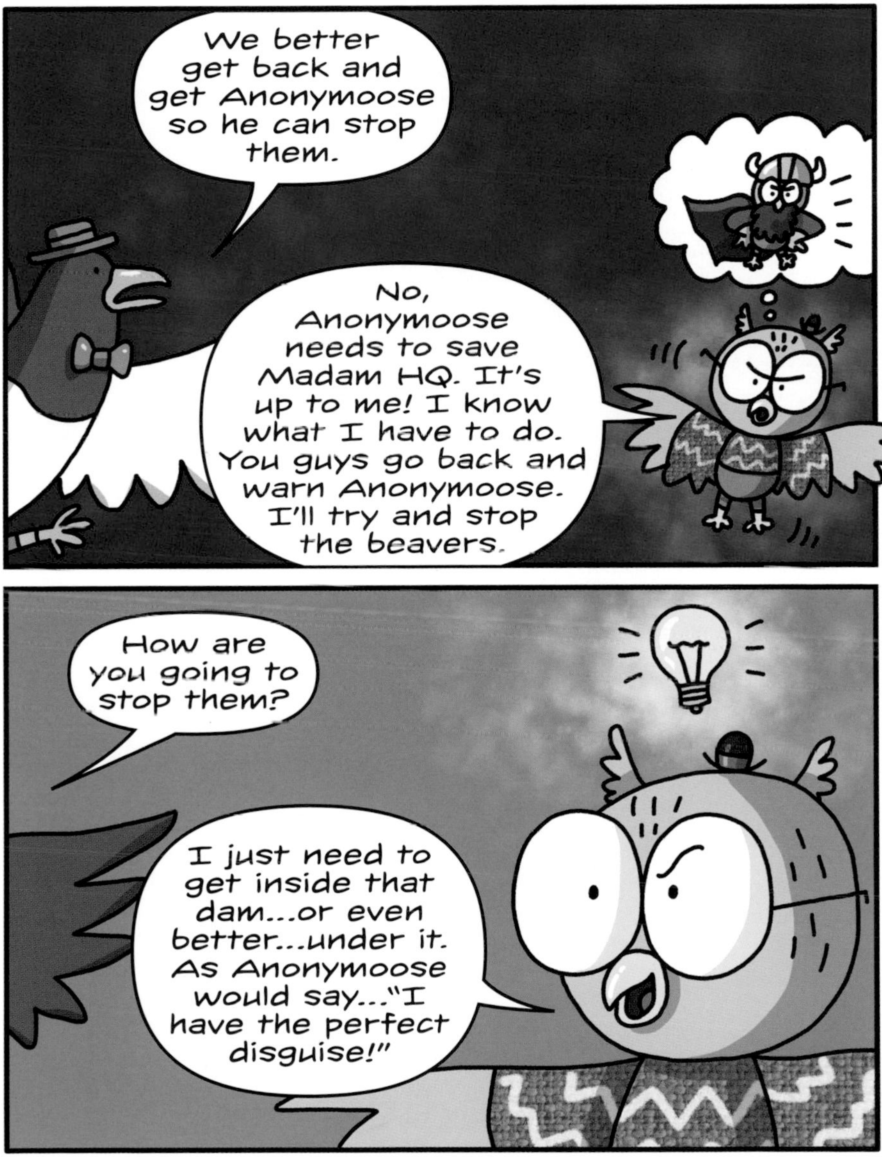
We better get back and get Anonymoose so he can stop them.
No, Anonymoose needs to save Madam HQ. It's up to me! I know what I have to do. You guys go back and warn Anonymoose. I'll try and stop the beavers.
How are you going to stop them?
I just need to get inside that dam...or even better...under it. As Anonymoose would say..."I have the perfect disguise!"

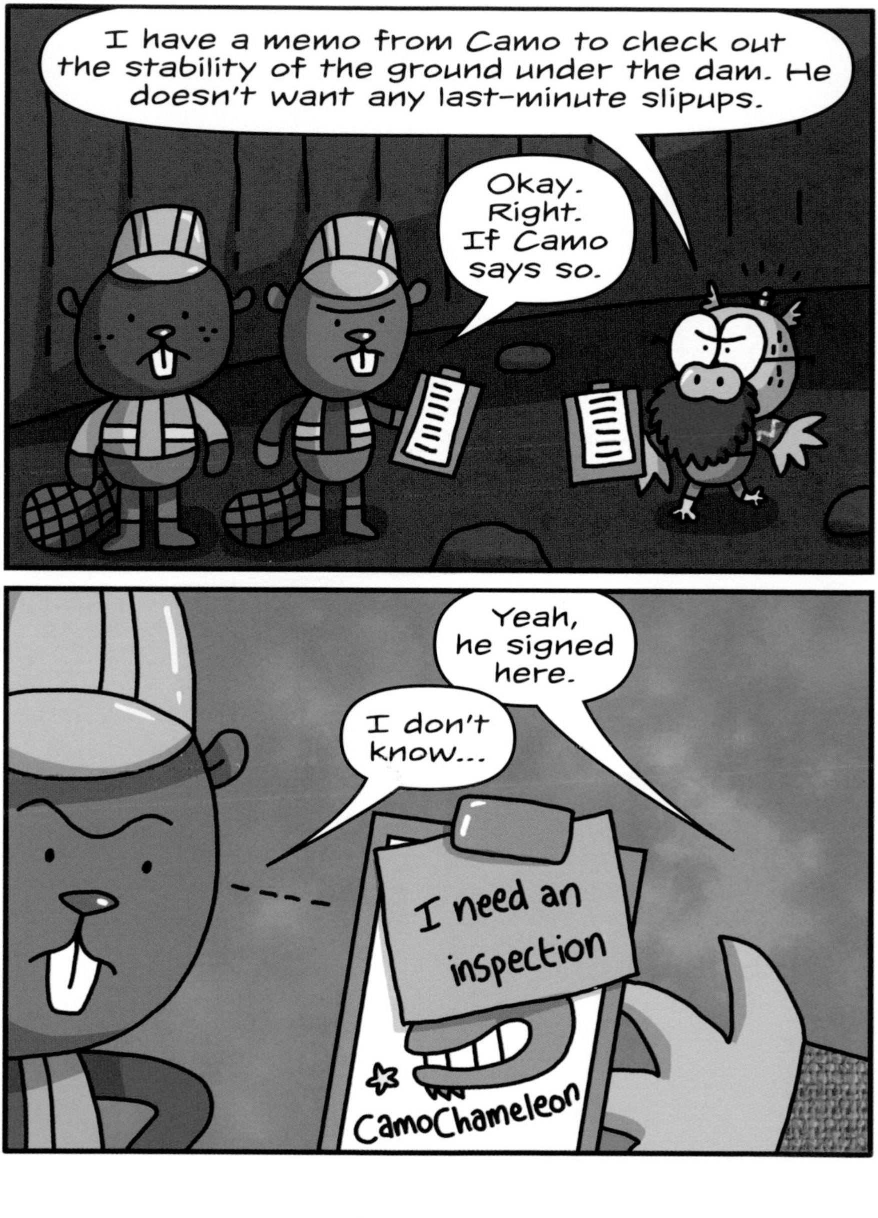
I have a memo from Camo to check out the stability of the ground under the dam. He doesn't want any last-minute slipups.
Okay. Right. If Camo says so.
Yeah, he signed here.
I don't know...
I need an inspection
CamoChameleon

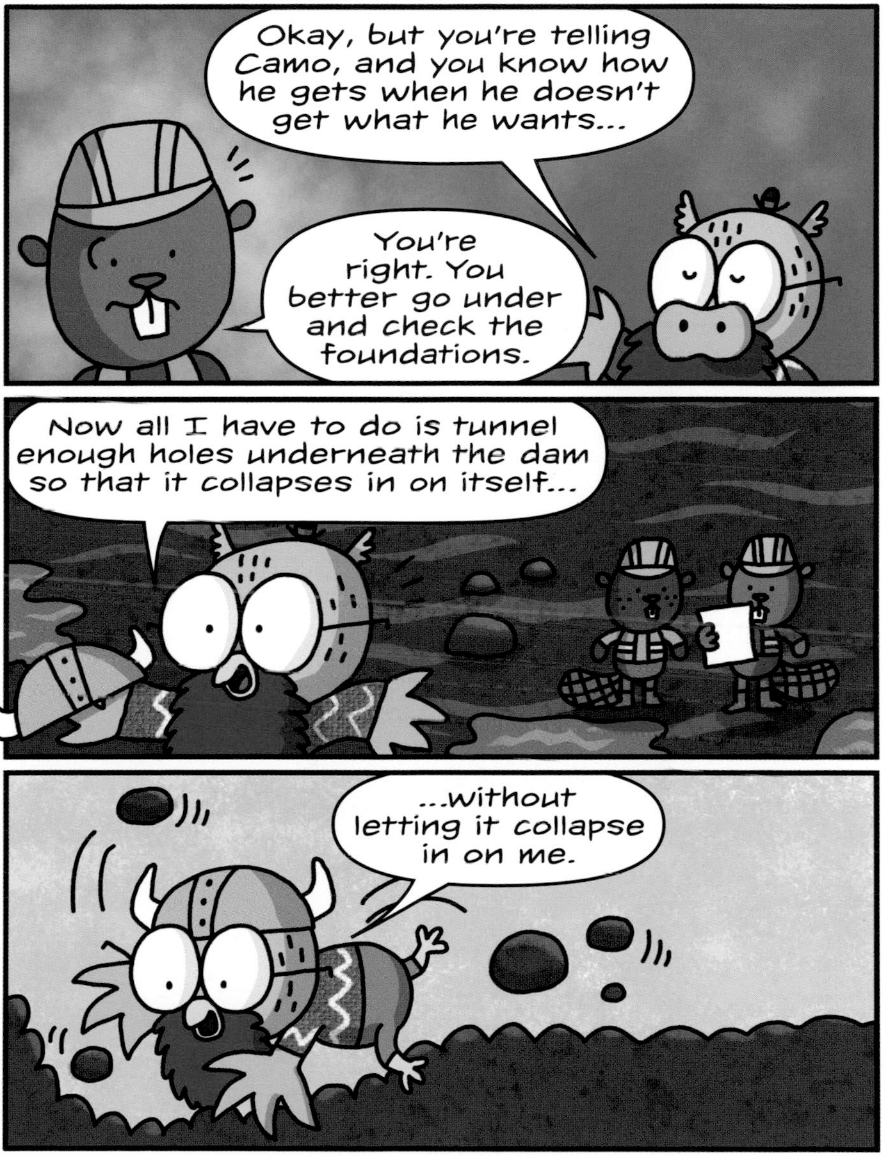
Okay, but you're telling Camo, and you know how he gets when he doesn't get what he wants...
You're right. You better go under and check the foundations.
Now all I have to do is tunnel enough holes underneath the dam so that it collapses in on itself...
...without letting it collapse in on me.

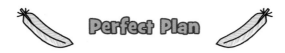

Chapter 7

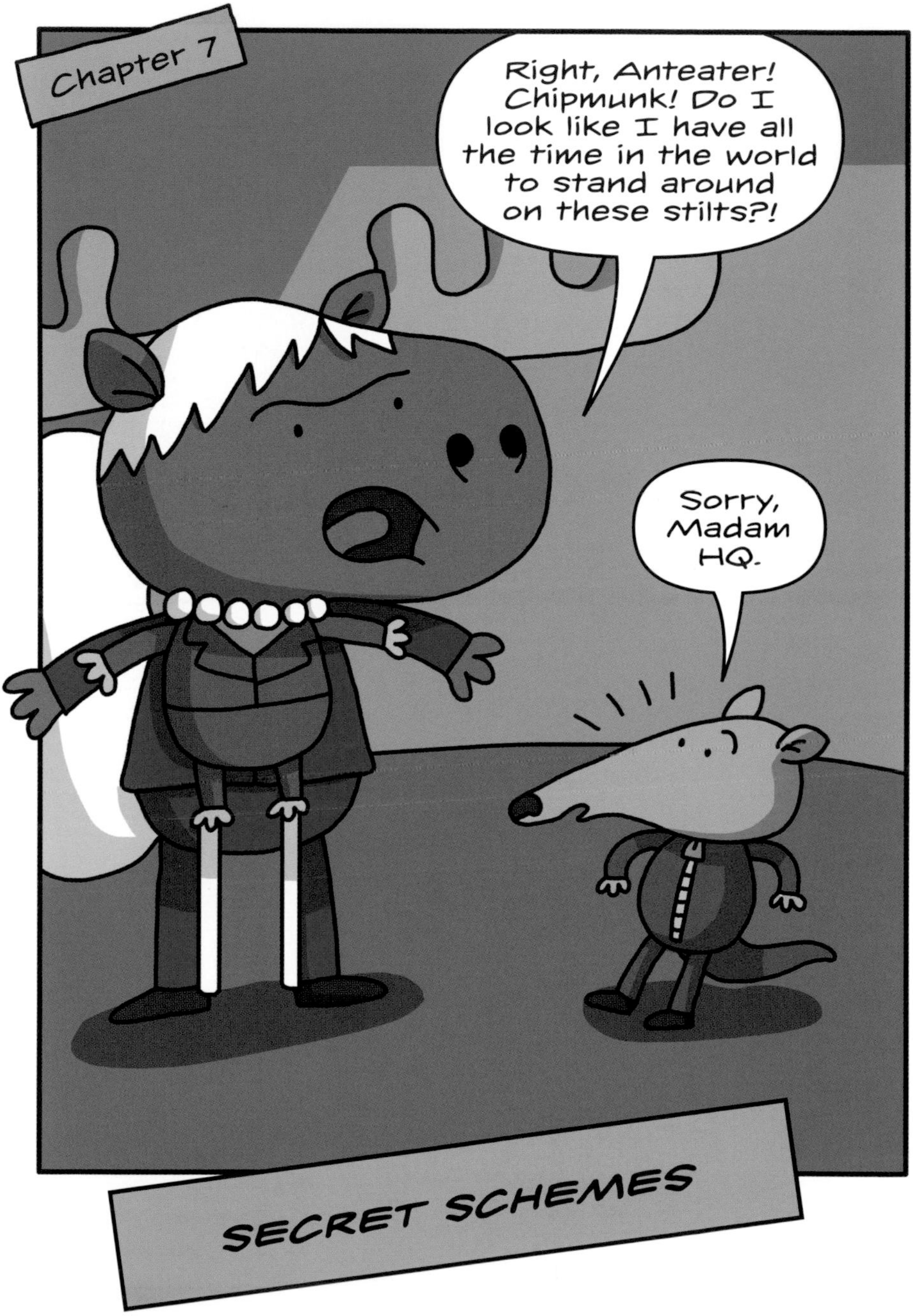
Right, Anteater! Chipmunk! Do I look like I have all the time in the world to stand around on these stilts?!
Sorry, Madam HQ.

SECRET SCHEMES

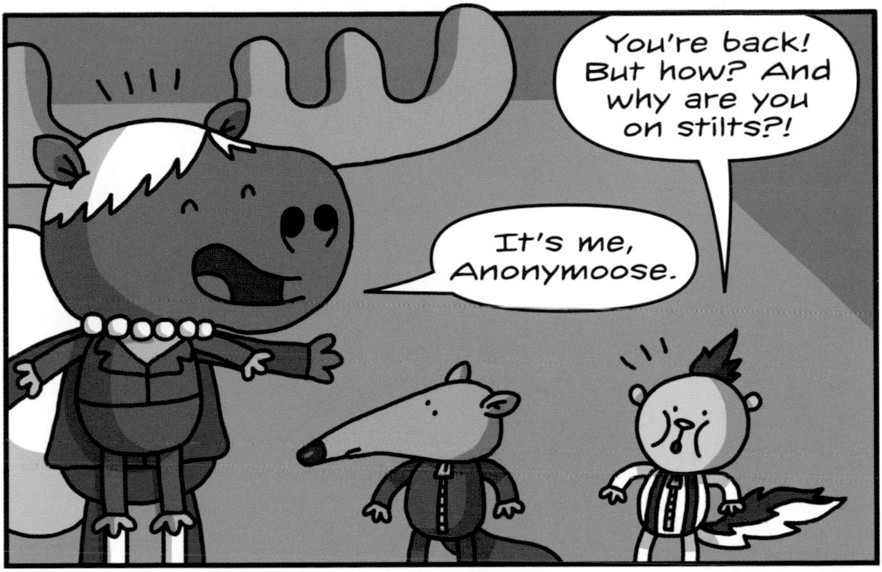
It's me, Anonymoose.
You're back! But how? And why are you on stilts?!

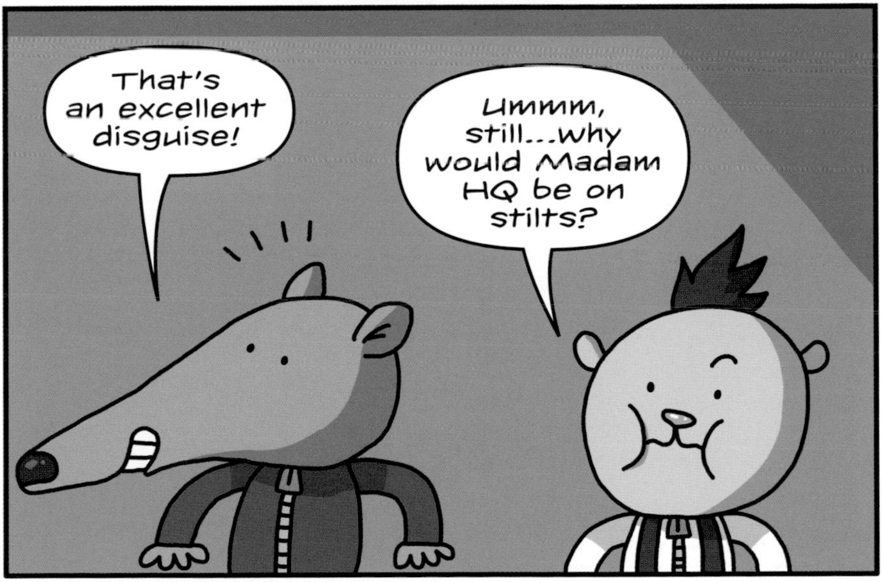
That's an excellent disguise!
Ummm, still...why would Madam HQ be on stilts?

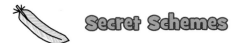

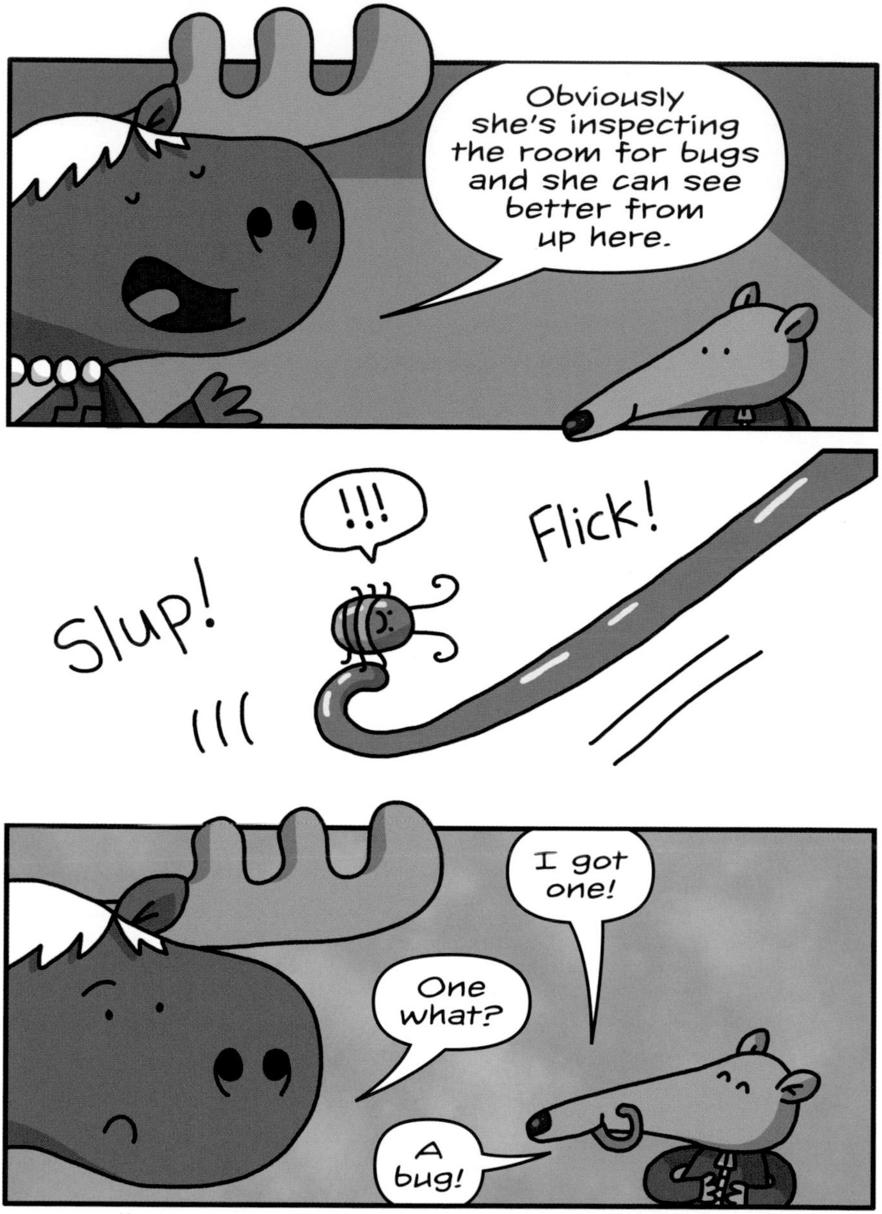
Obviously she's inspecting the room for bugs and she can see better from up here.
!!!
Flick!
Slup!
I got one!
One what?
A bug!

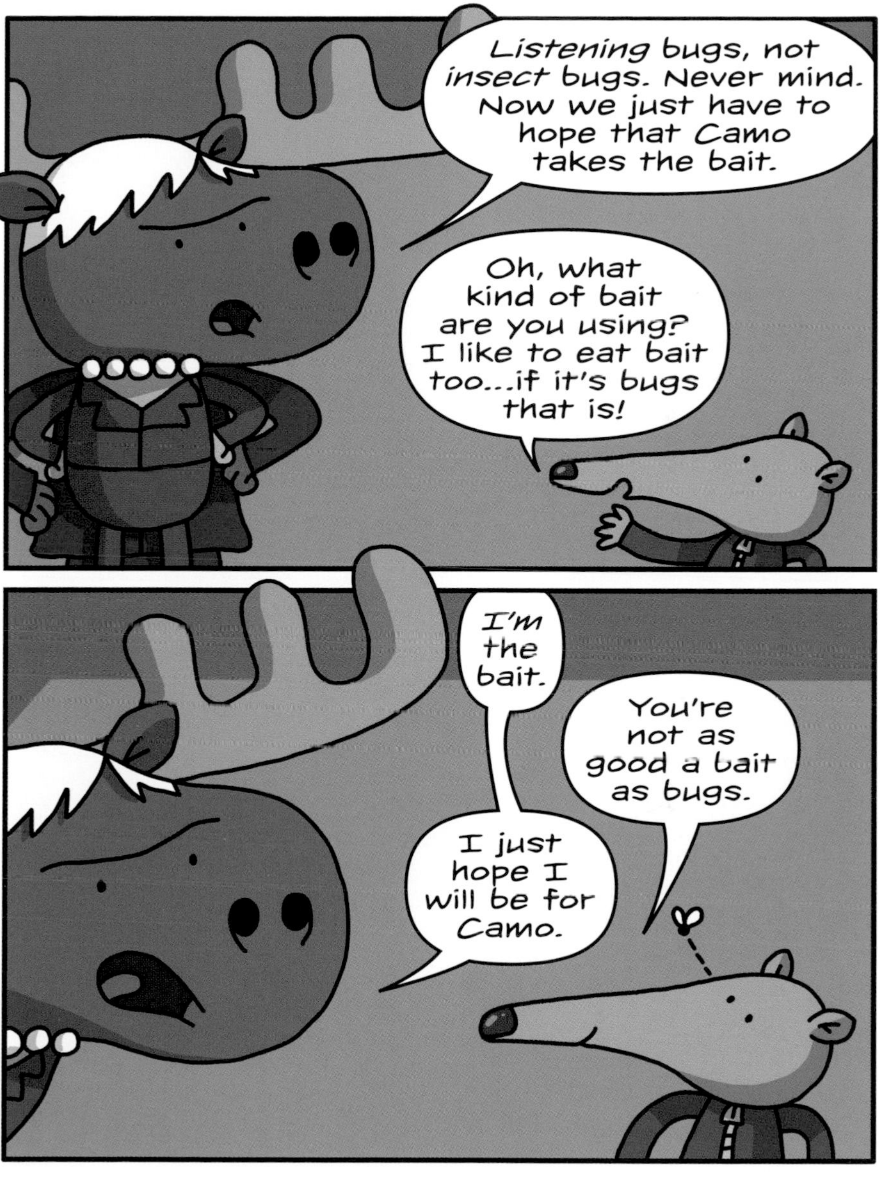
Listening bugs, not *insect* bugs. Never mind. Now we just have to hope that Camo takes the bait.
Oh, what kind of bait are you using? I like to eat bait too...if it's bugs that is!
I'm the bait.
You're not as good a bait as bugs.
I just hope I will be for Camo.

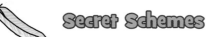

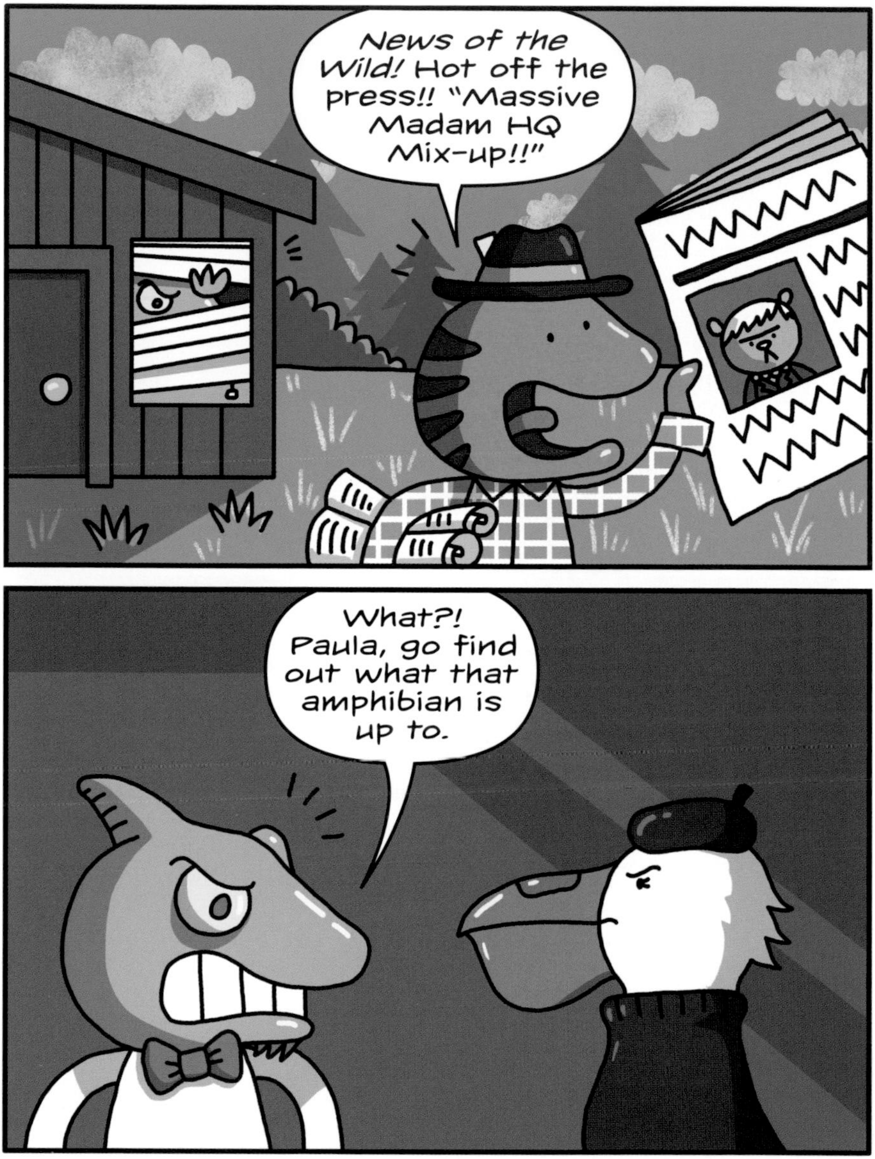
News of the Wild! Hot off the press!! "Massive Madam HQ Mix-up!!"
What?! Paula, go find out what that amphibian is up to.

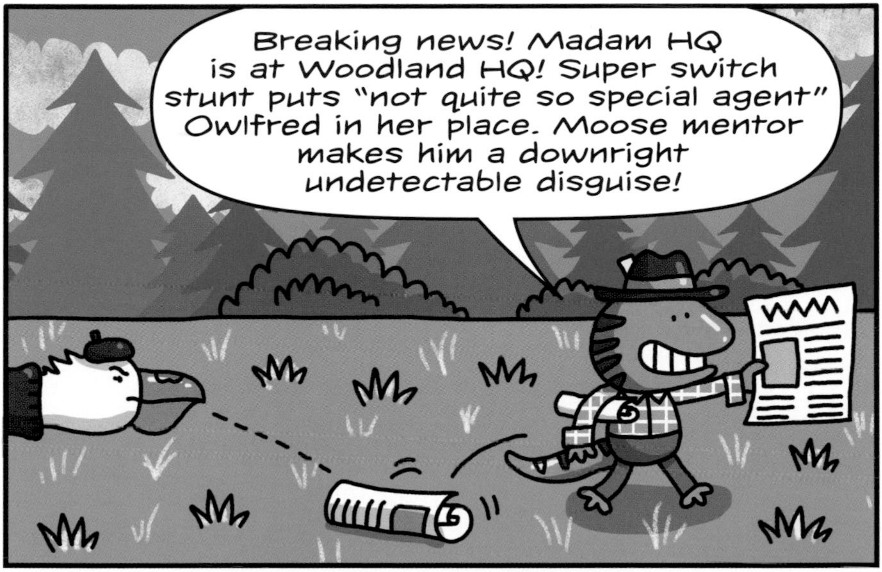
Breaking news! Madam HQ is at Woodland HQ! Super switch stunt puts "not quite so special agent" Owlfred in her place. Moose mentor makes him a downright undetectable disguise!

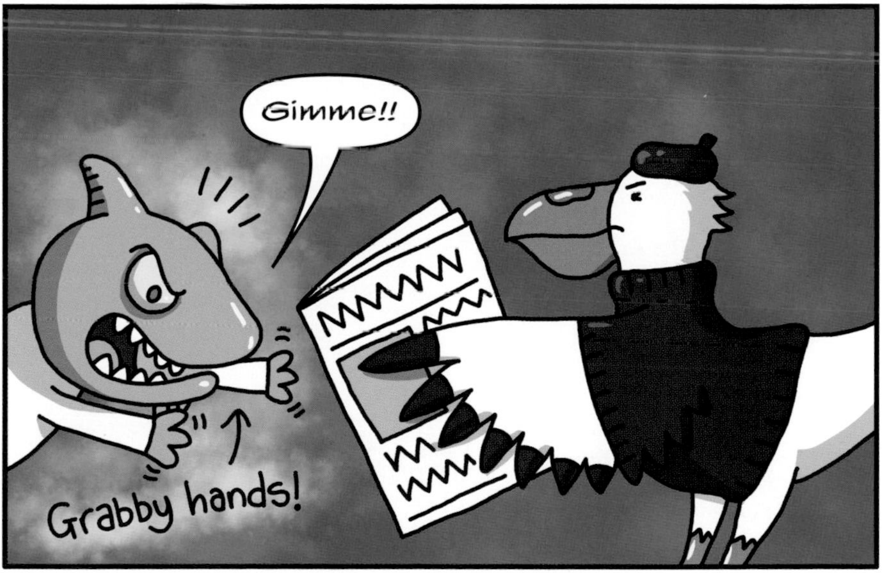
Gimme!!
Grabby hands!

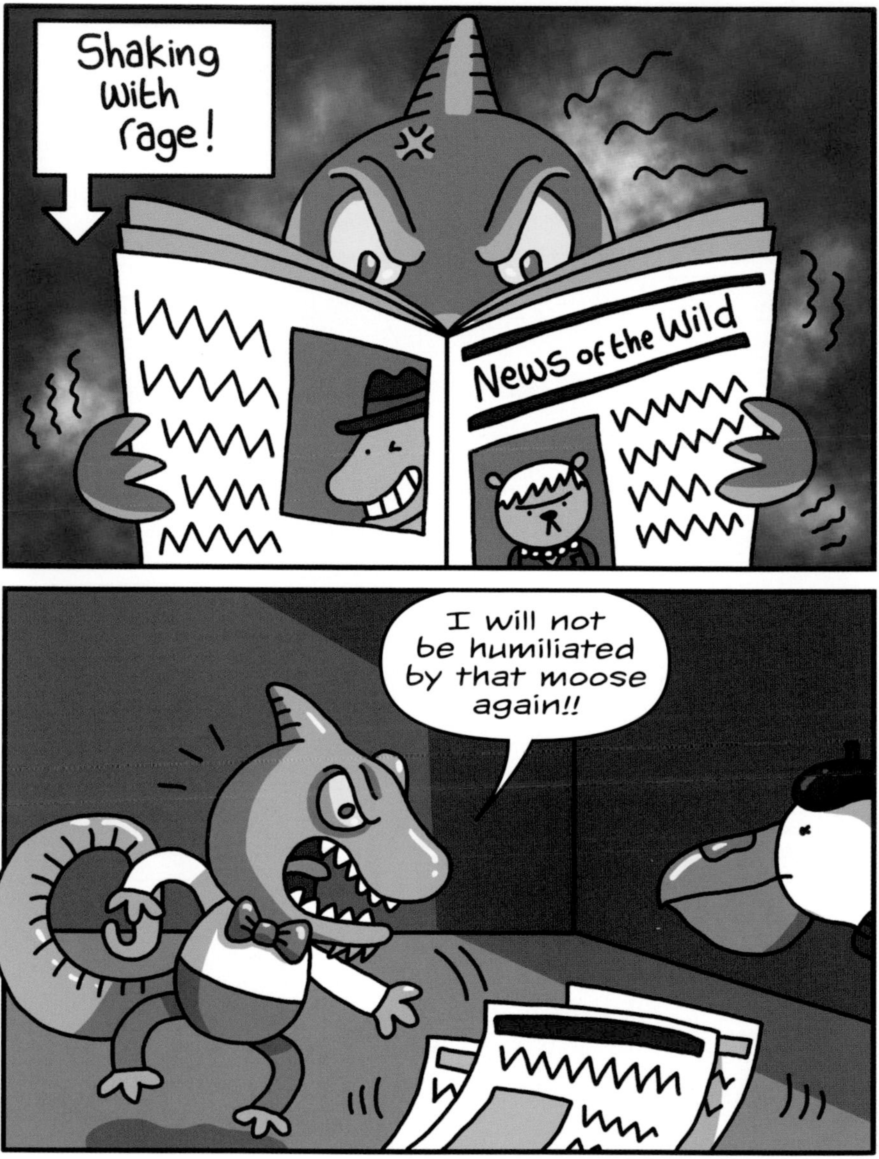
Shaking with rage!
News of the Wild
I will not be humiliated by that moose again!!

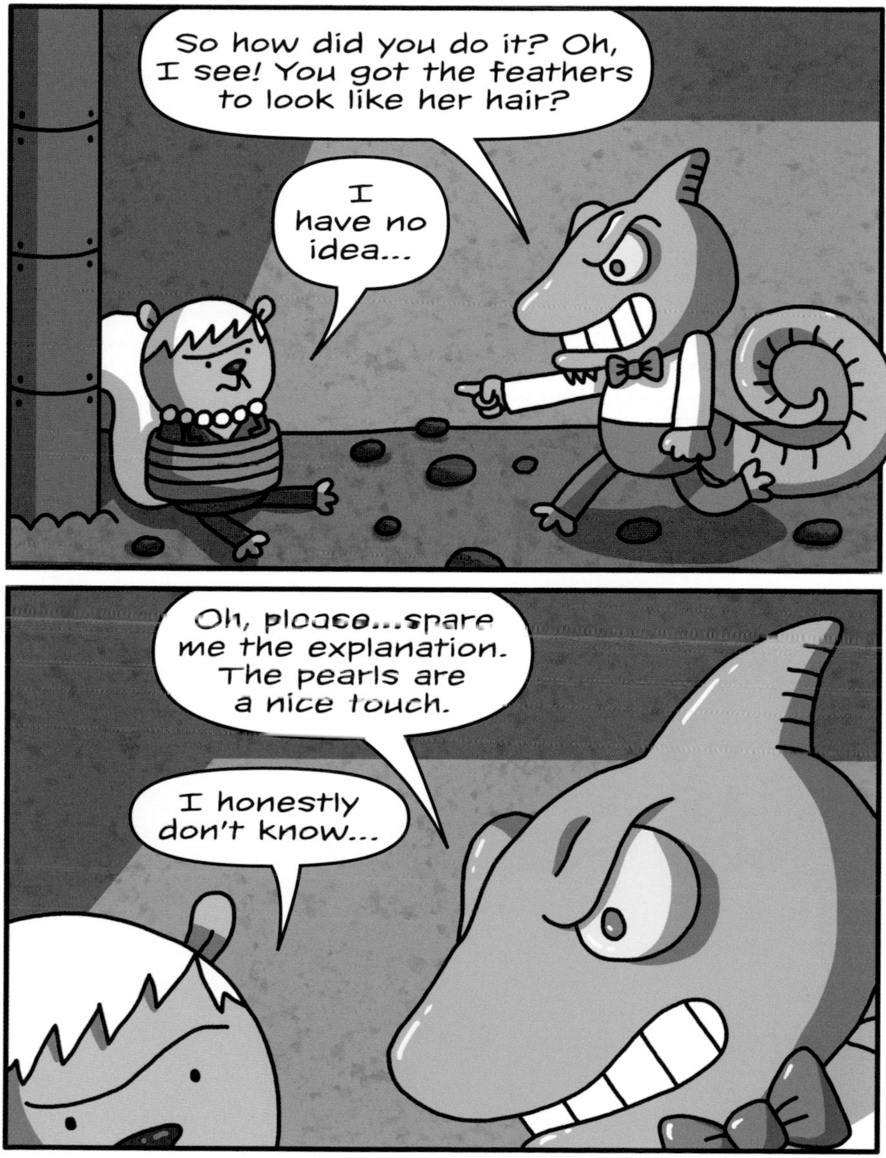
So how did you do it? Oh, I see! You got the feathers to look like her hair?
I have no idea...
Oh, please...spare me the explanation. The pearls are a nice touch.
I honestly don't know...

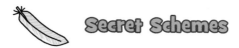

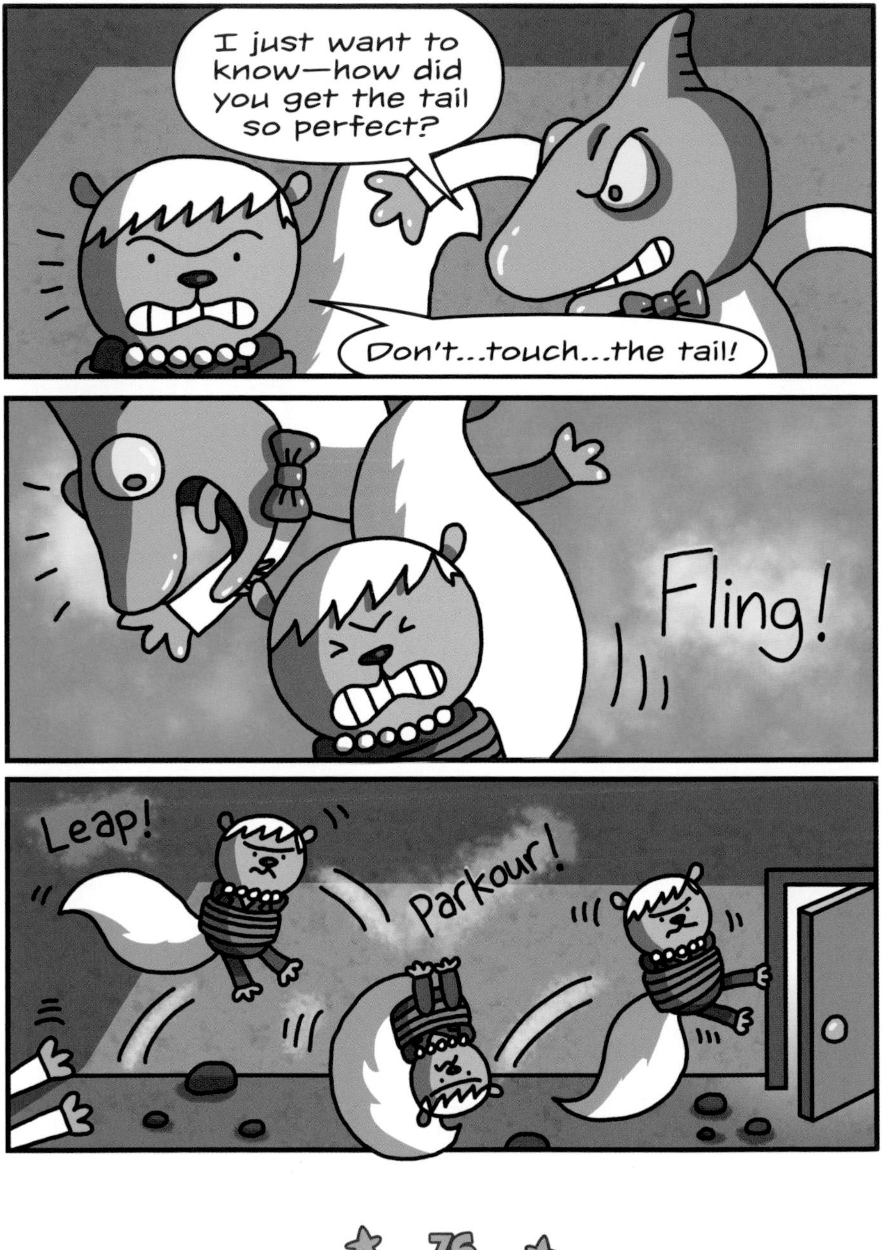
I just want to know—how did you get the tail so perfect?
Don't...touch...the tail!
Fling!
Leap!
Parkour!

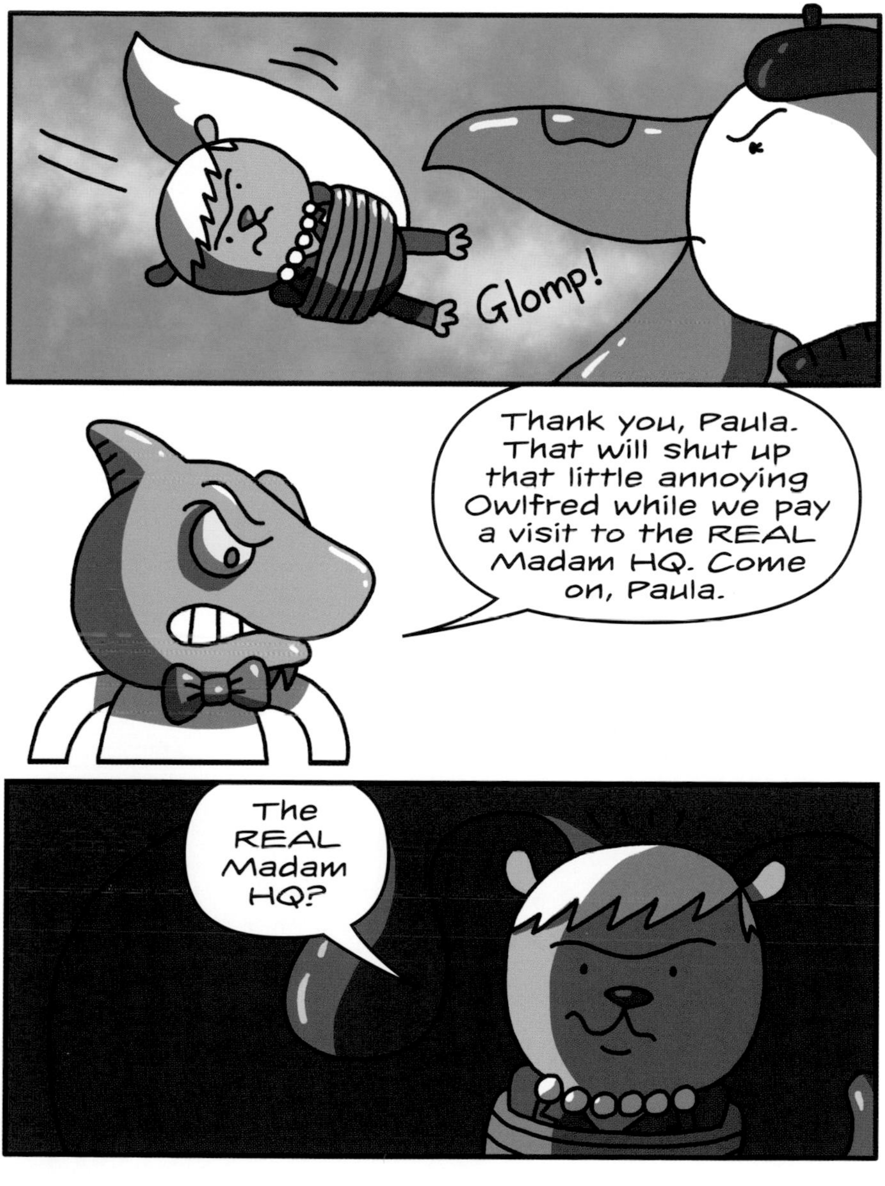
Glomp!
Thank you, Paula. That will shut up that little annoying Owlfred while we pay a visit to the REAL Madam HQ. Come on, Paula.
The REAL Madam HQ?

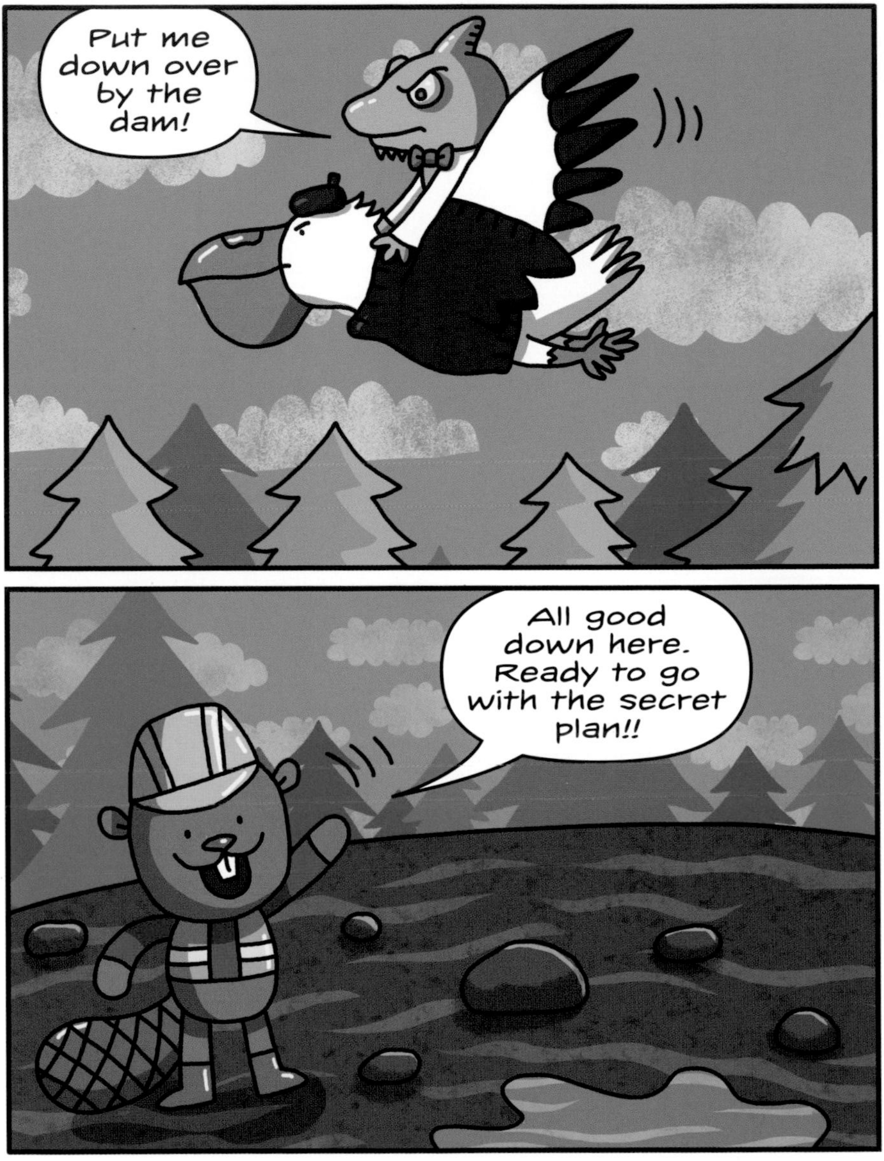
Put me down over by the dam!
All good down here. Ready to go with the secret plan!!

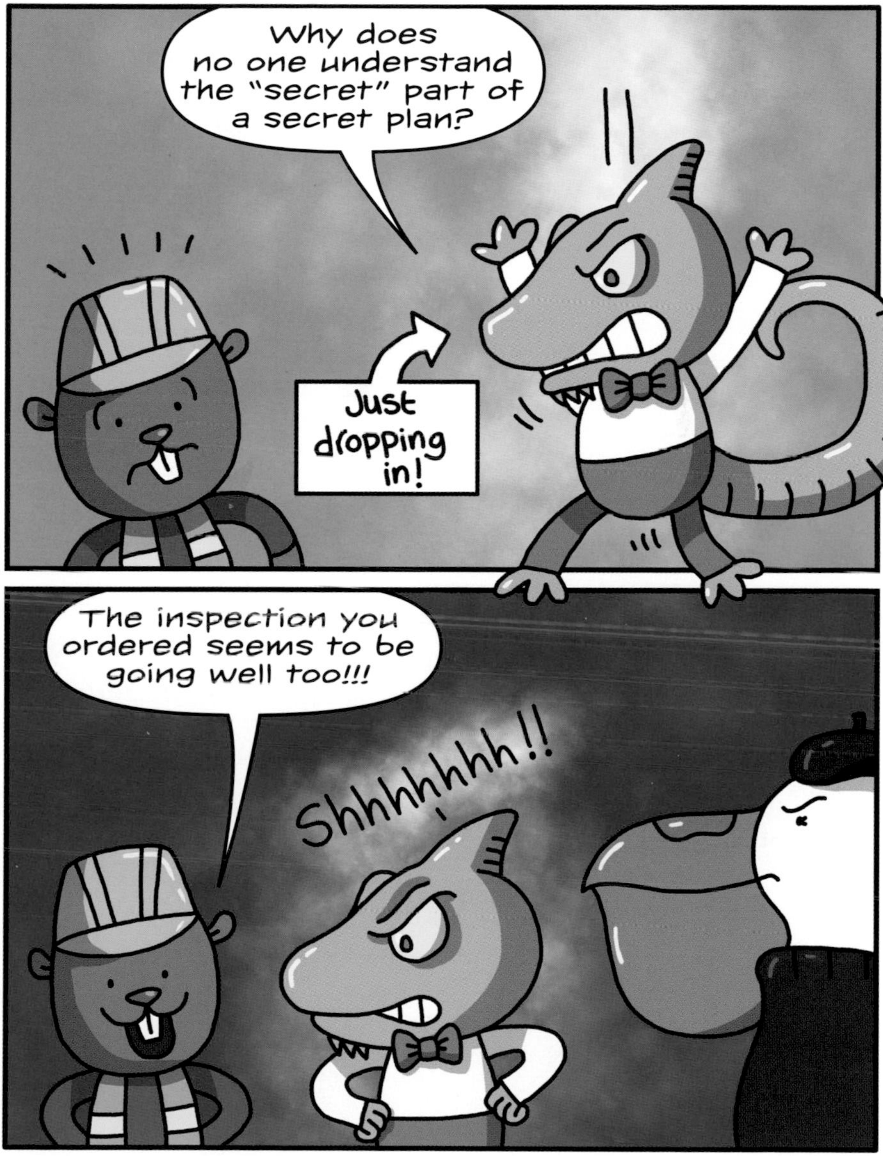
Why does no one understand the "secret" part of a secret plan?
Just dropping in!
The inspection you ordered seems to be going well too!!!
Shhhhhhh!!

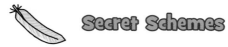

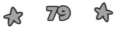

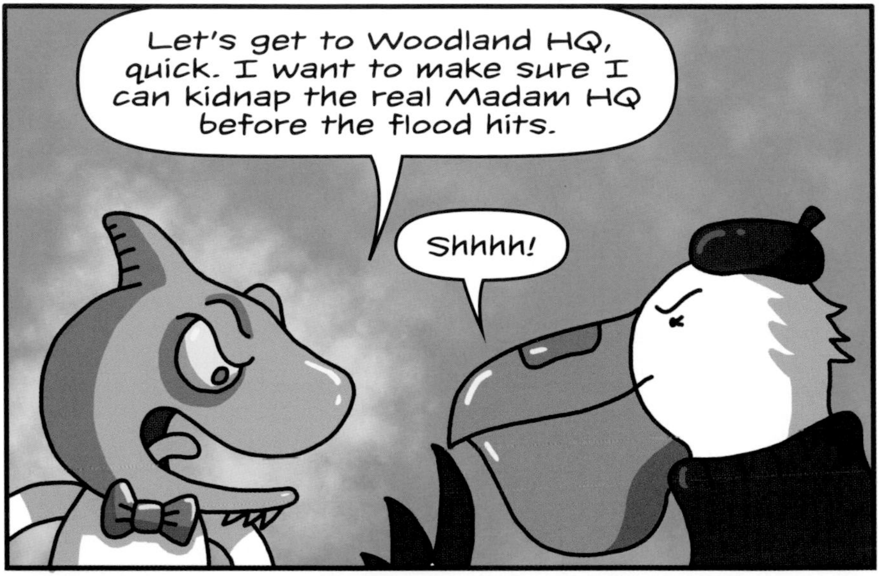
Let's get to Woodland HQ, quick. I want to make sure I can kidnap the real Madam HQ before the flood hits.
Shhhh!

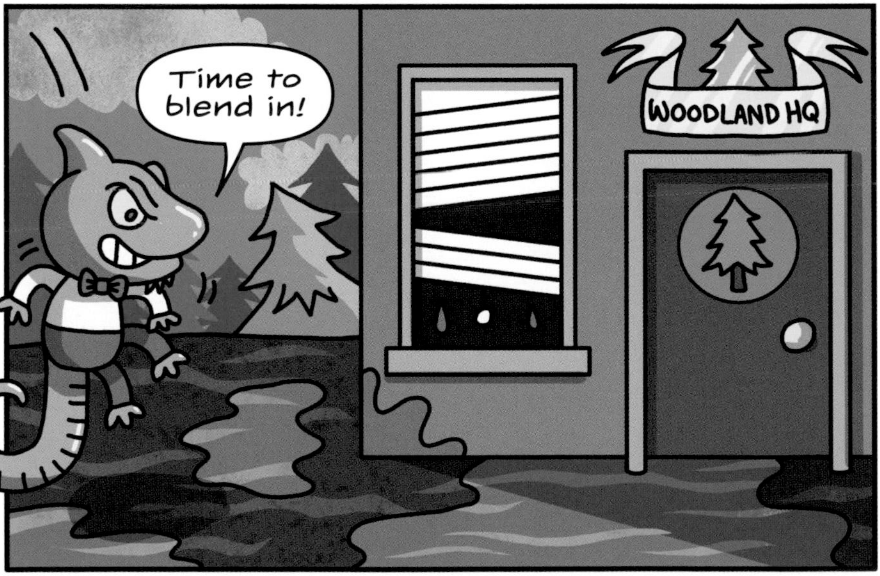
Time to blend in!
WOODLAND HQ

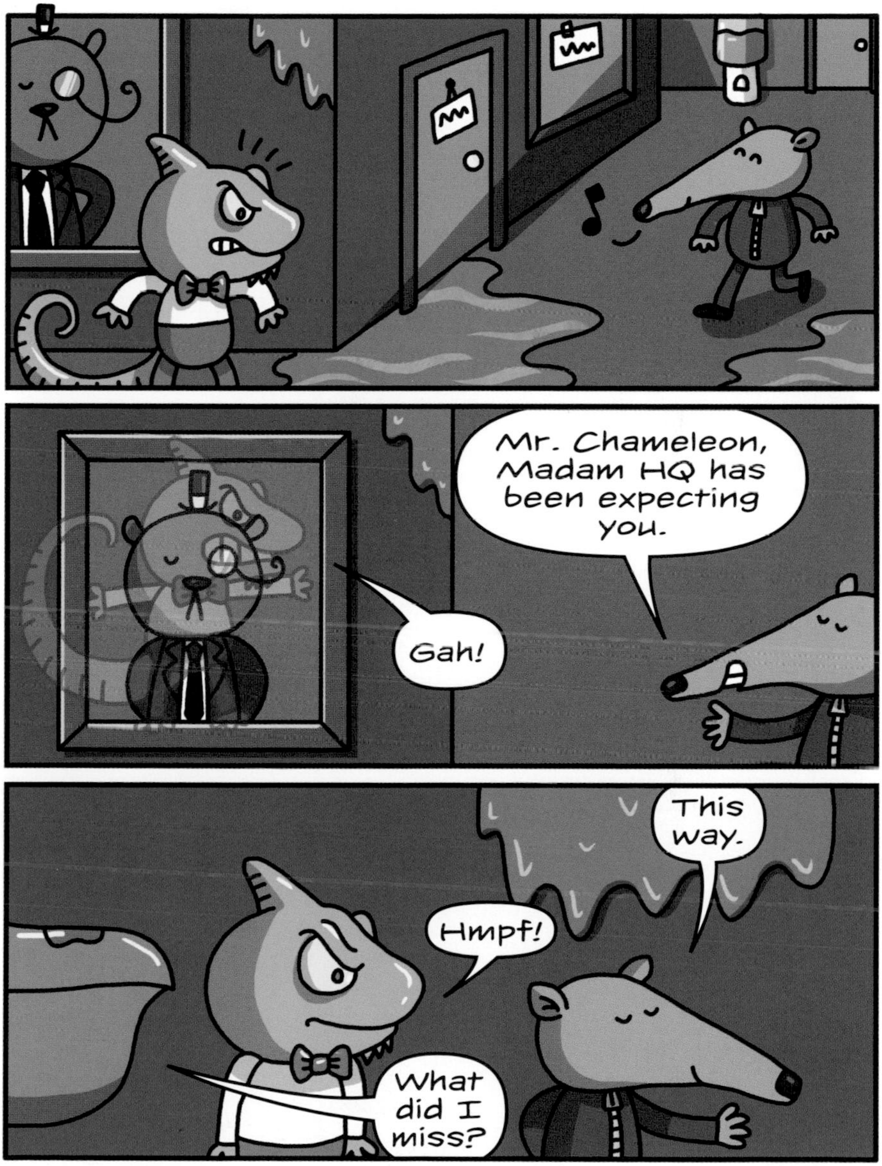
Mr. Chameleon, Madam HQ has been expecting you.
Gah!
This way.
Hmpf!
What did I miss?

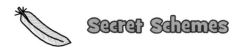

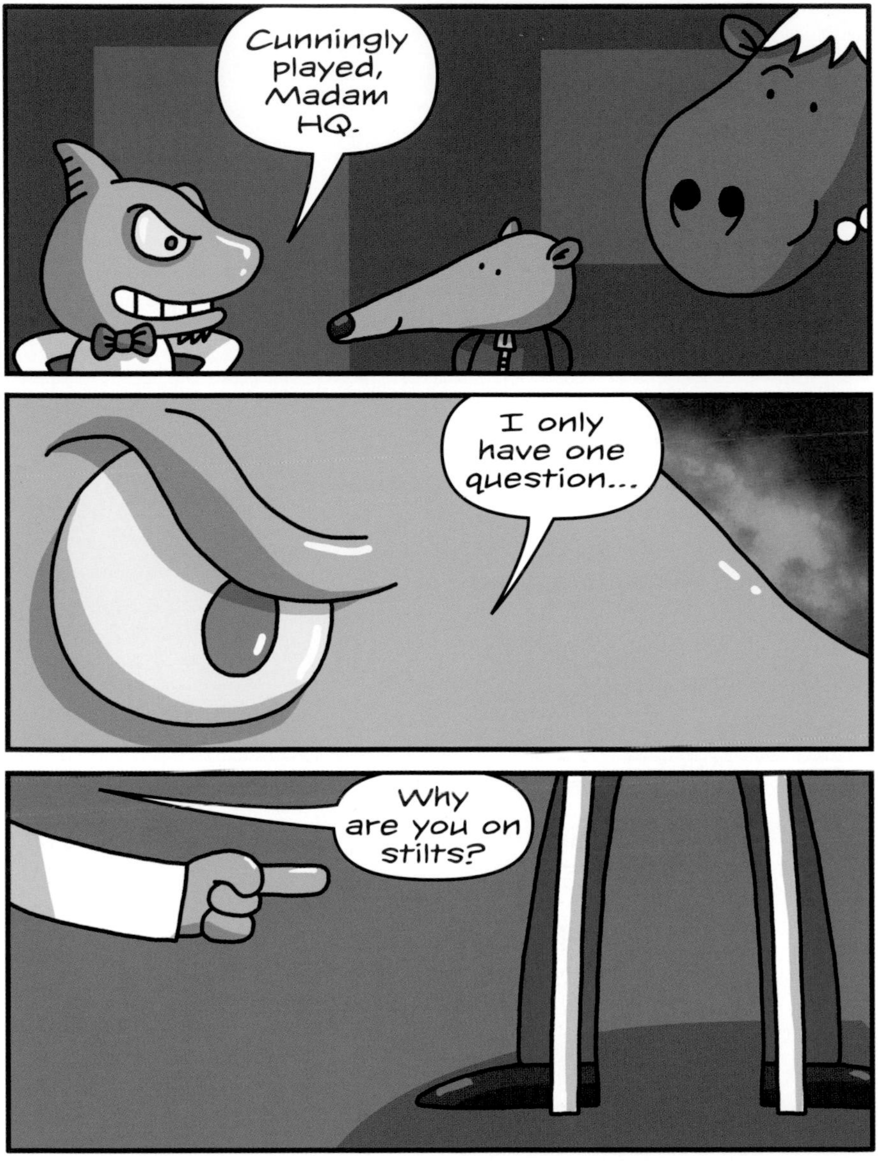
Cunningly played, Madam HQ.
I only have one question...
Why are you on stilts?

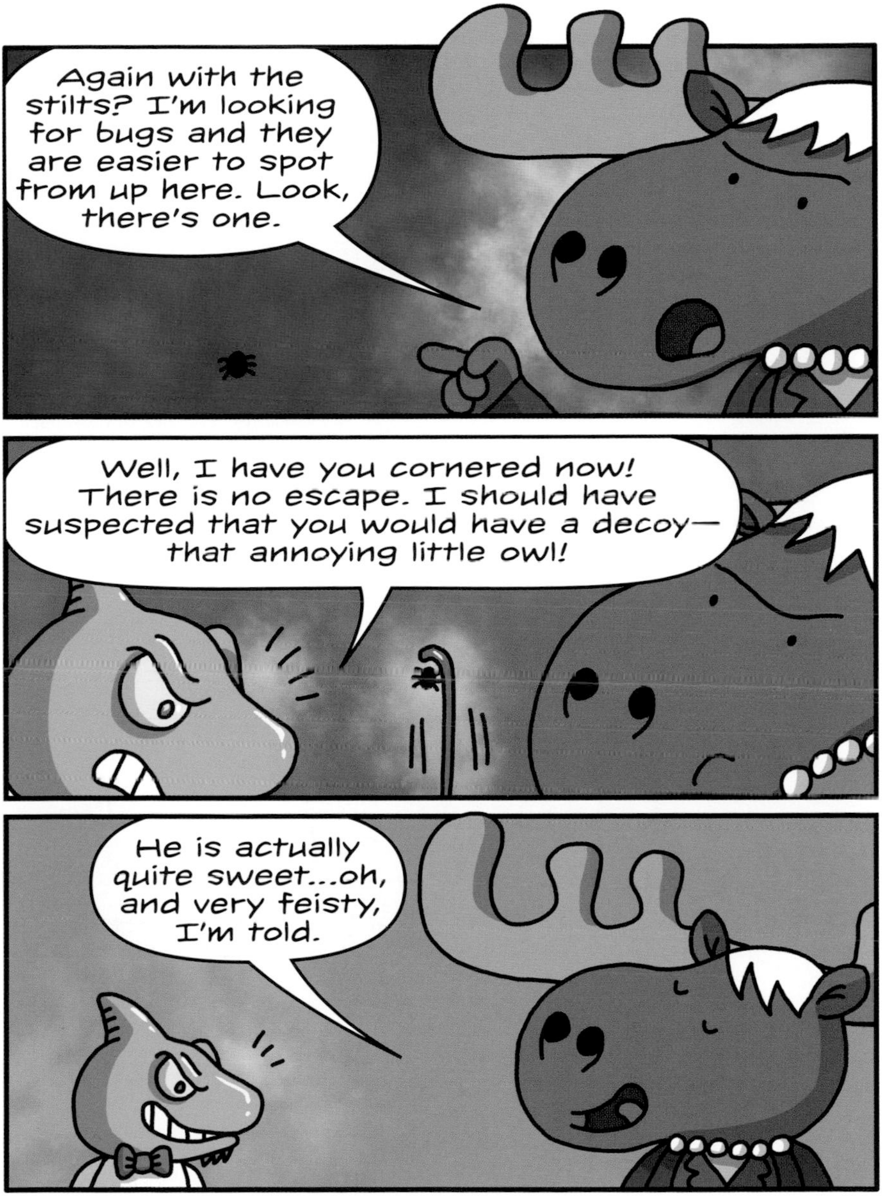
Again with the stilts? I'm looking for bugs and they are easier to spot from up here. Look, there's one.
Well, I have you cornered now! There is no escape. I should have suspected that you would have a decoy—that annoying little owl!
He is actually quite sweet...oh, and very feisty, I'm told.

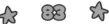

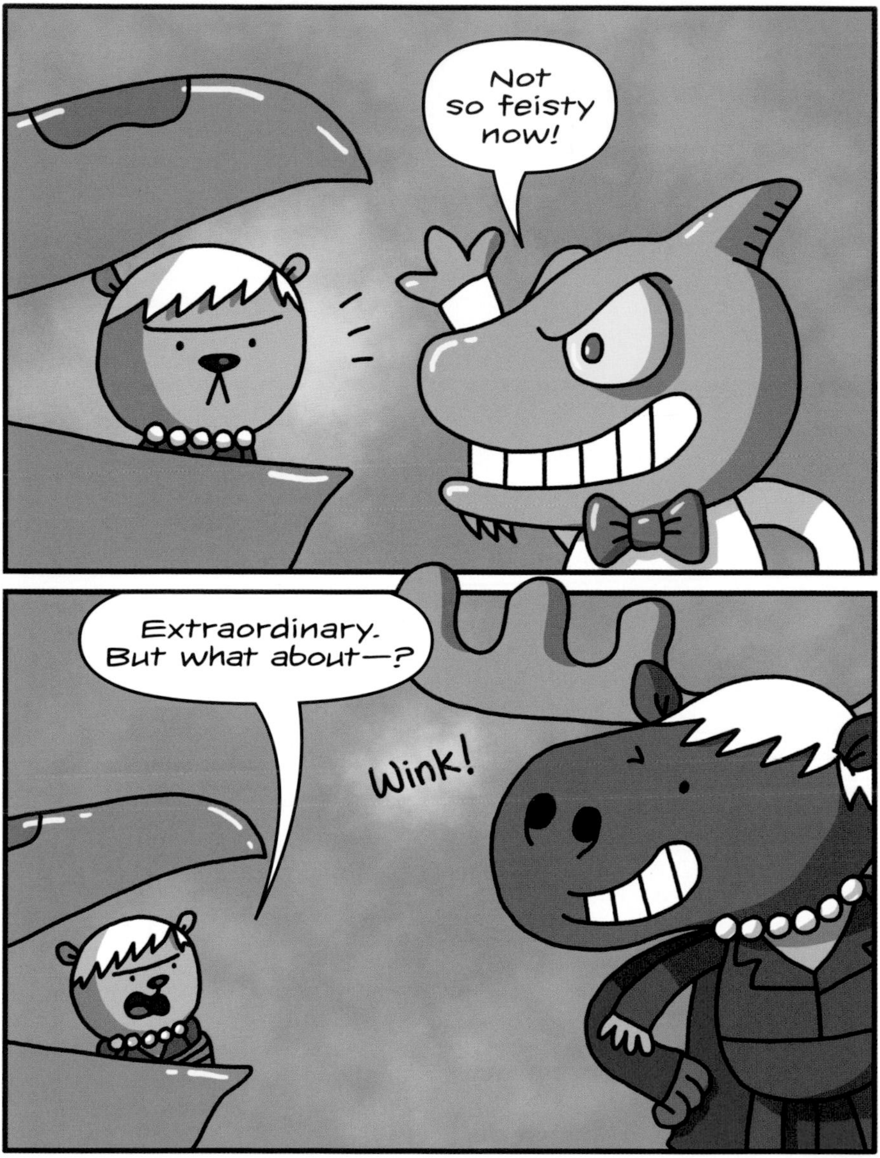
Not so feisty now!
Extraordinary. But what about—?
Wink!

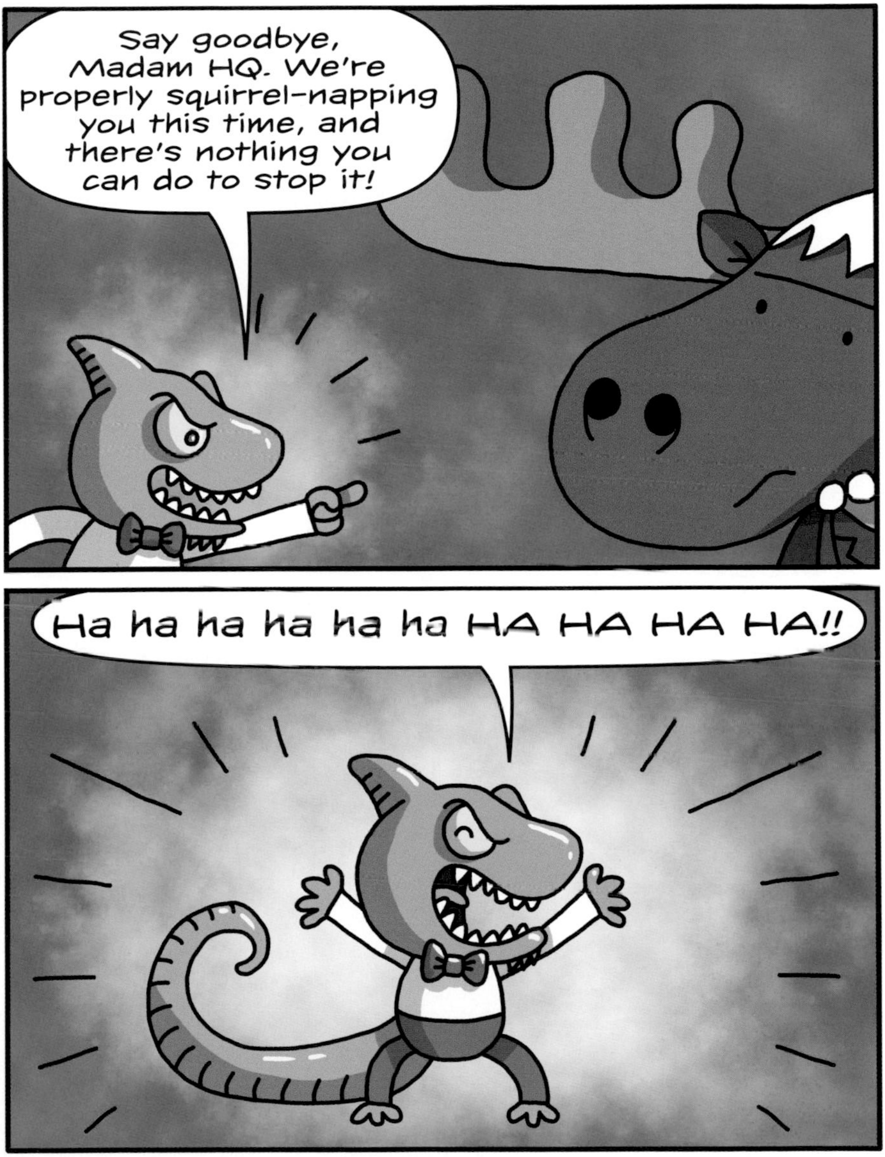
Say goodbye, Madam HQ. We're properly squirrel-napping you this time, and there's nothing you can do to stop it!
Ha ha ha ha ha ha HA HA HA HA!!

Chapter 8

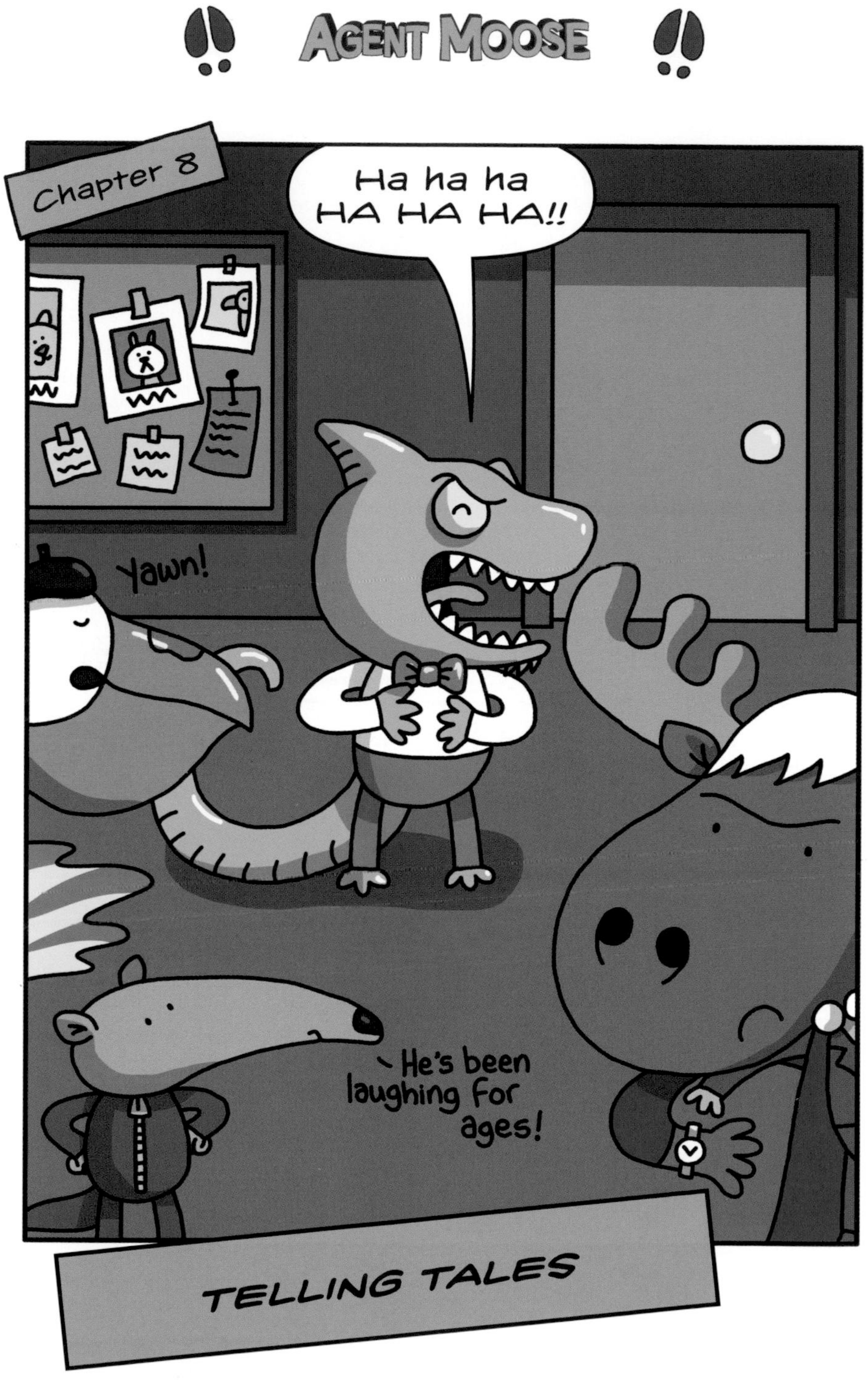
Ha ha ha HA HA HA!!
Yawn!
He's been laughing for ages!

TELLING TALES

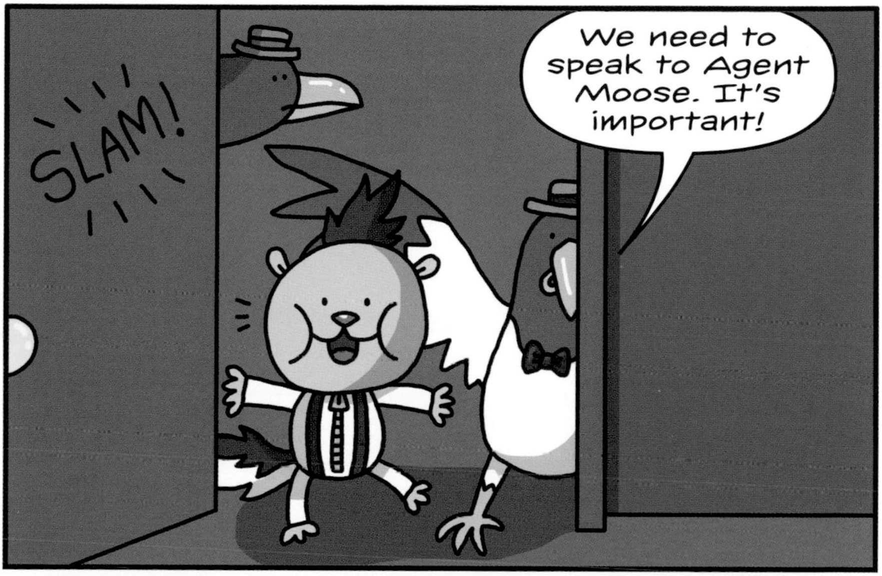
SLAM!
We need to speak to Agent Moose. It's important!

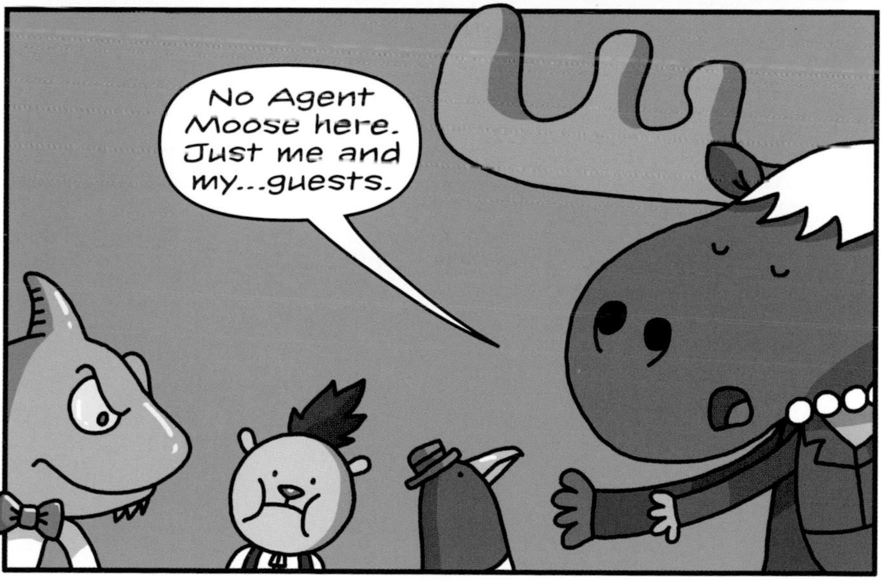
No Agent Moose here. Just me and my...guests.

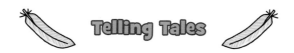

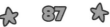

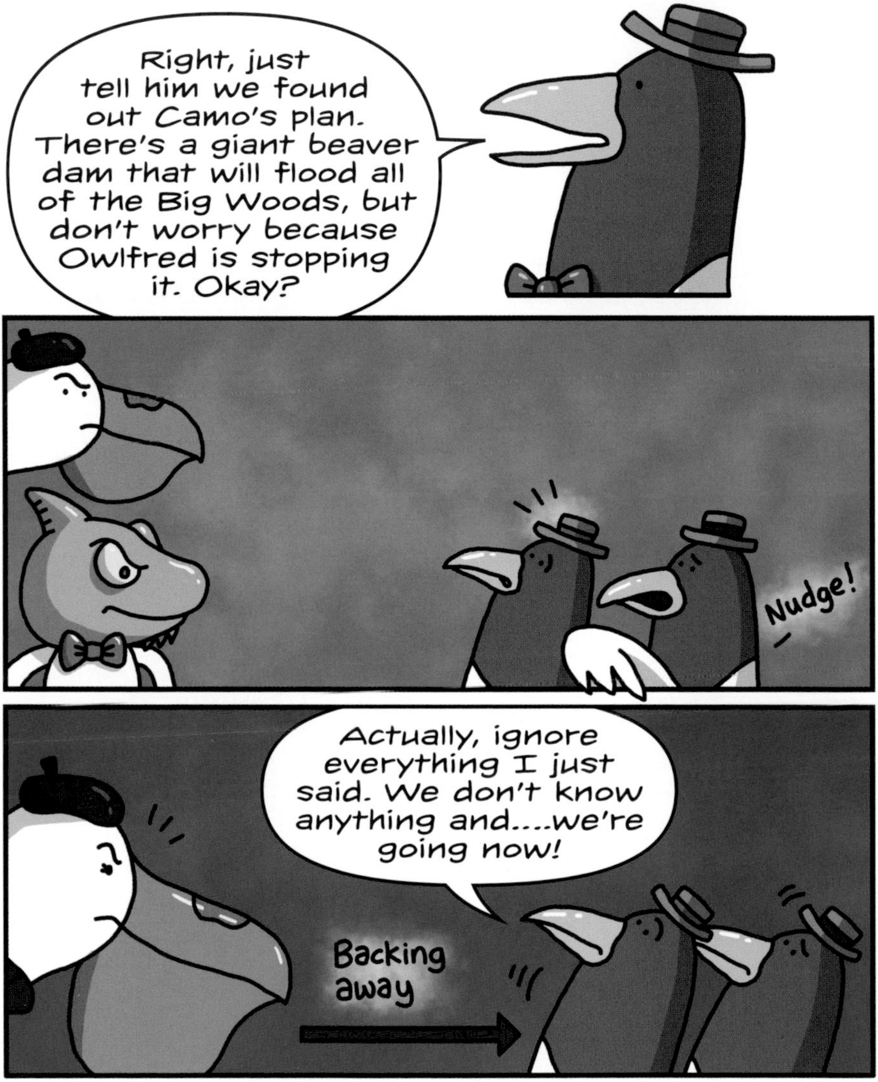
Right, just tell him we found out Camo's plan. There's a giant beaver dam that will flood all of the Big Woods, but don't worry because Owlfred is stopping it. Okay?
Nudge!
Actually, ignore everything I just said. We don't know anything and....we're going now!
Backing away

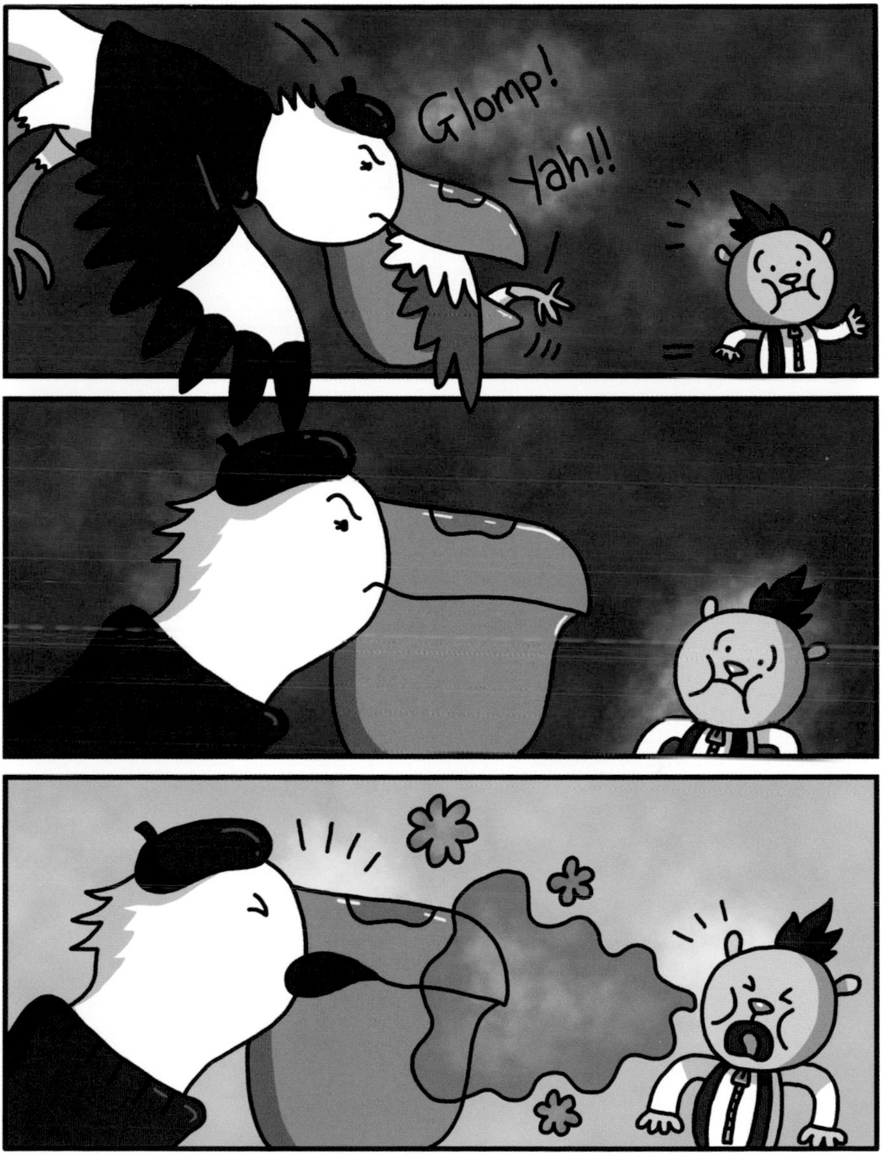
Glomp!
Yah!!

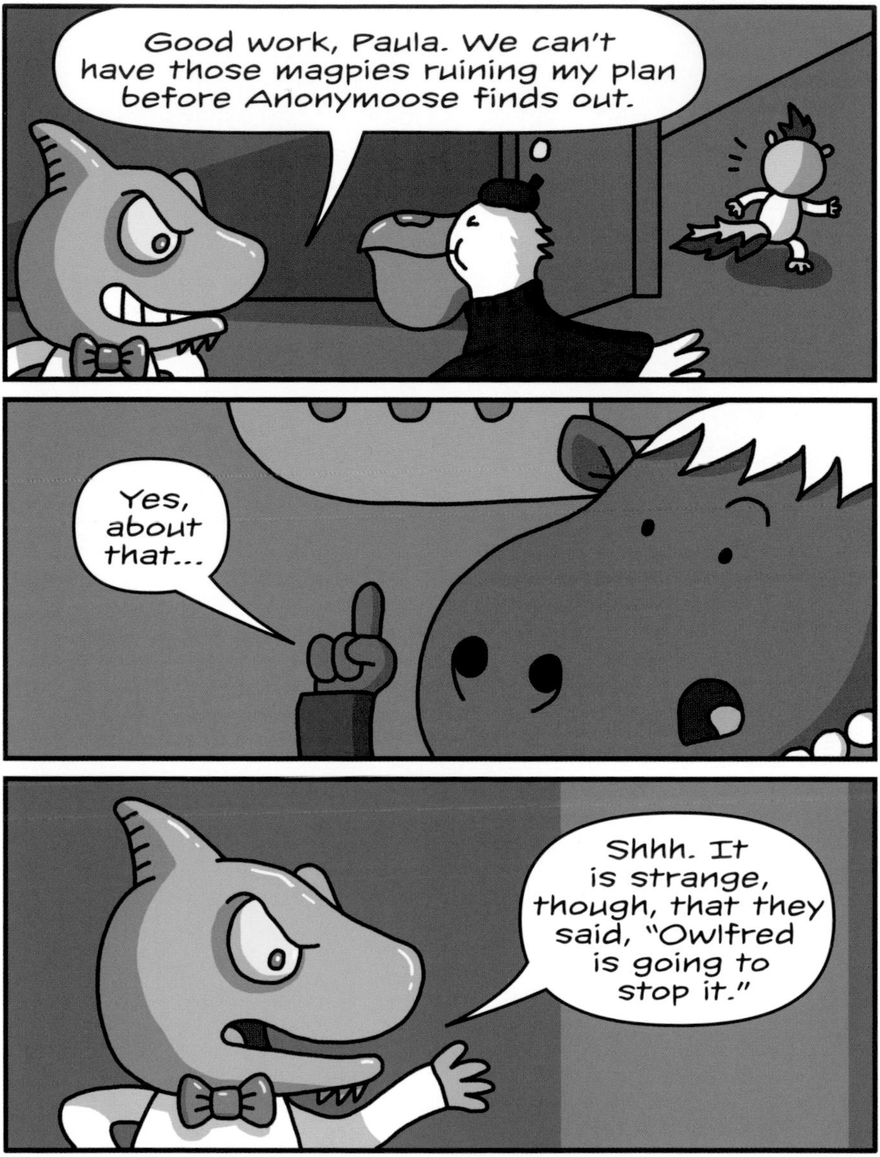
Good work, Paula. We can't have those magpies ruining my plan before Anonymoose finds out.
Yes, about that...
Shhh. It is strange, though, that they said, "Owlfred is going to stop it."

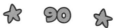

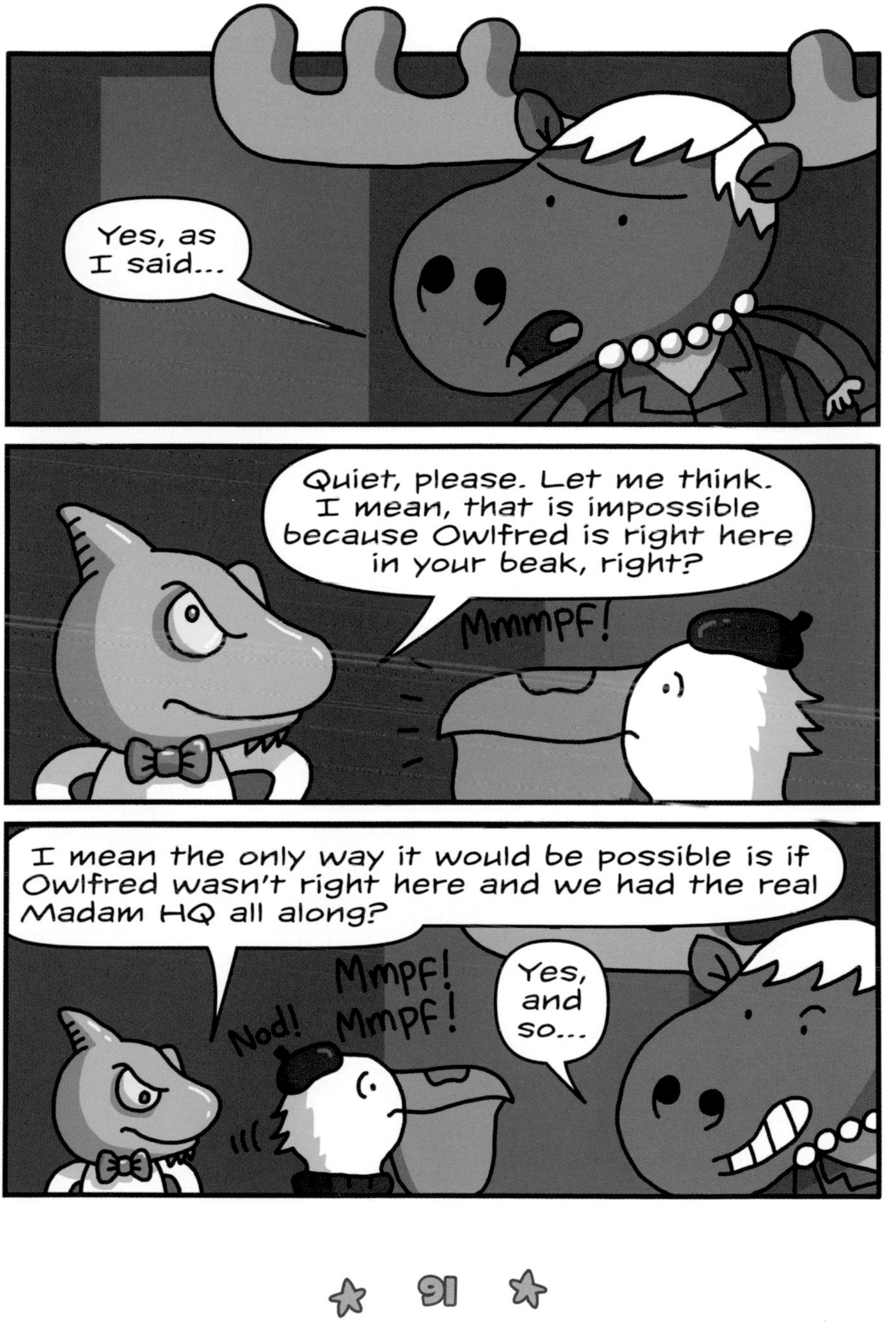
Yes, as I said...
Quiet, please. Let me think. I mean, that is impossible because Owlfred is right here in your beak, right?
Mmmpf!
I mean the only way it would be possible is if Owlfred wasn't right here and we had the real Madam HQ all along?
Nod!
Mmpf! Mmpf!
Yes, and so...

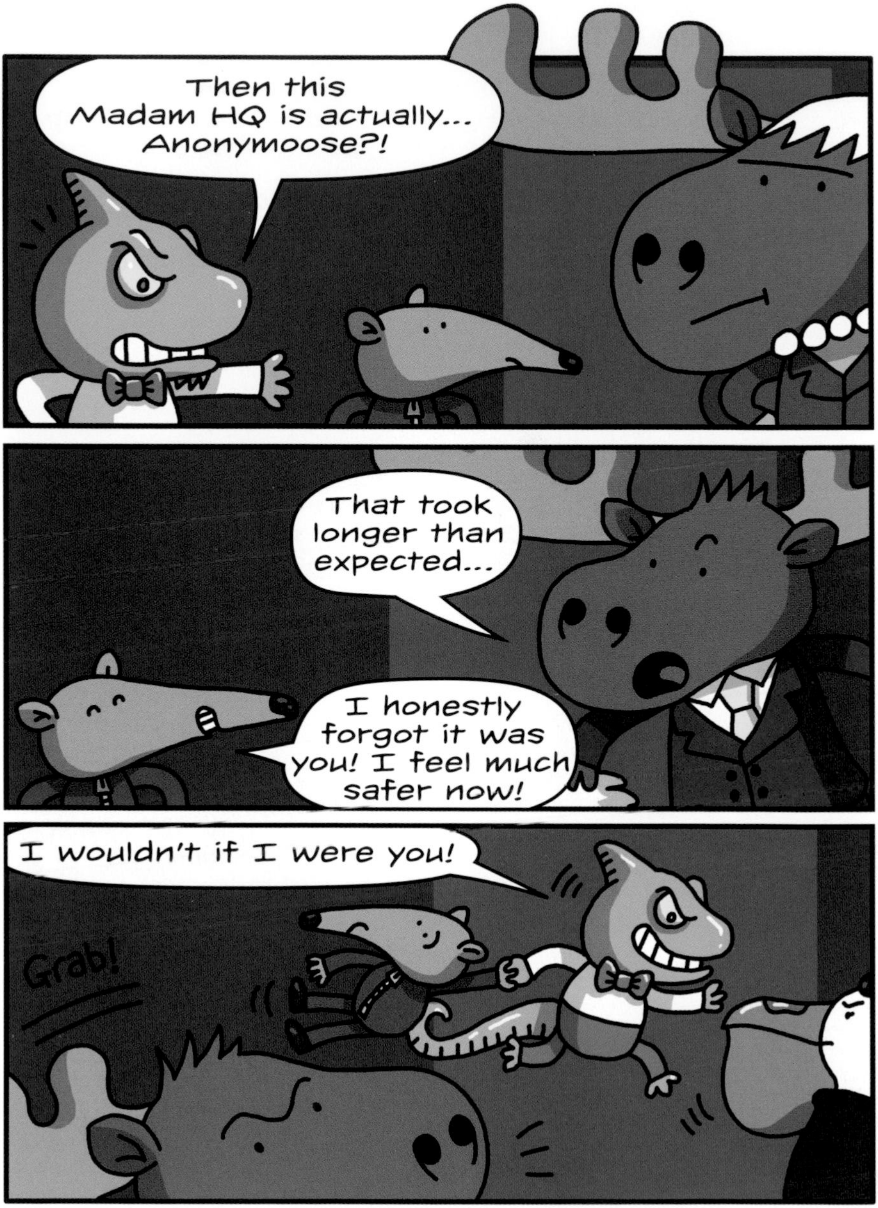
Then this Madam HQ is actually... Anonymoose?!
That took longer than expected...
I honestly forgot it was you! I feel much safer now!
I wouldn't if I were you!
Grab!

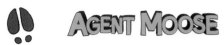

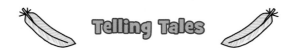

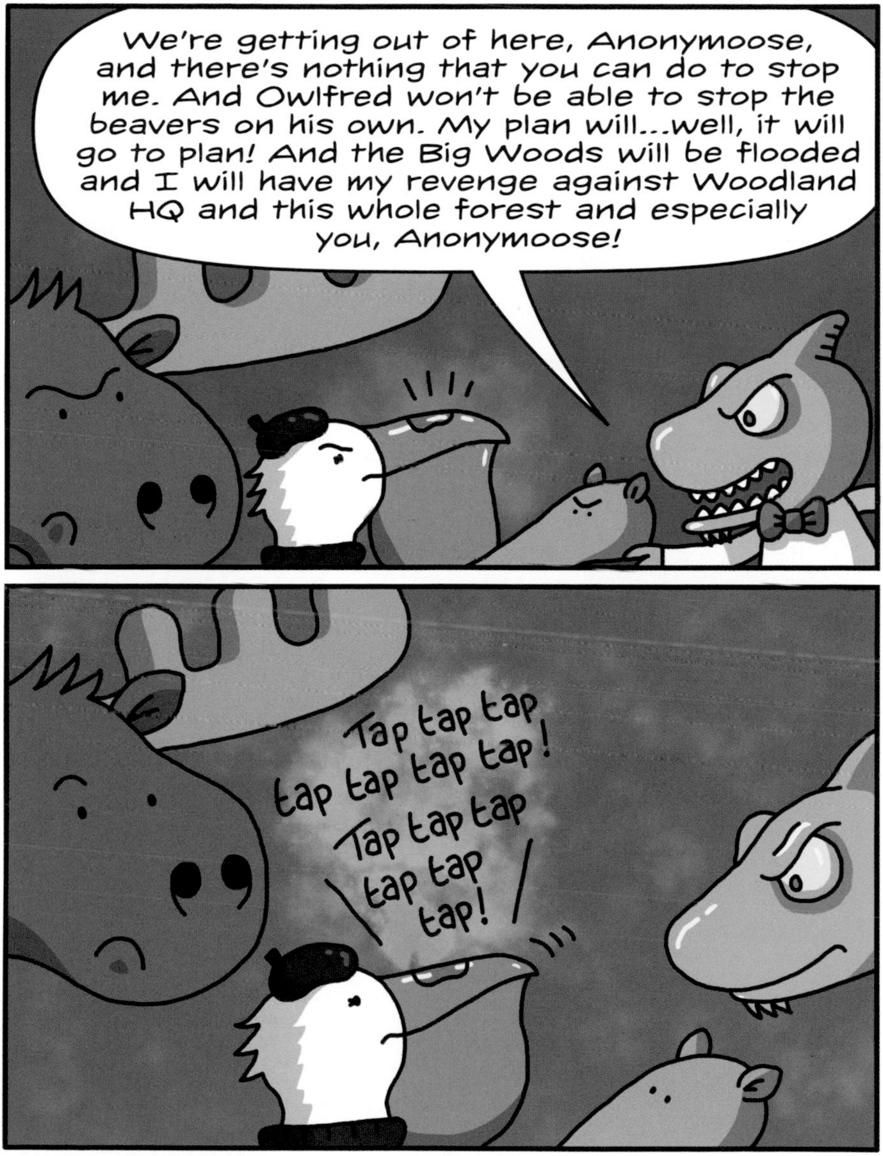
We're getting out of here, Anonymoose, and there's nothing that you can do to stop me. And Owlfred won't be able to stop the beavers on his own. My plan will...well, it will go to plan! And the Big Woods will be flooded and I will have my revenge against Woodland HQ and this whole forest and especially you, Anonymoose!
Tap tap tap tap tap tap tap!
Tap tap tap tap tap tap!

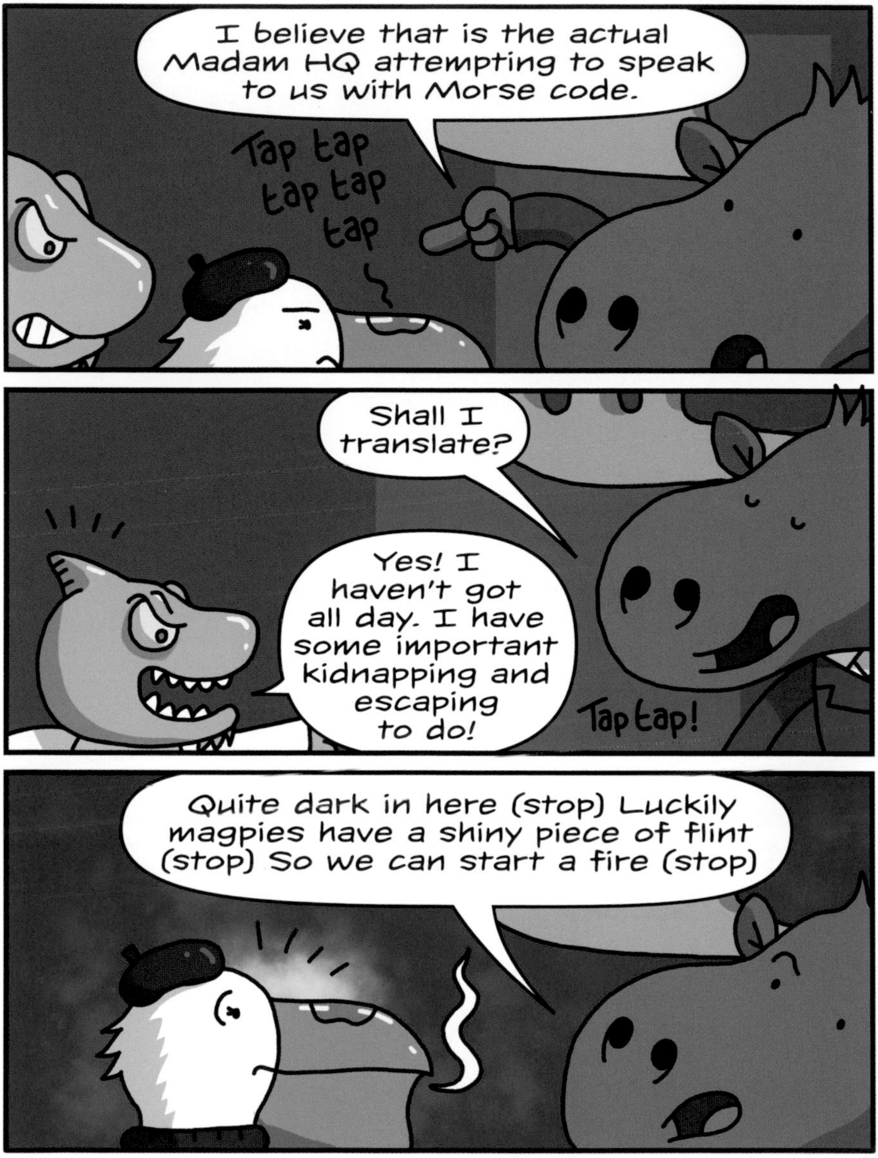
I believe that is the actual Madam HQ attempting to speak to us with Morse code.
Tap tap tap tap tap
Shall I translate?
Yes! I haven't got all day. I have some important kidnapping and escaping to do!
Tap tap!
Quite dark in here (stop) Luckily magpies have a shiny piece of flint (stop) So we can start a fire (stop)

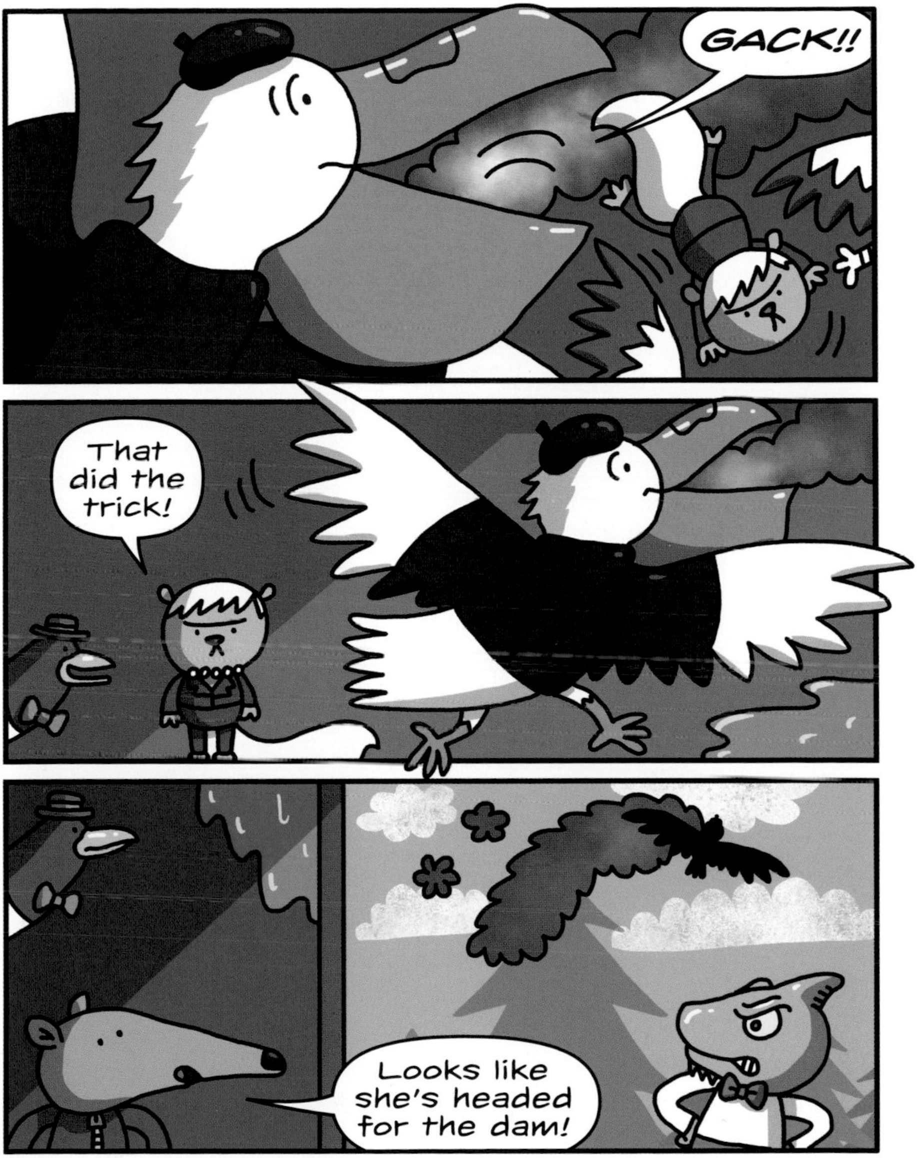
GACK!!
That did the trick!
Looks like she's headed for the dam!

Chapter 9

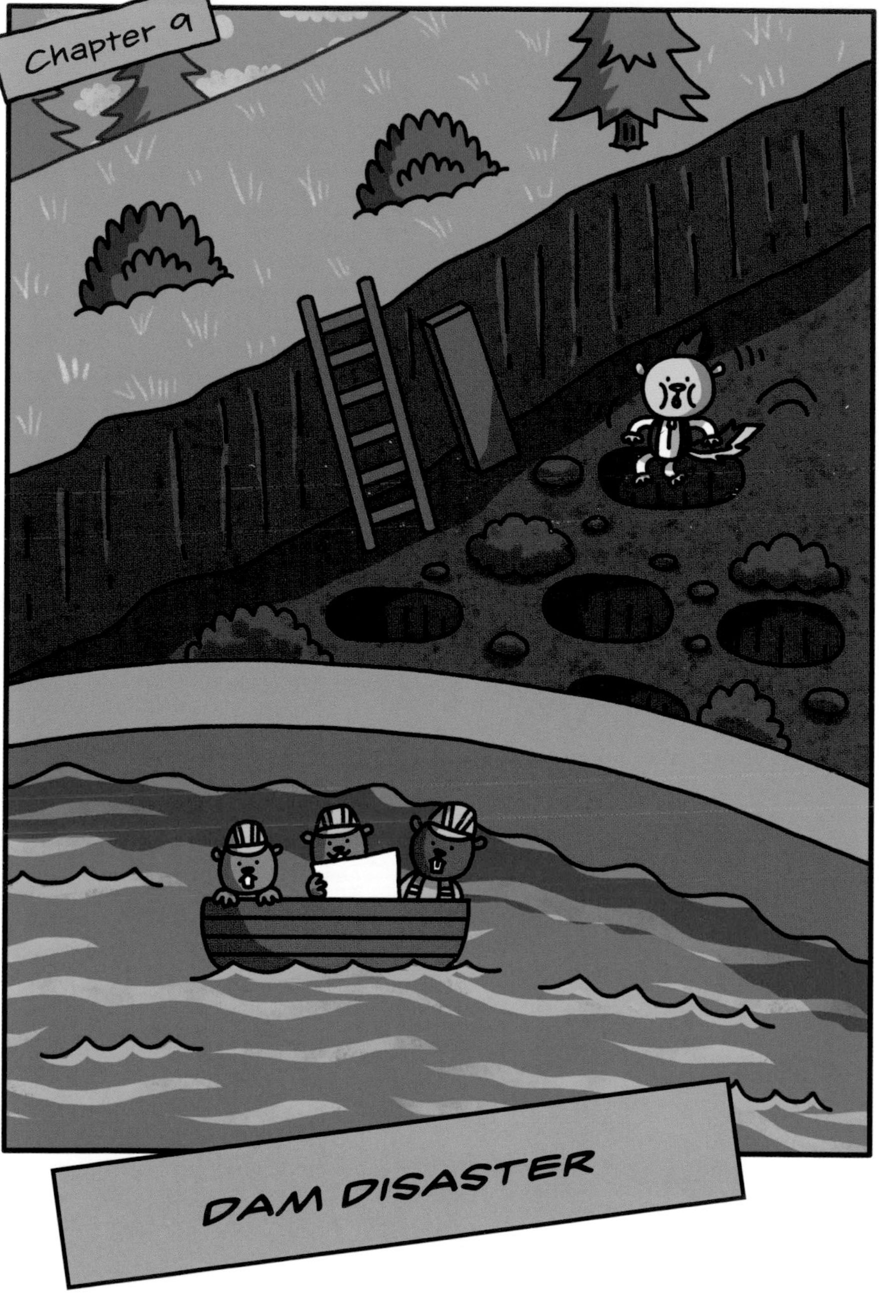

DAM DISASTER

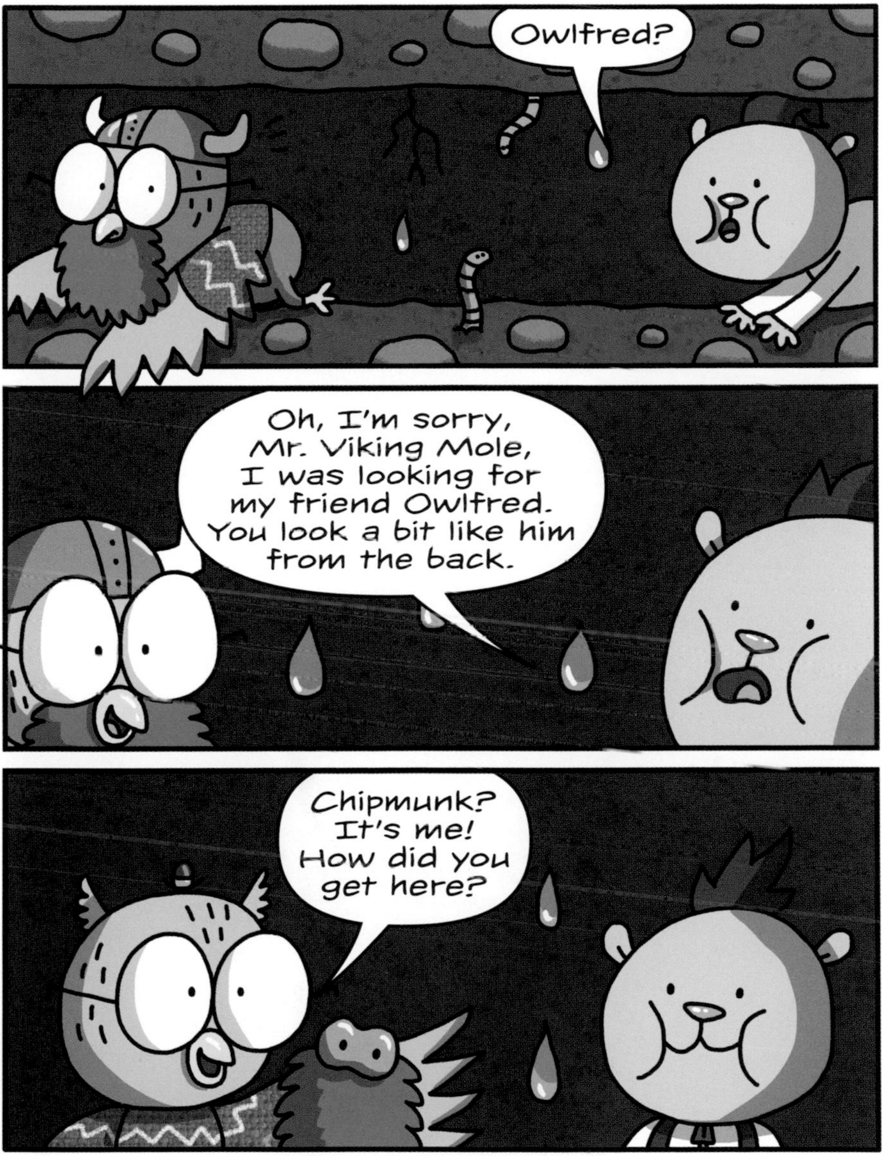
Owlfred?
Oh, I'm sorry, Mr. Viking Mole, I was looking for my friend Owlfred. You look a bit like him from the back.
Chipmunk? It's me! How did you get here?

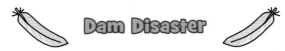

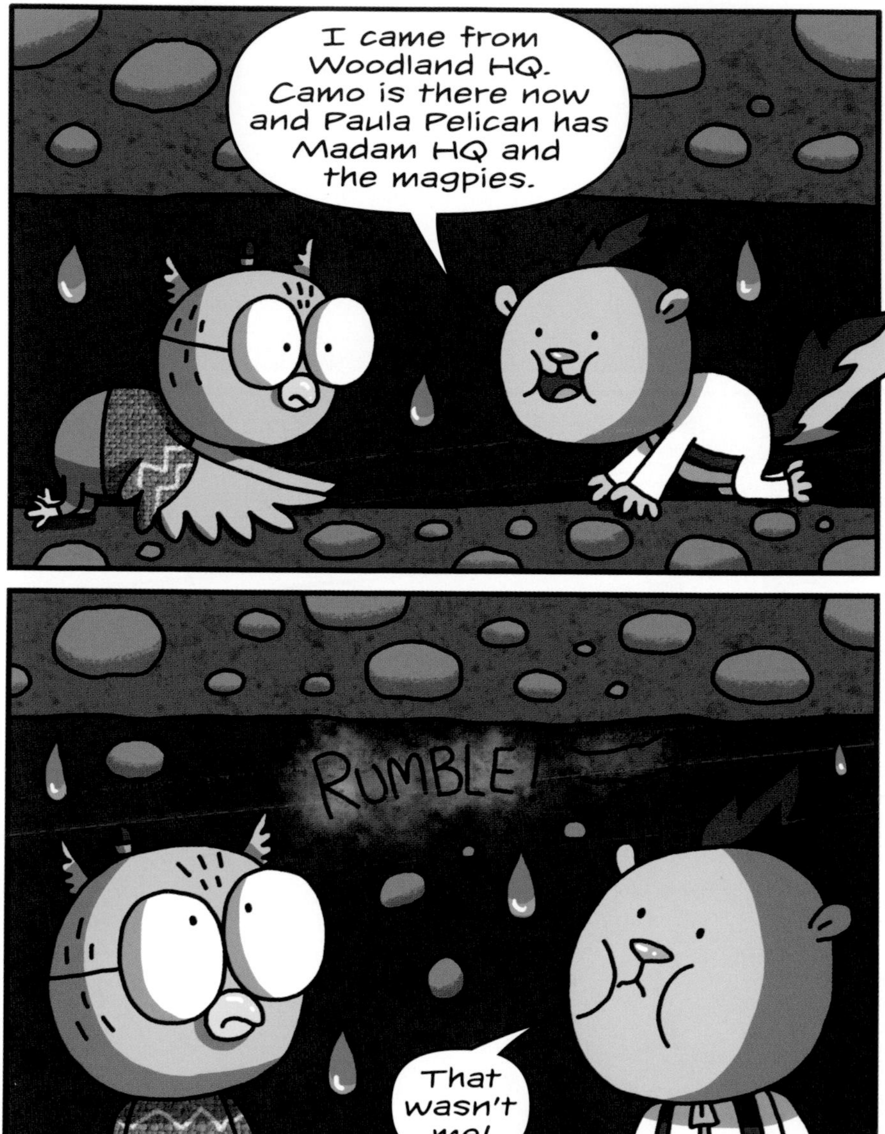
I came from Woodland HQ. Camo is there now and Paula Pelican has Madam HQ and the magpies.
RUMBLE!
That wasn't me!

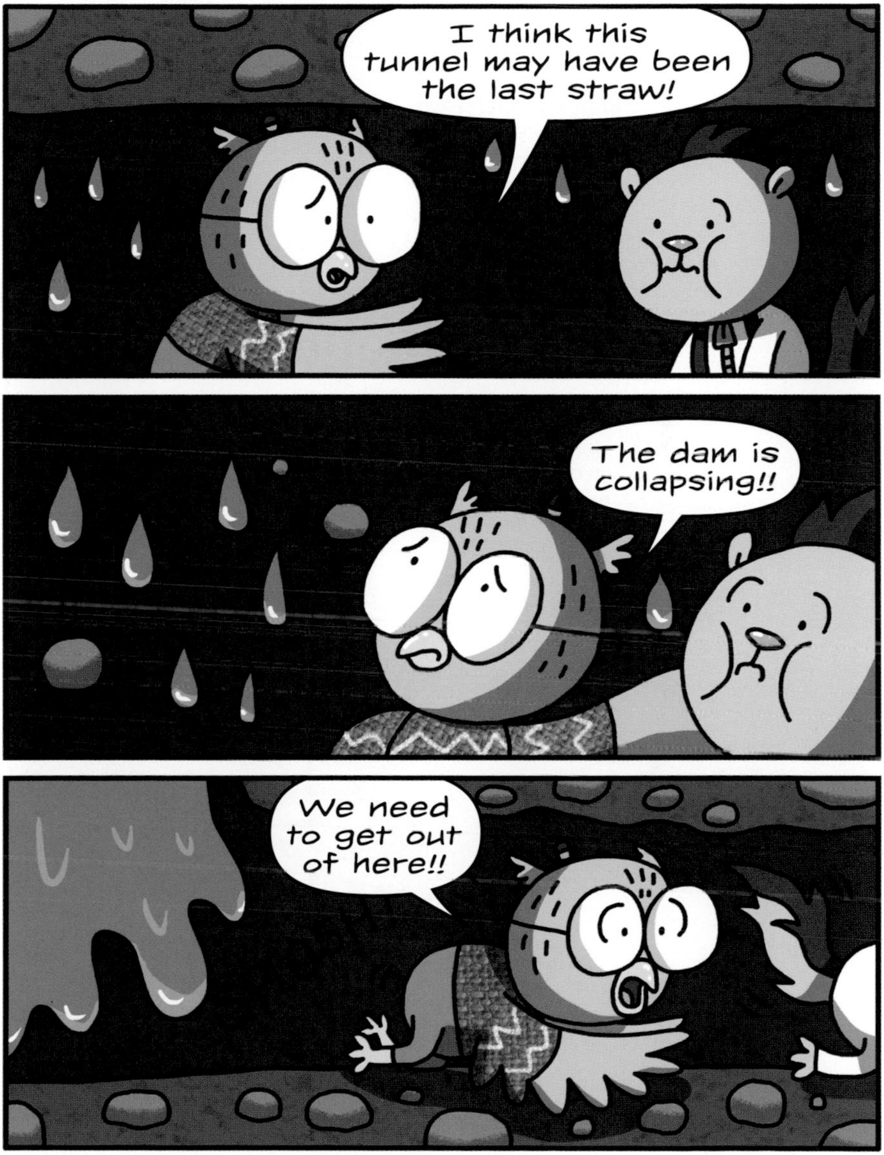
I think this tunnel may have been the last straw!
The dam is collapsing!!
We need to get out of here!!

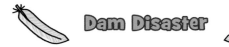

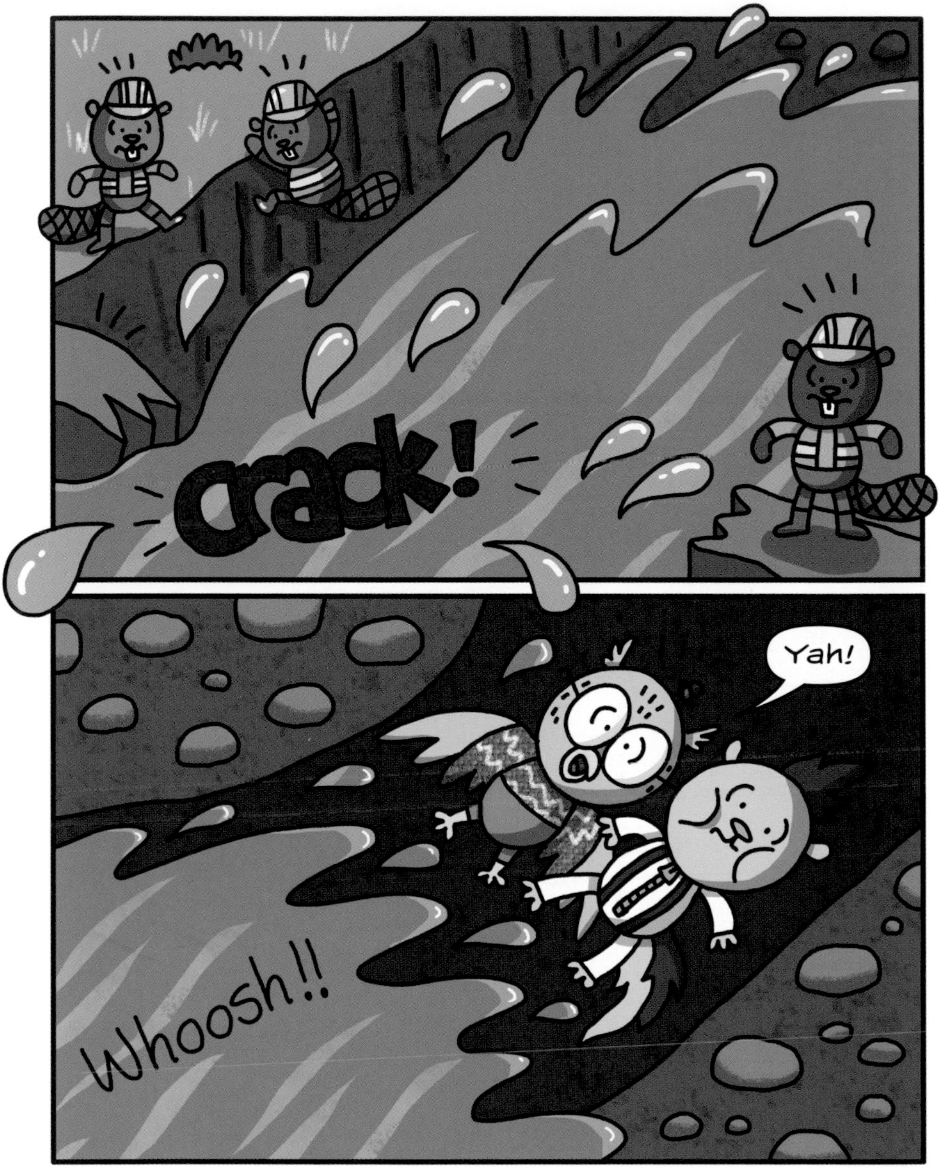
Crack!
Yah!
Whoosh!!

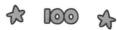

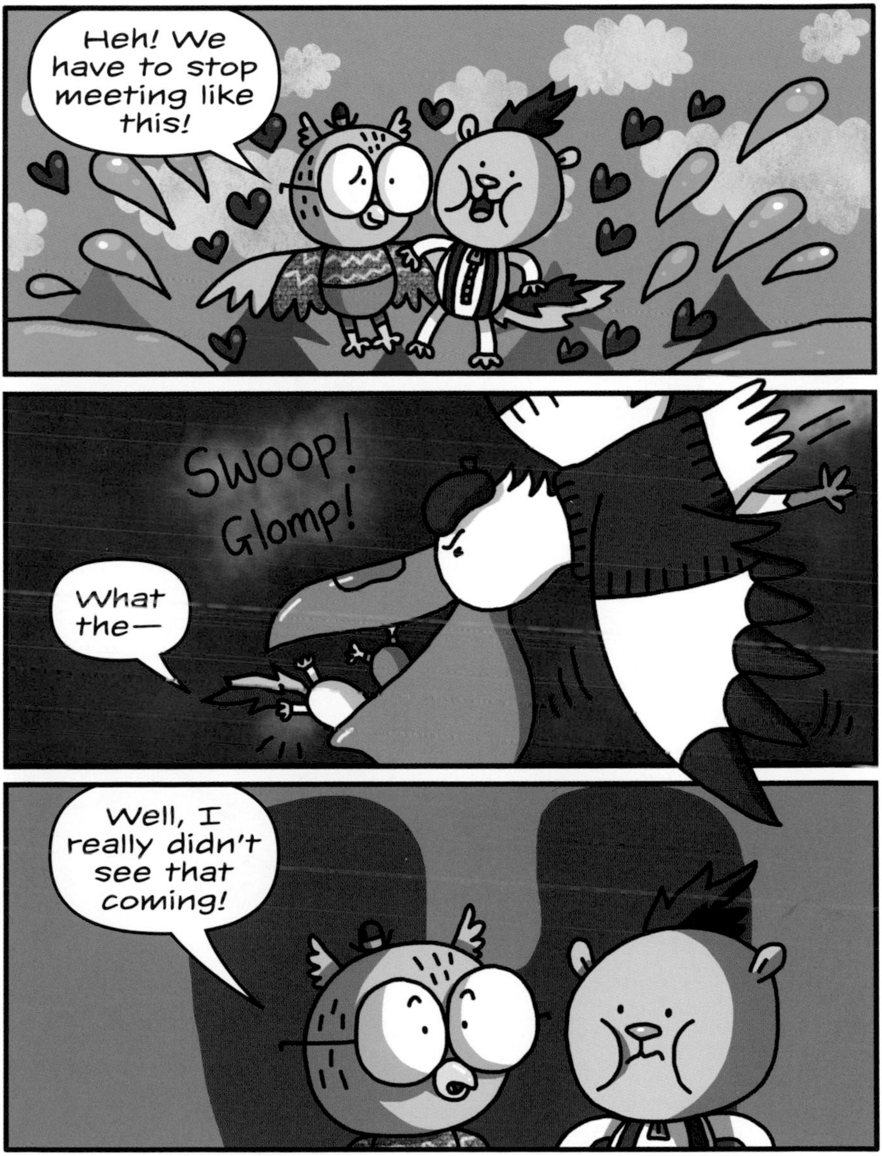
Heh! We have to stop meeting like this!
SWOOP! Glomp!
What the—
Well, I really didn't see that coming!

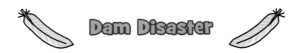

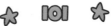

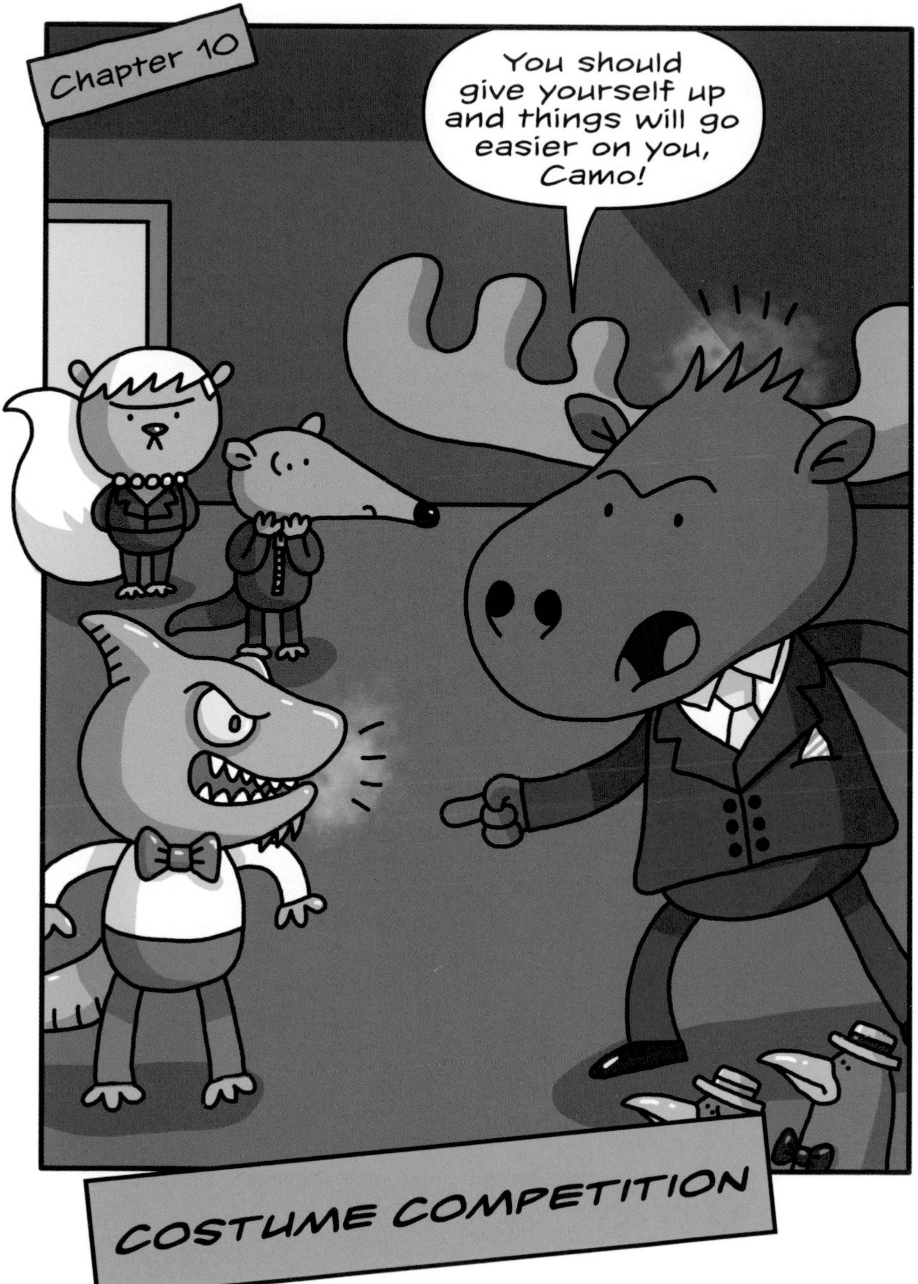
Chapter 10
You should give yourself up and things will go easier on you, Camo!
COSTUME COMPETITION

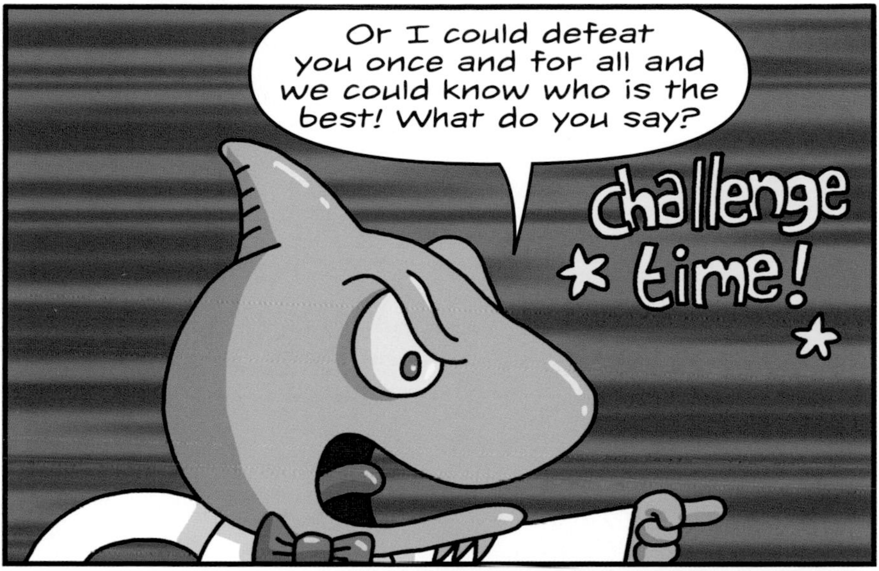
Or I could defeat you once and for all and we could know who is the best! What do you say?
challenge time!

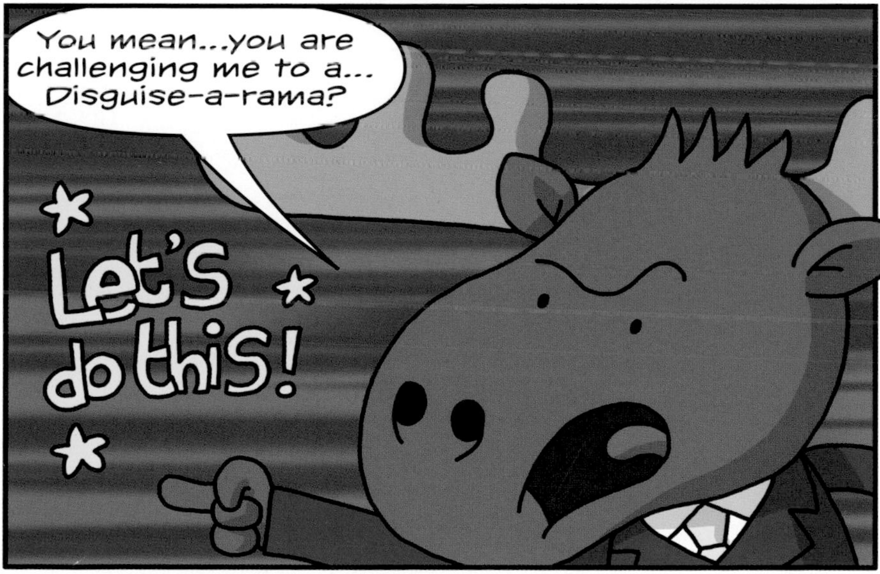
You mean...you are challenging me to a... Disguise-a-rama?
Let's do this!

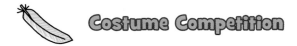

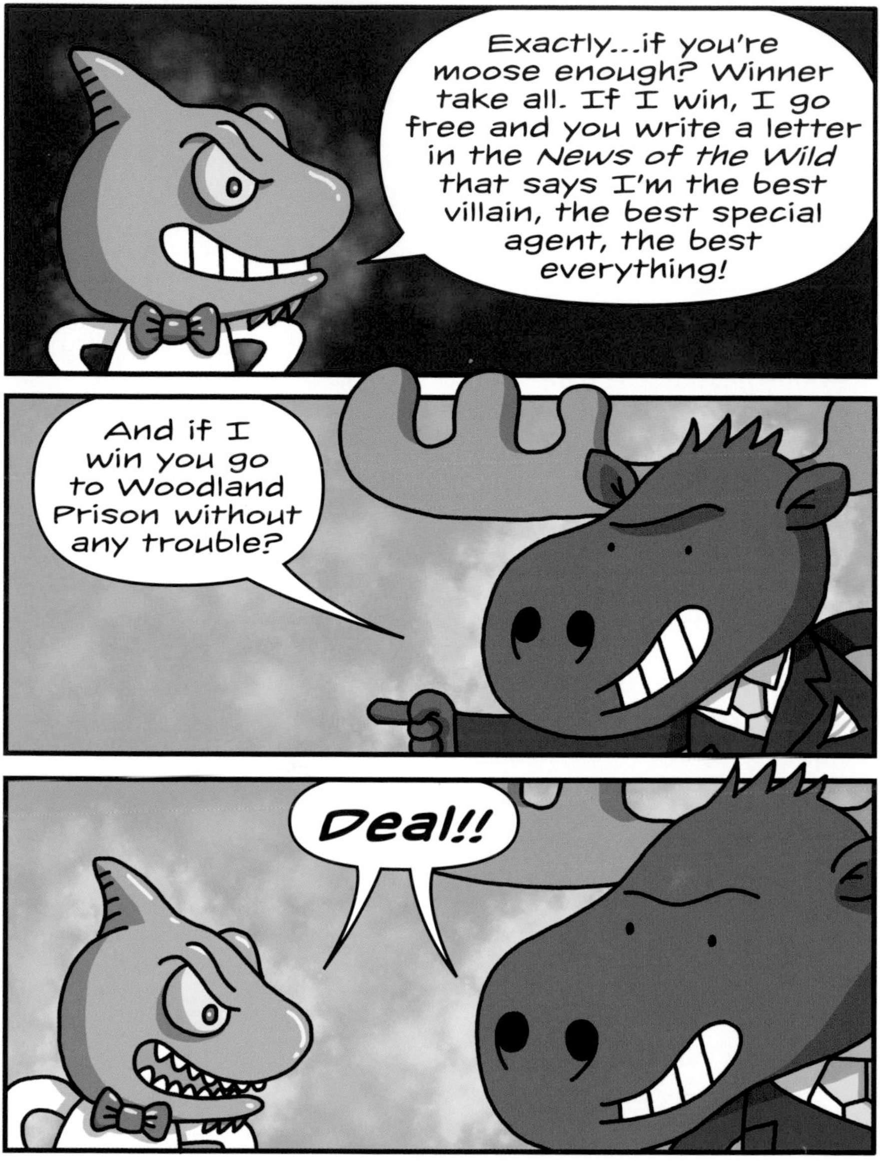
Exactly...if you're moose enough? Winner take all. If I win, I go free and you write a letter in the *News of the Wild* that says I'm the best villain, the best special agent, the best everything!
And if I win you go to Woodland Prison without any trouble?
Deal!!

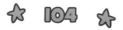

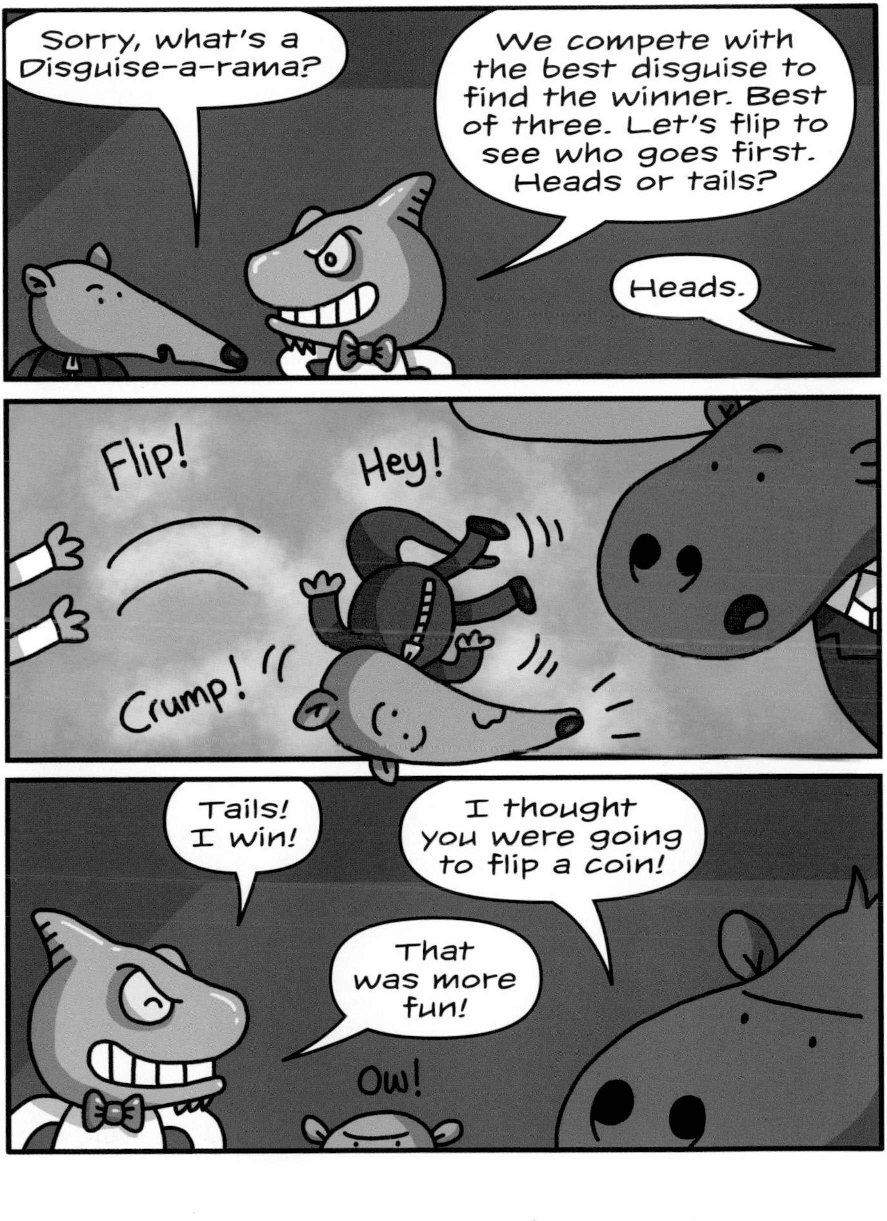
Sorry, what's a Disguise-a-rama?
We compete with the best disguise to find the winner. Best of three. Let's flip to see who goes first. Heads or tails?
Heads.
Flip!
Hey!
Crump!
Tails! I win!
I thought you were going to flip a coin!
That was more fun!
Ow!

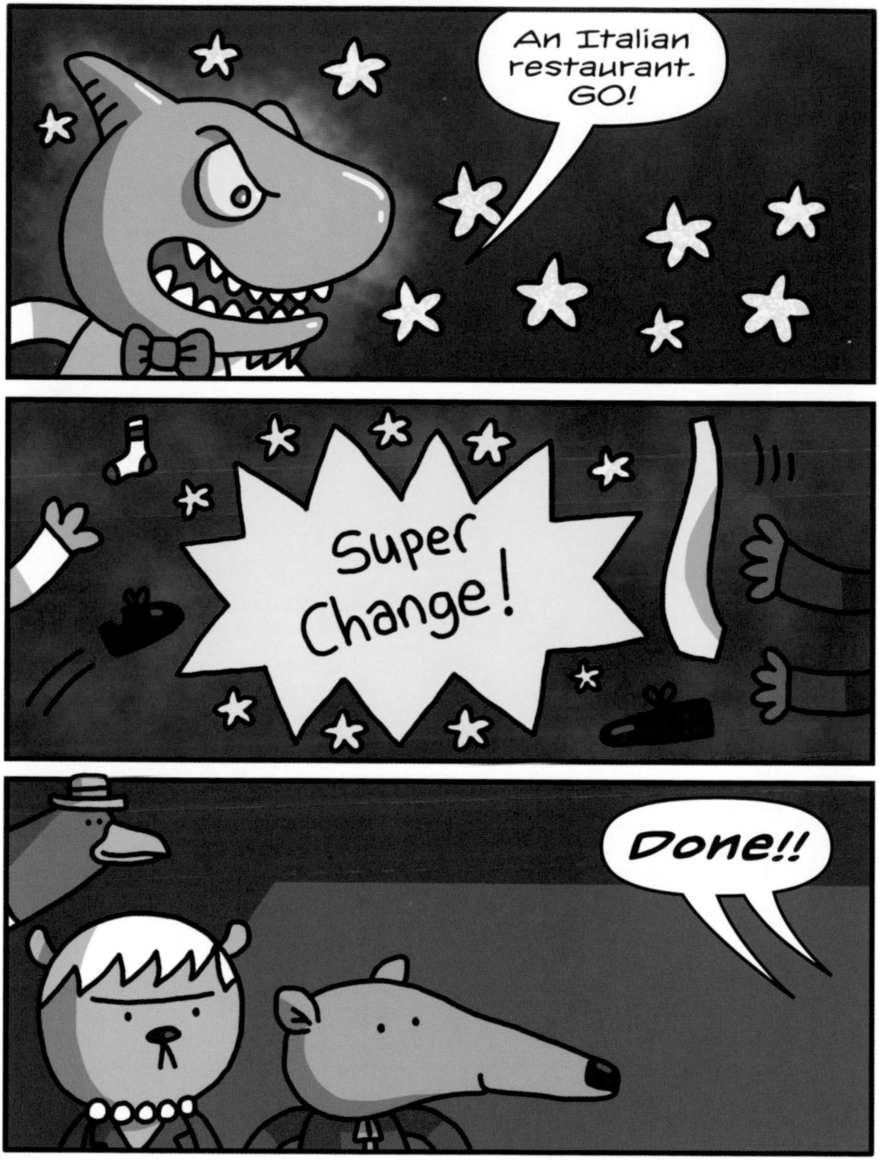
An Italian restaurant. GO!
Super Change!
Done!!

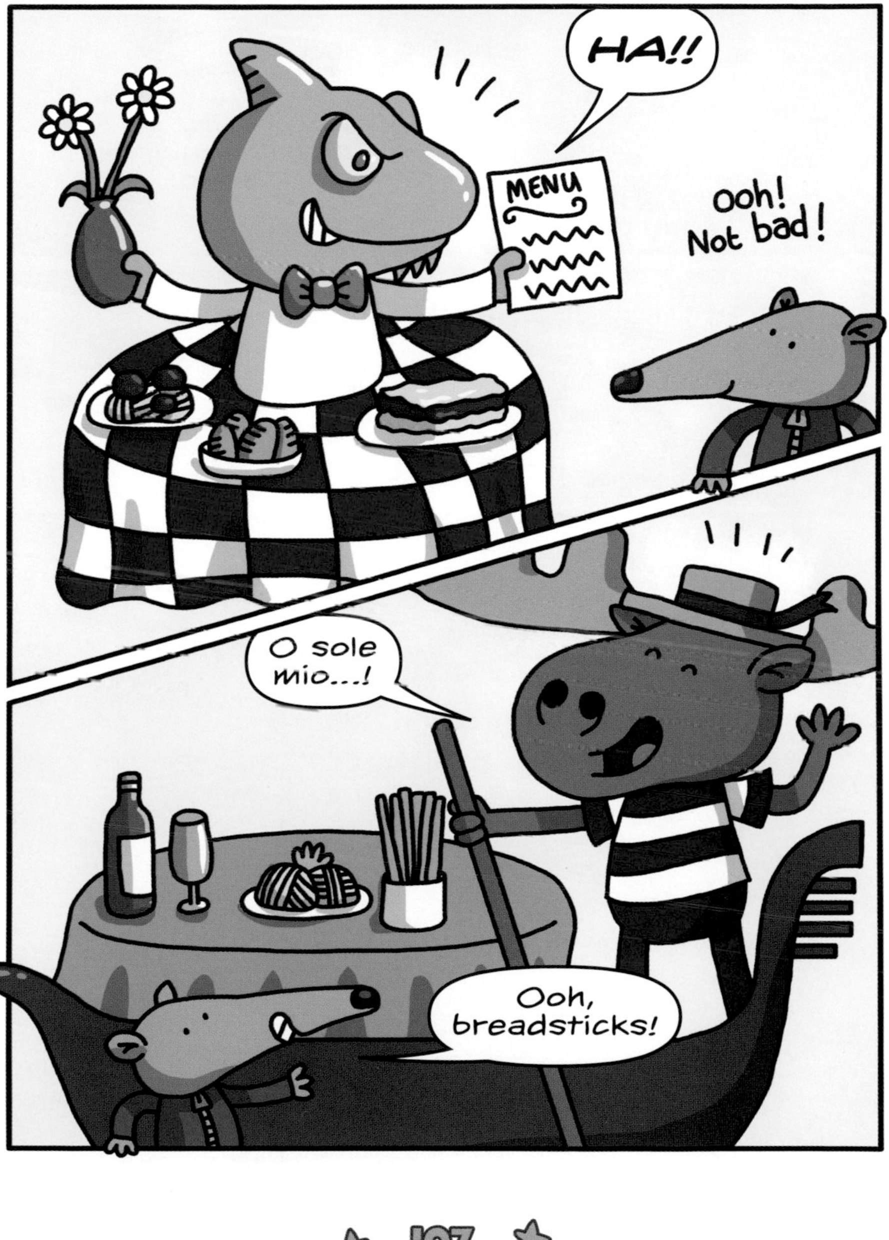
HA!!
MENU
Ooh! Not bad!
O sole mio...!
Ooh, breadsticks!

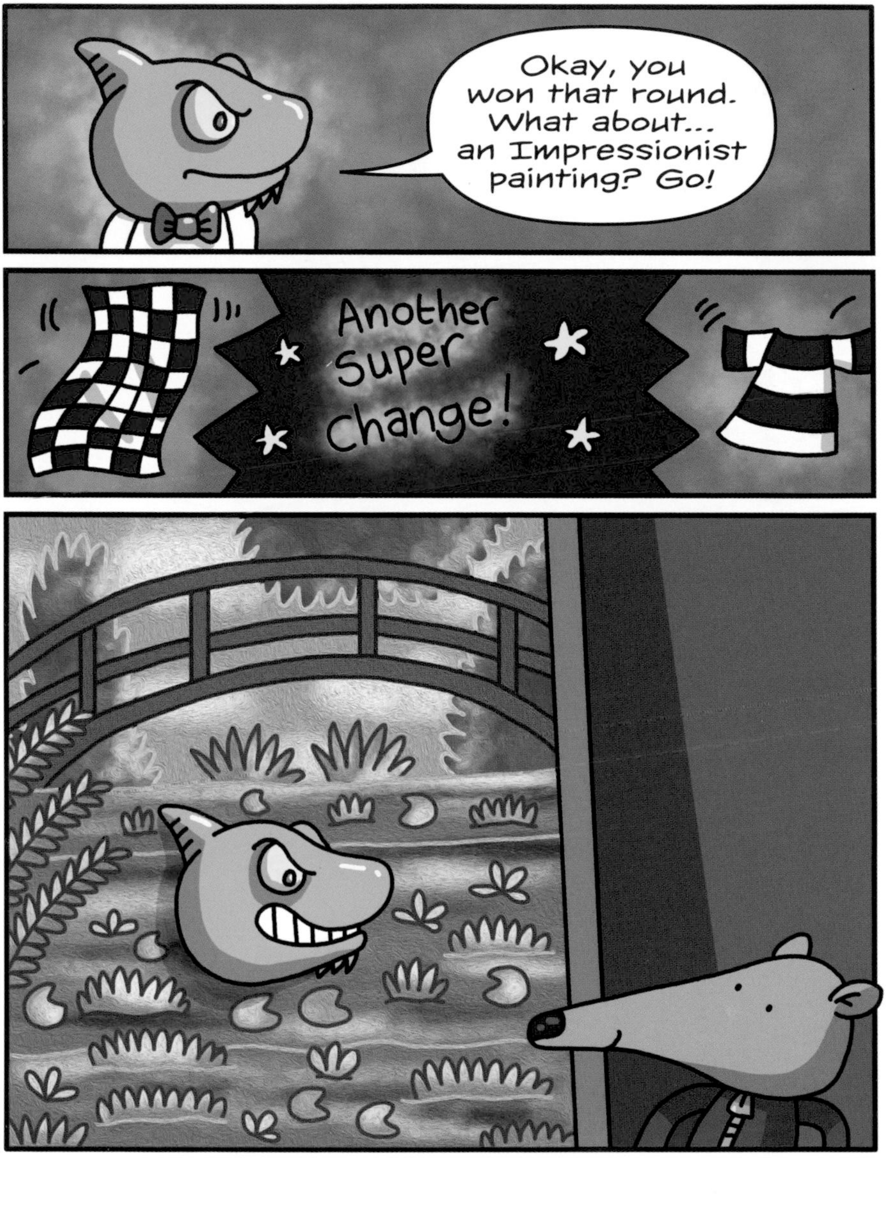
Okay, you won that round. What about... an Impressionist painting? Go!
Another Super Change!

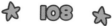

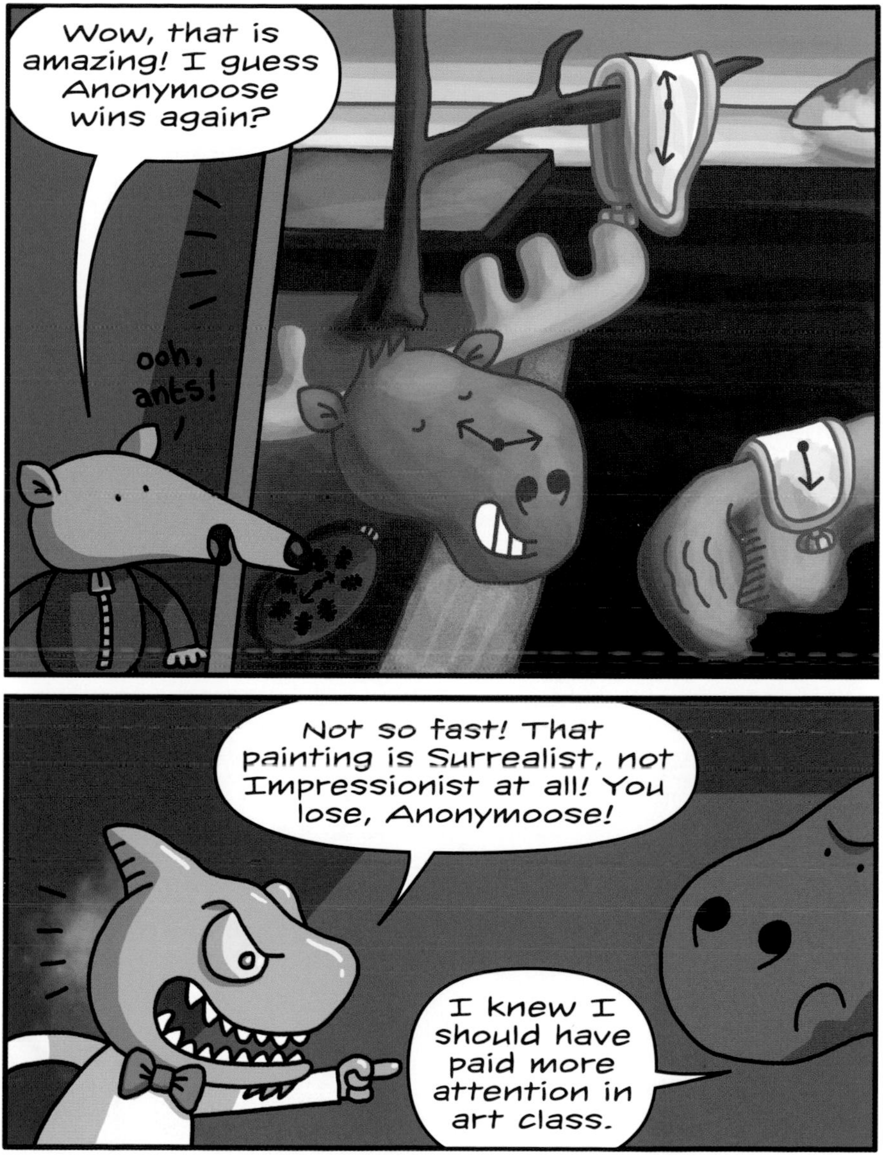
Wow, that is amazing! I guess Anonymoose wins again?
ooh, ants!
Not so fast! That painting is Surrealist, not Impressionist at all! You lose, Anonymoose!
I knew I should have paid more attention in art class.

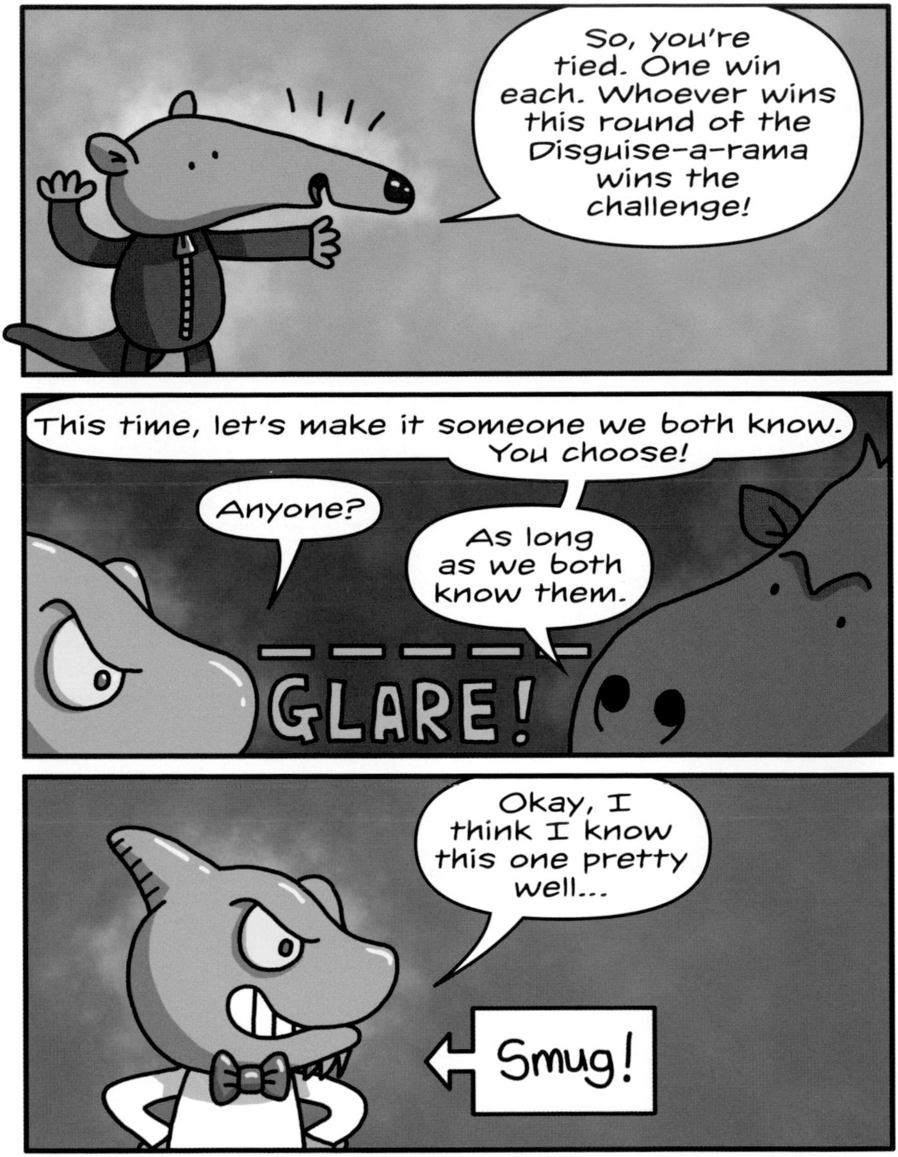
So, you're tied. One win each. Whoever wins this round of the Disguise-a-rama wins the challenge!
This time, let's make it someone we both know. You choose!
Anyone?
As long as we both know them.
GLARE!
Okay, I think I know this one pretty well...
Smug!

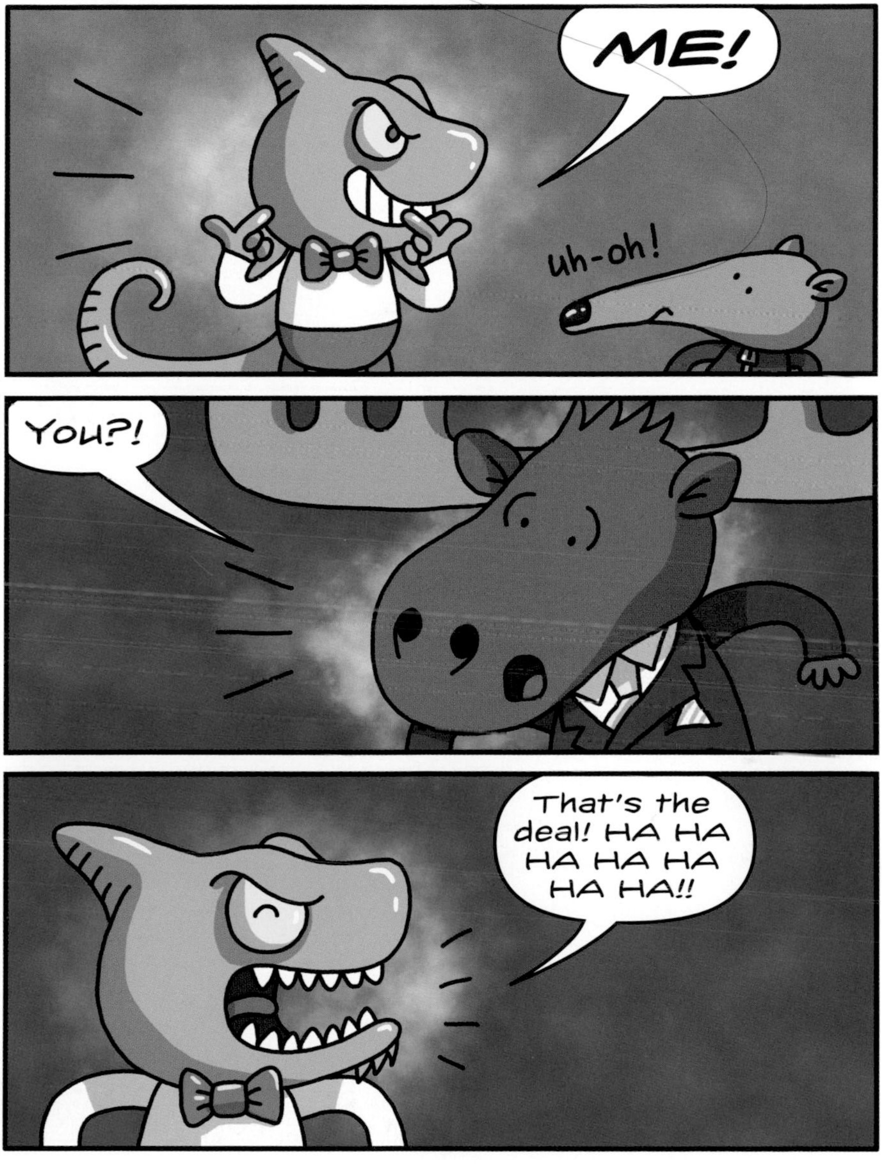
ME!
uh-oh!
YOU?!
That's the deal! HA HA HA HA HA HA HA!!

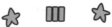

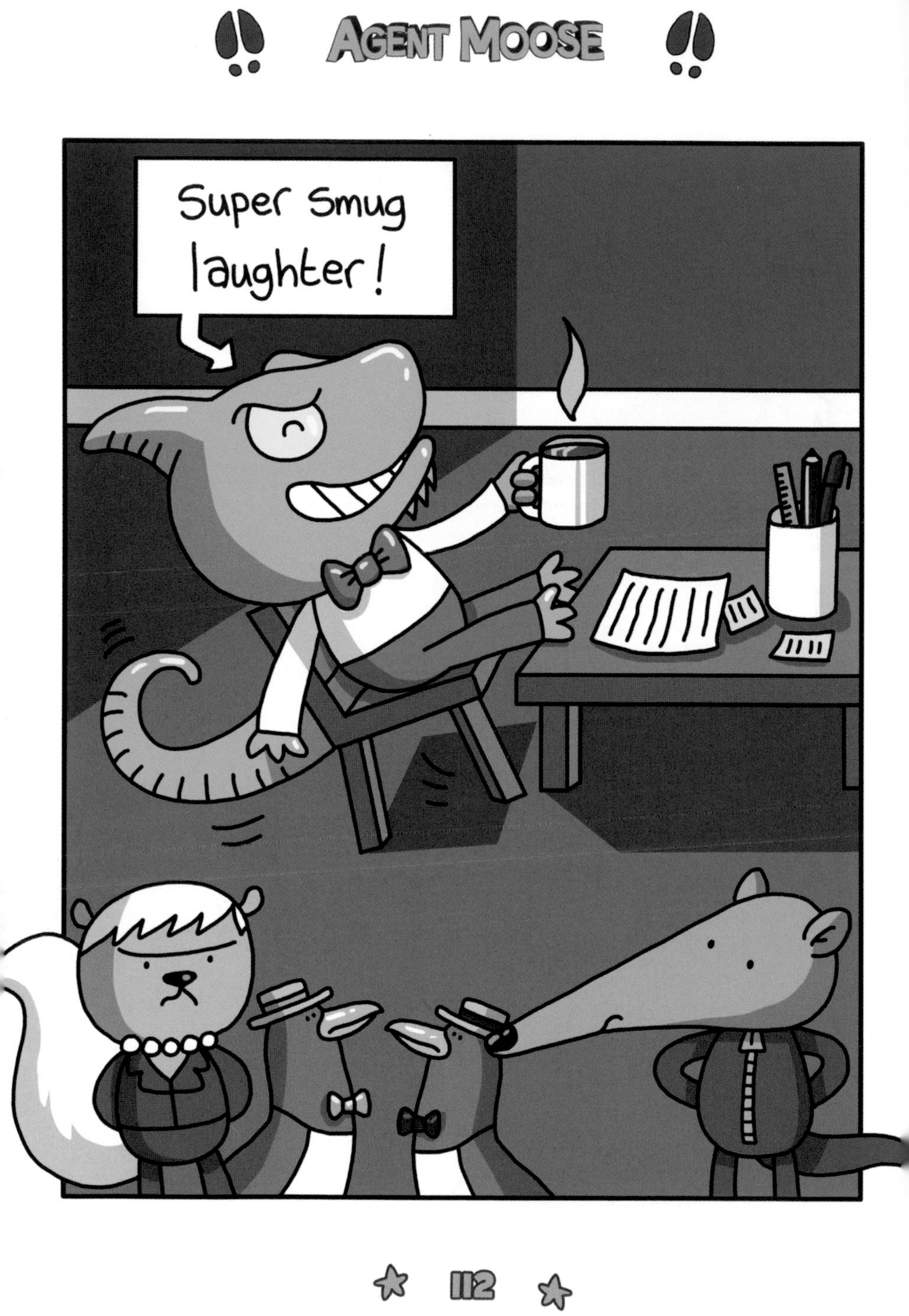
Super Smug laughter!

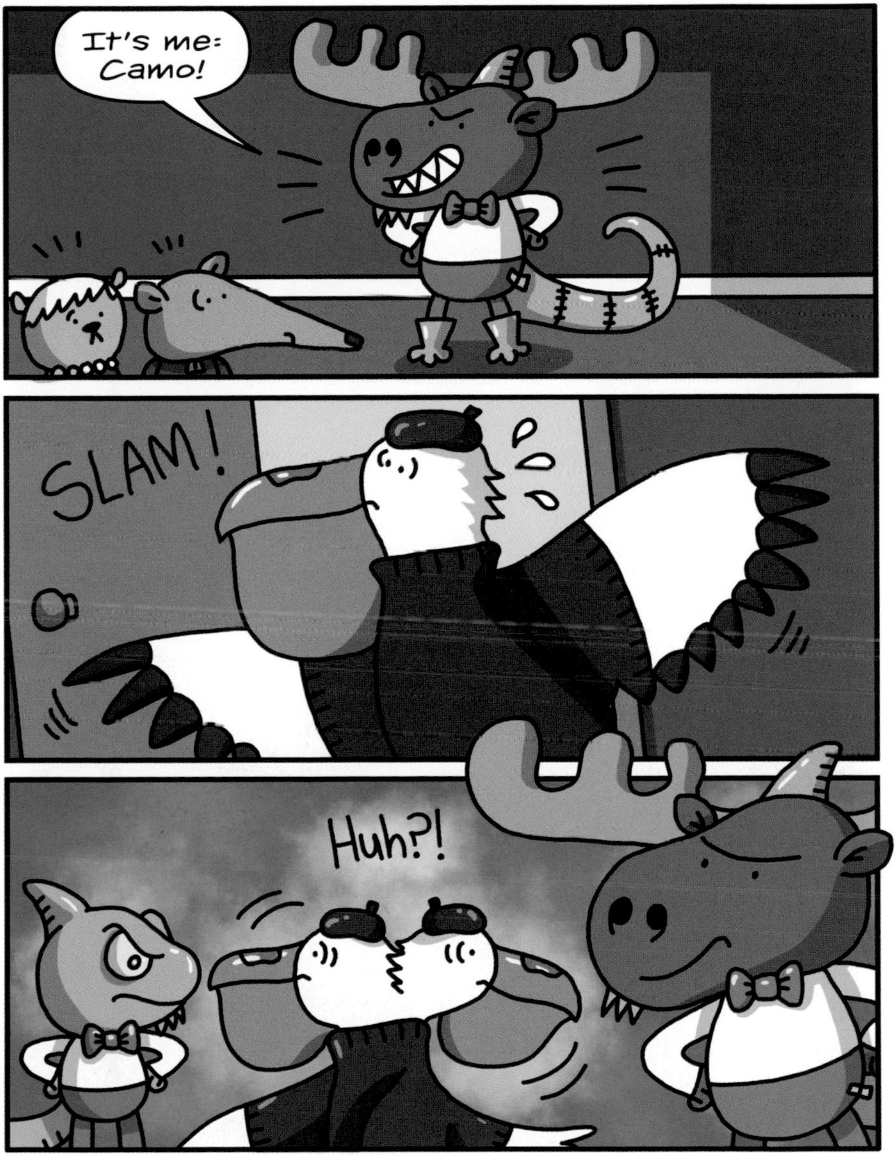
It's me: Camo!
SLAM!
Huh?!

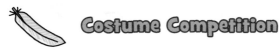

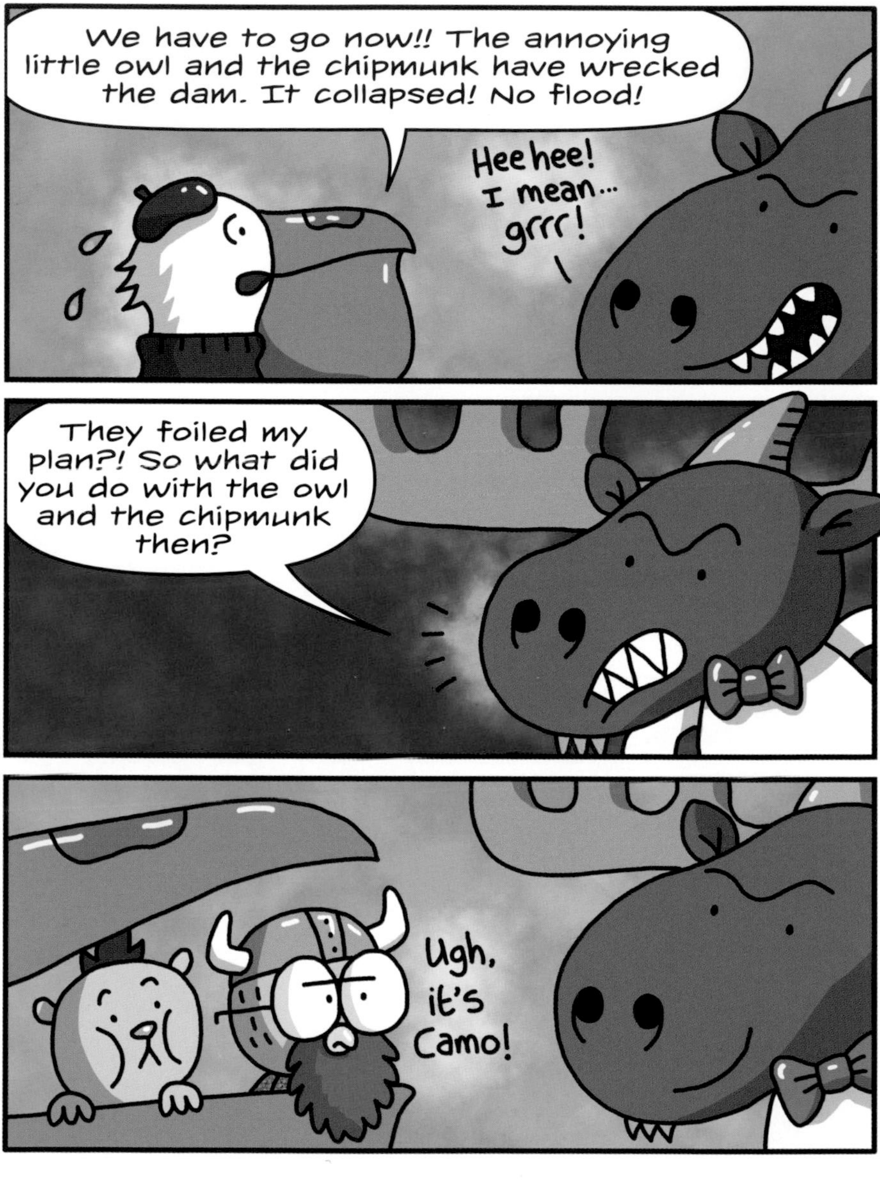
We have to go now!! The annoying little owl and the chipmunk have wrecked the dam. It collapsed! No flood!
Hee hee! I mean... grrr!
They foiled my plan?! So what did you do with the owl and the chipmunk then?
Ugh, it's Camo!

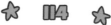

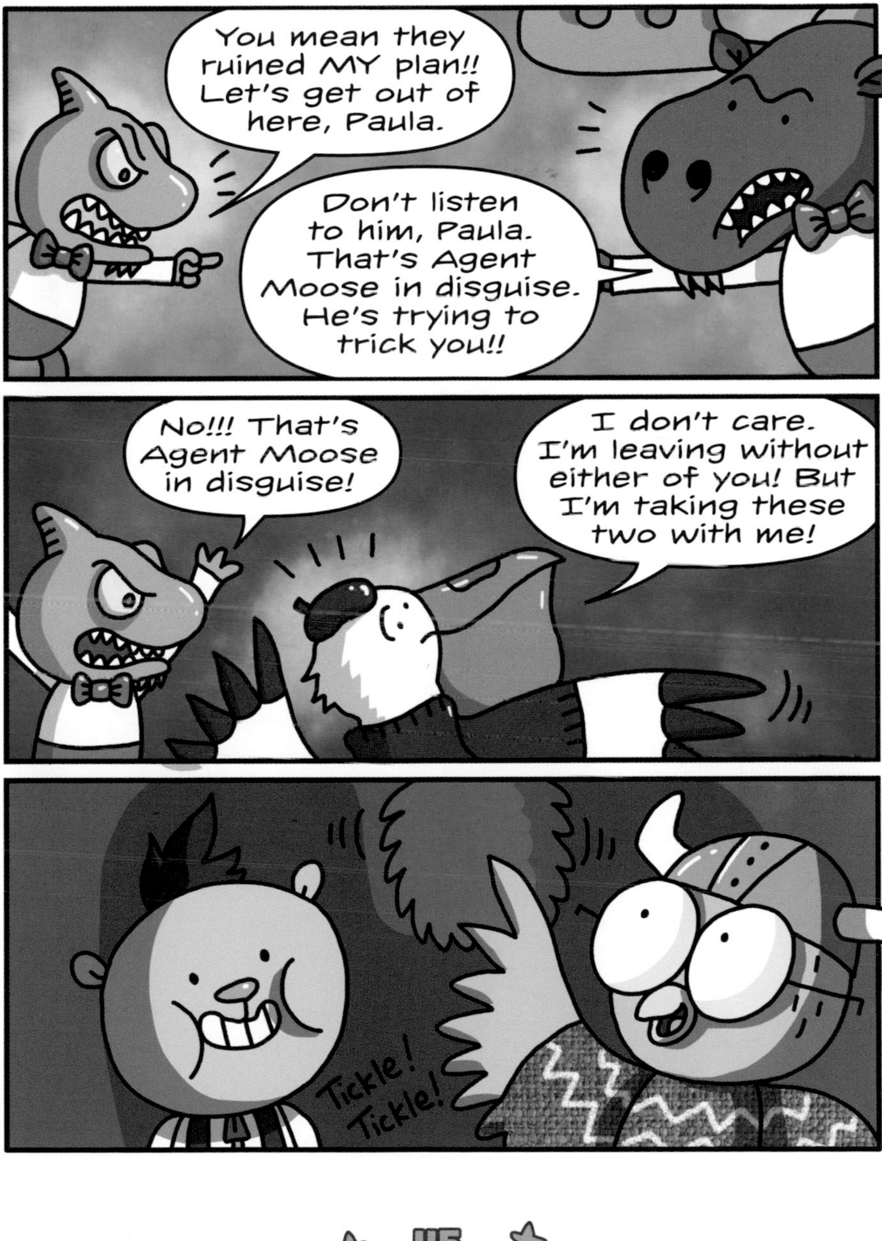
You mean they ruined MY plan!! Let's get out of here, Paula.
Don't listen to him, Paula. That's Agent Moose in disguise. He's trying to trick you!!
No!!! That's Agent Moose in disguise!
I don't care. I'm leaving without either of you! But I'm taking these two with me!
Tickle! Tickle!

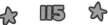

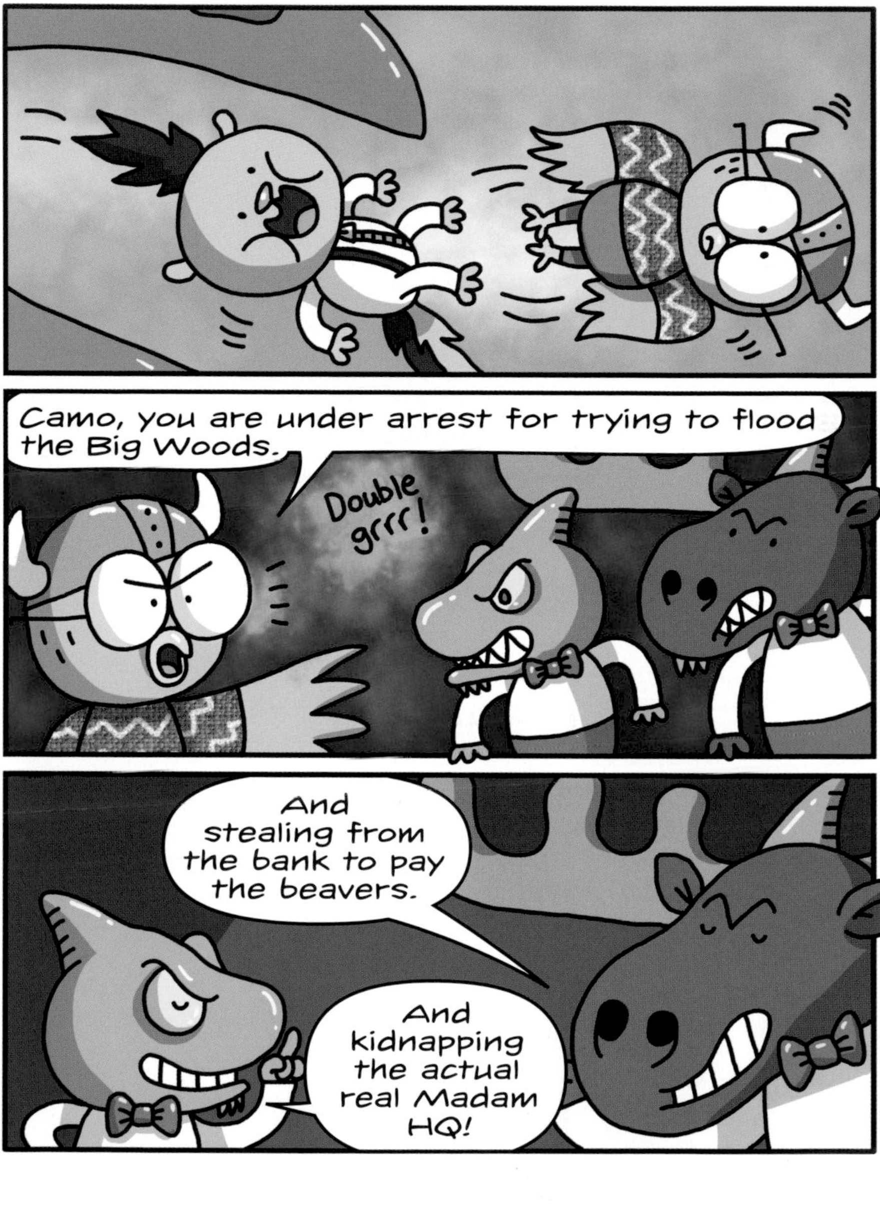
Camo, you are under arrest for trying to flood the Big Woods.
Double grrr!
And stealing from the bank to pay the beavers.
And kidnapping the actual real Madam HQ!

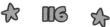

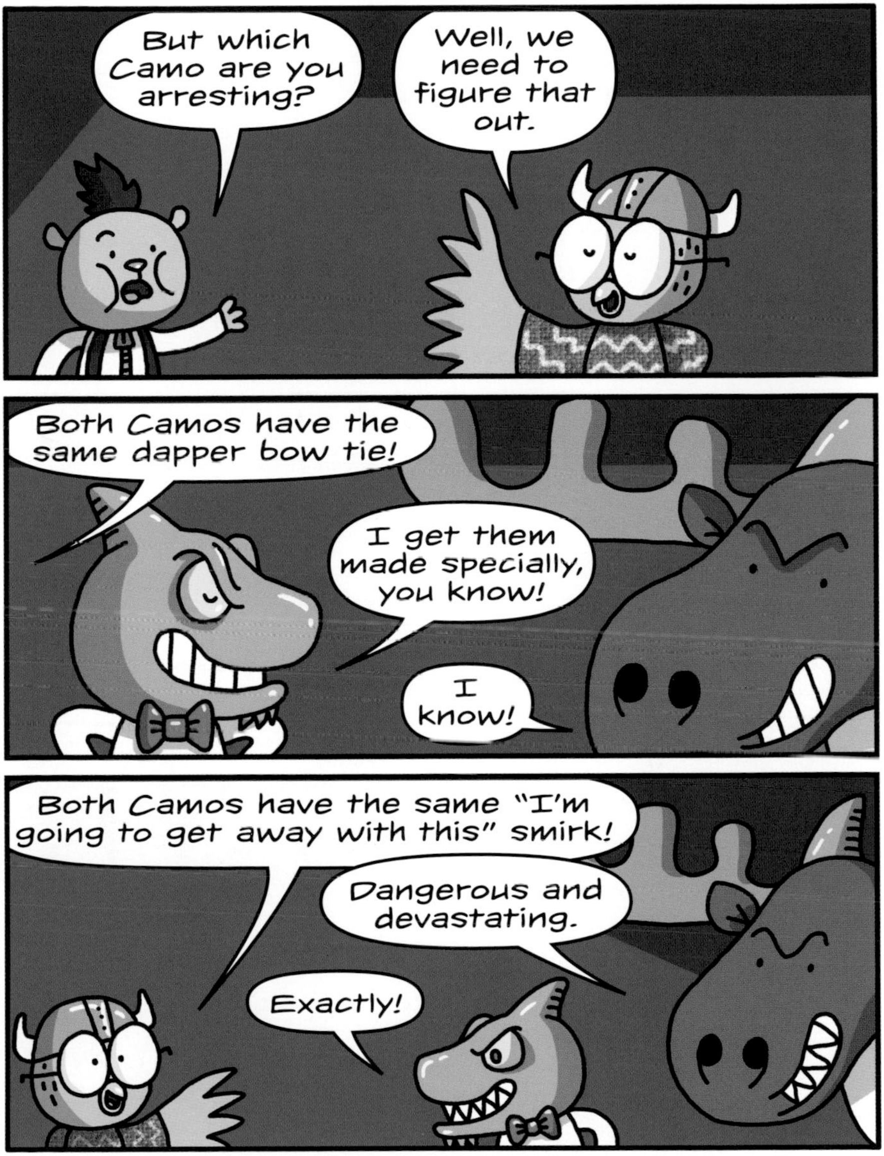
But which Camo are you arresting?
Well, we need to figure that out.
Both Camos have the same dapper bow tie!
I get them made specially, you know!
I know!
Both Camos have the same "I'm going to get away with this" smirk!
Dangerous and devastating.
Exactly!

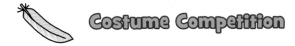

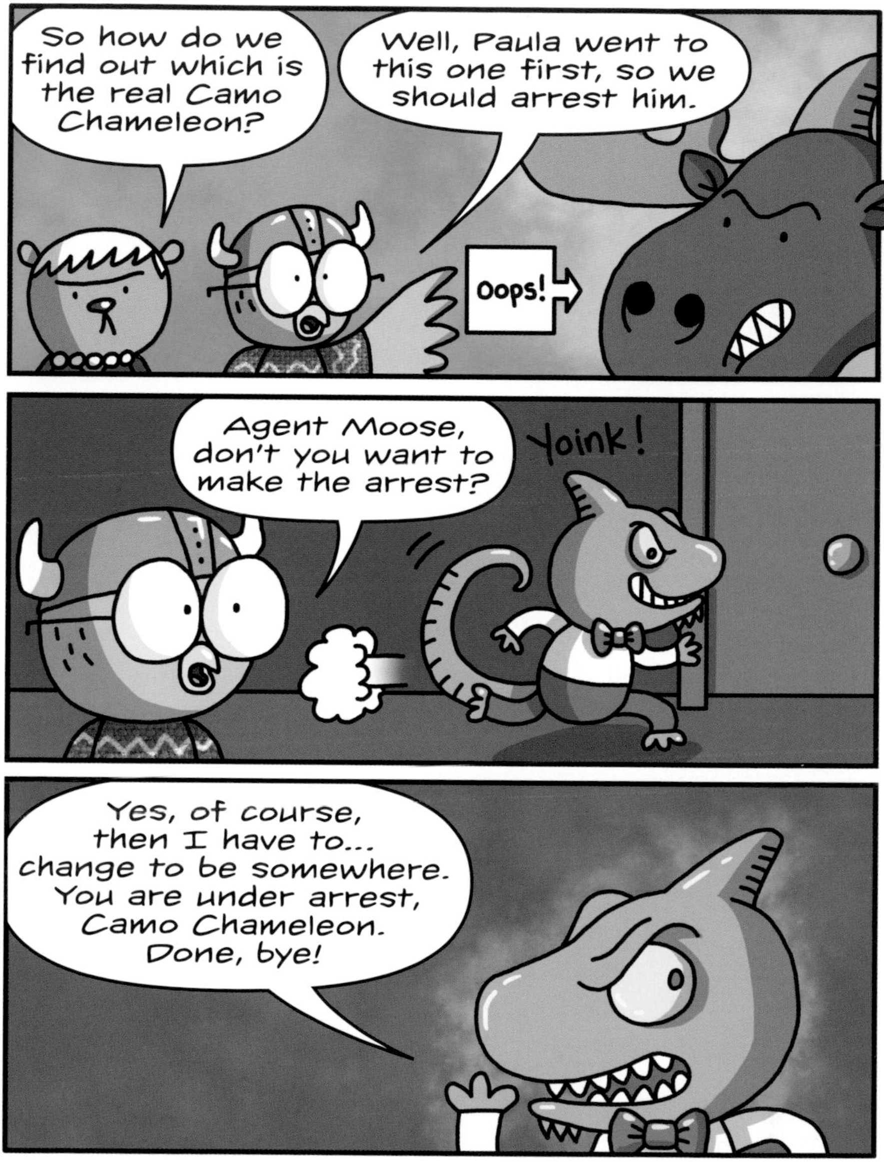
So how do we find out which is the real Camo Chameleon?
Well, Paula went to this one first, so we should arrest him.
Oops!
Agent Moose, don't you want to make the arrest?
Yoink!
Yes, of course, then I have to... change to be somewhere. You are under arrest, Camo Chameleon. Done, bye!

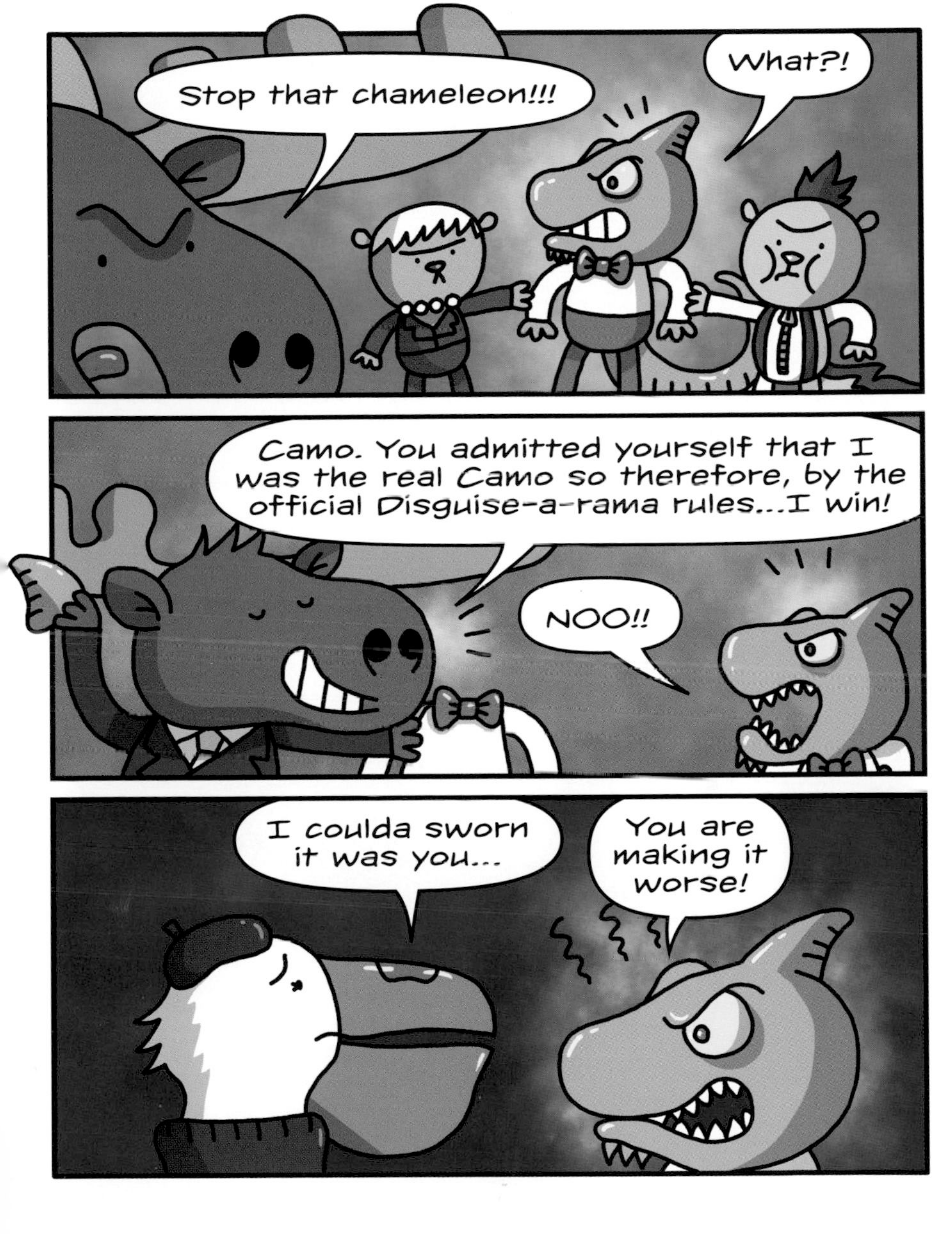
Stop that chameleon!!!
What?!
Camo. You admitted yourself that I was the real Camo so therefore, by the official Disguise-a-rama rules...I win!
NOO!!
I coulda sworn it was you...
You are making it worse!

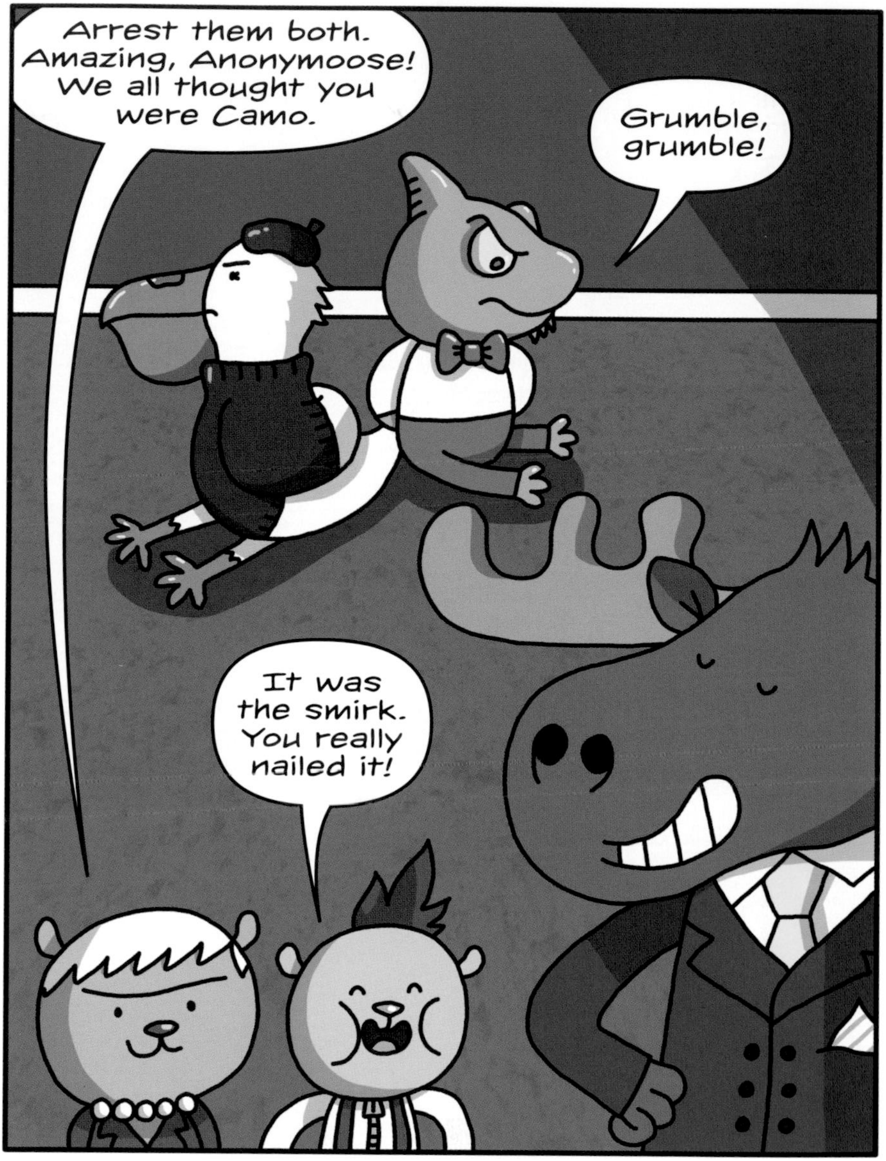
Arrest them both. Amazing, Anonymoose! We all thought you were Camo.
Grumble, grumble!
It was the smirk. You really nailed it!

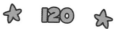

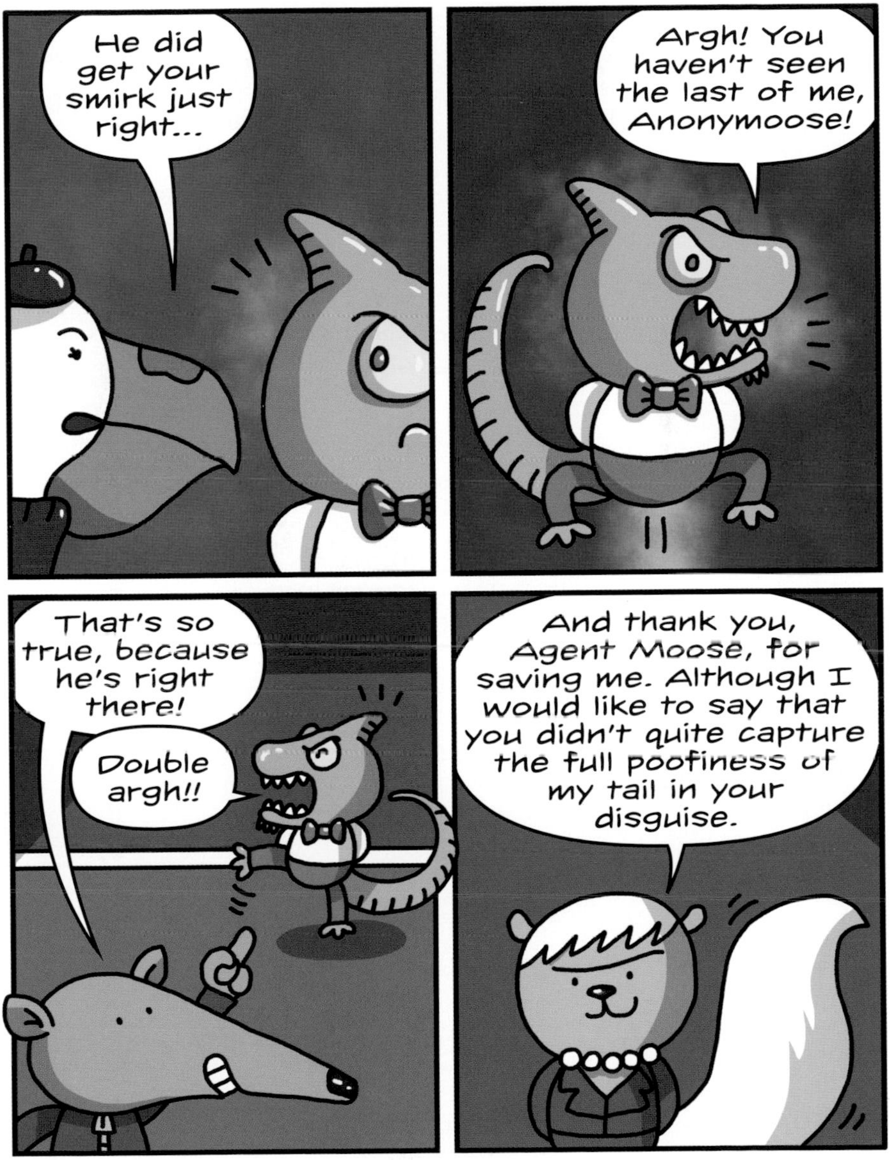
He did get your smirk just right...
Argh! You haven't seen the last of me, Anonymoose!
That's so true, because he's right there!
Double argh!!
And thank you, Agent Moose, for saving me. Although I would like to say that you didn't quite capture the full poofiness of my tail in your disguise.

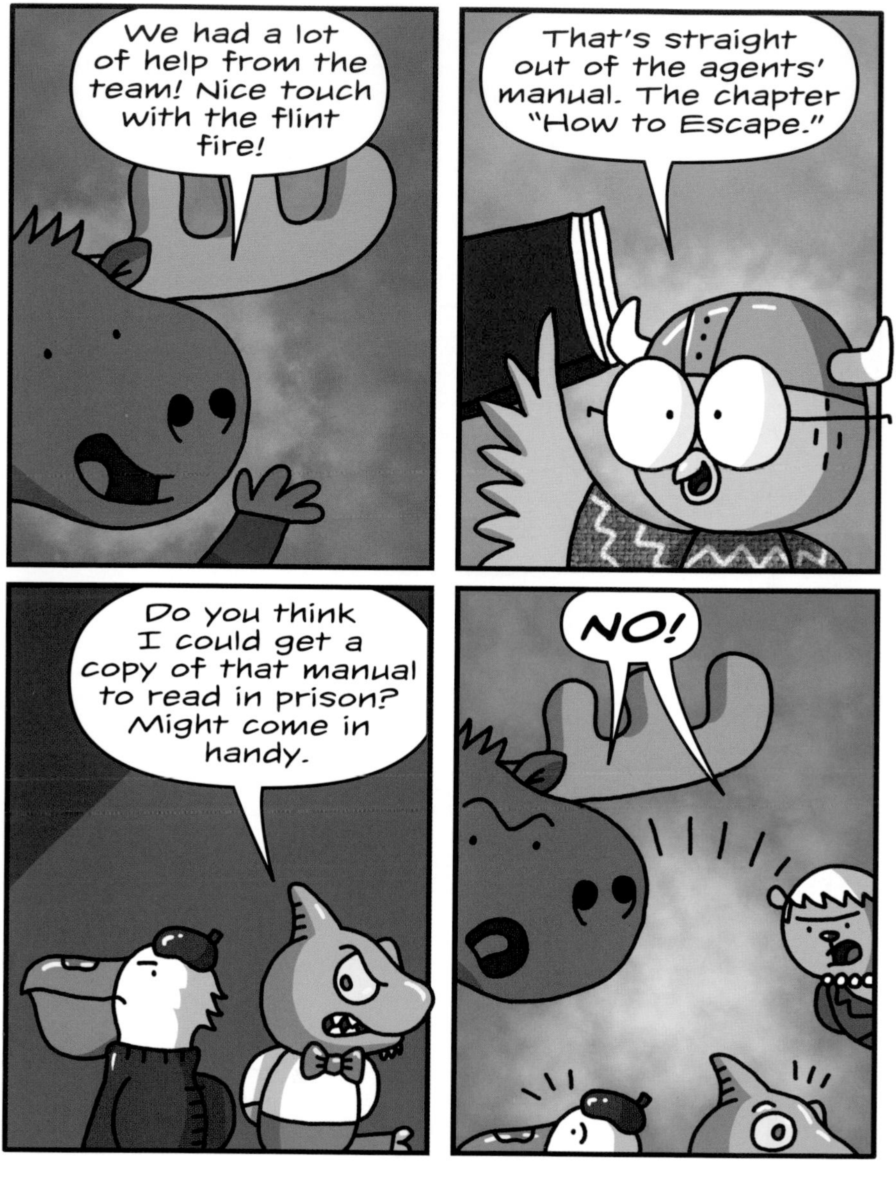
We had a lot of help from the team! Nice touch with the flint fire!
That's straight out of the agents' manual. The chapter "How to Escape."
Do you think I could get a copy of that manual to read in prison? Might come in handy.
NO!

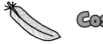

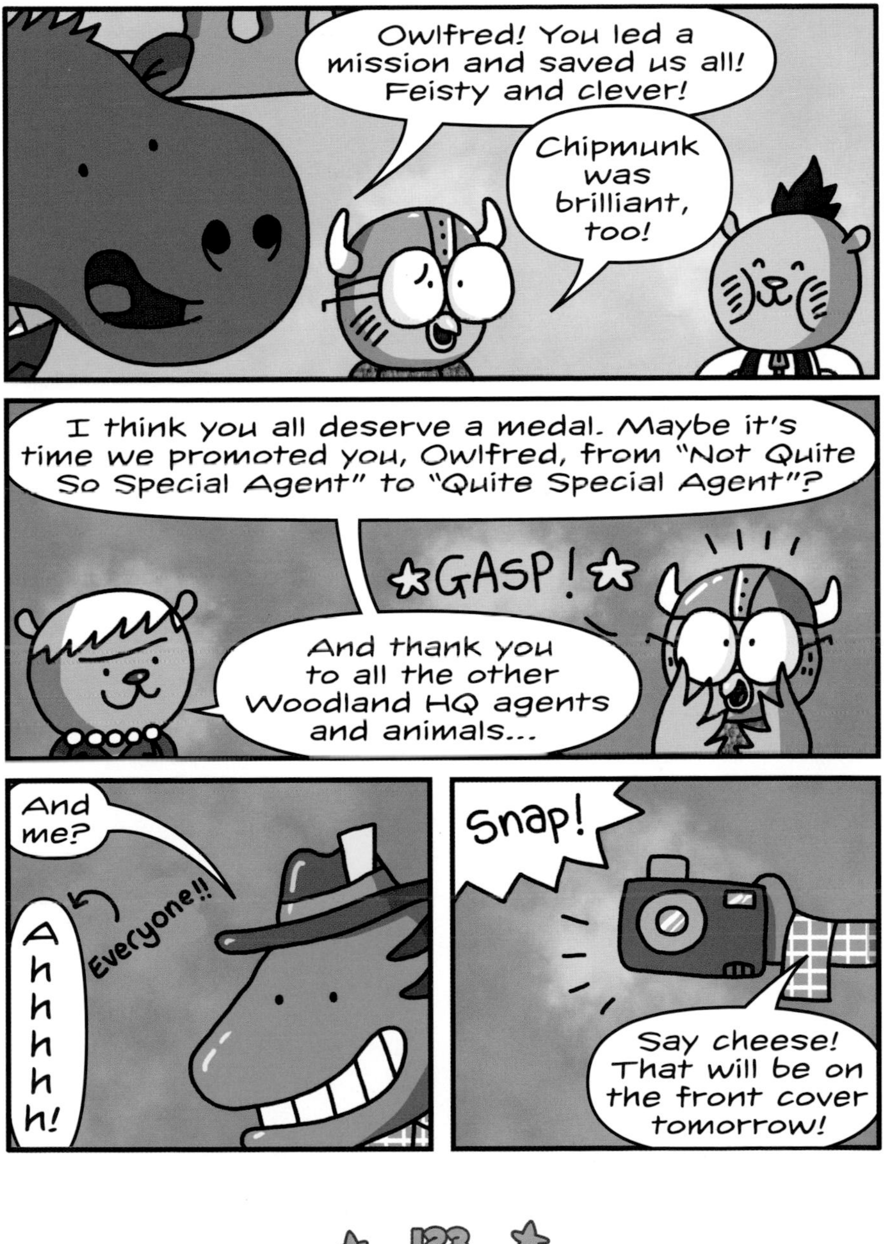
Owlfred! You led a mission and saved us all! Feisty and clever!
Chipmunk was brilliant, too!
I think you all deserve a medal. Maybe it's time we promoted you, Owlfred, from "Not Quite So Special Agent" to "Quite Special Agent"?
GASP!
And thank you to all the other Woodland HQ agents and animals...
And me?
Everyone!!
Ahhhhh!
Snap!
Say cheese! That will be on the front cover tomorrow!

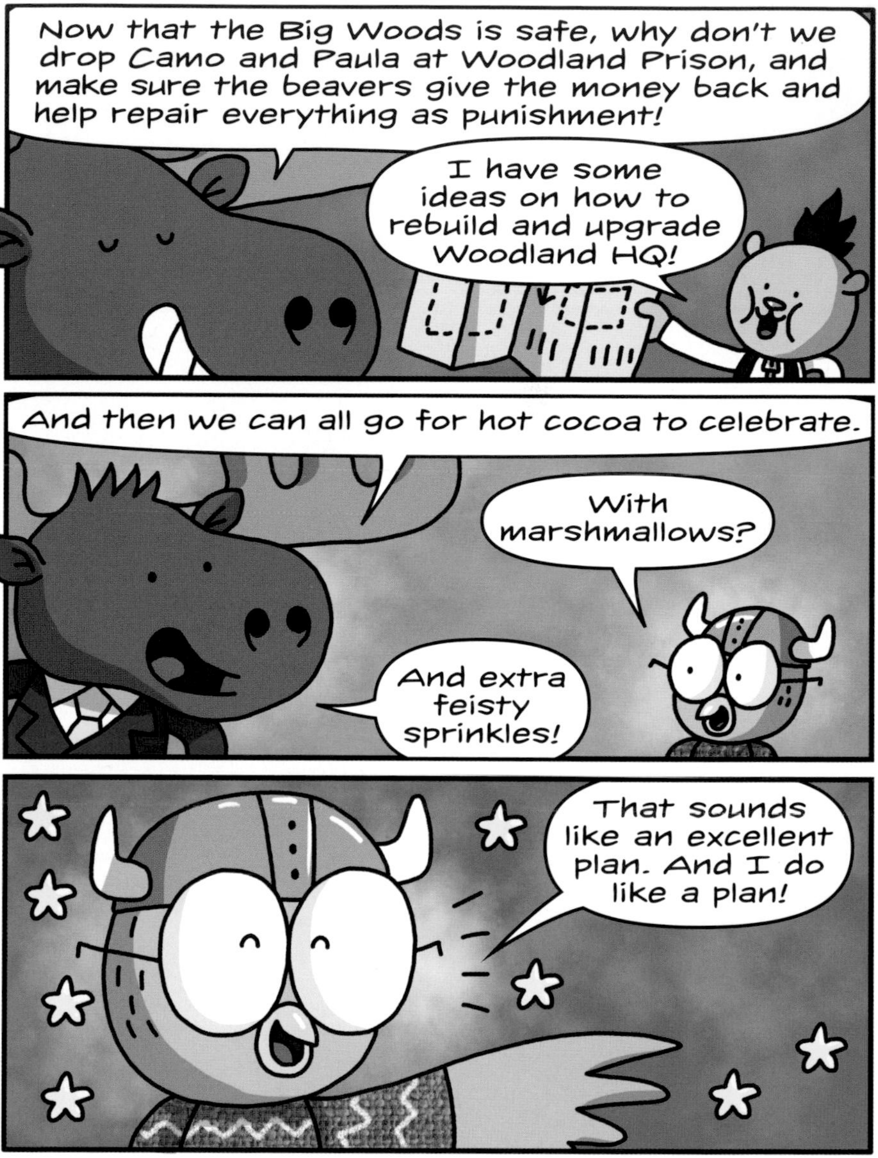
Now that the Big Woods is safe, why don't we drop Camo and Paula at Woodland Prison, and make sure the beavers give the money back and help repair everything as punishment!
I have some ideas on how to rebuild and upgrade Woodland HQ!
And then we can all go for hot cocoa to celebrate.
With marshmallows?
And extra feisty sprinkles!
That sounds like an excellent plan. And I do like a plan!

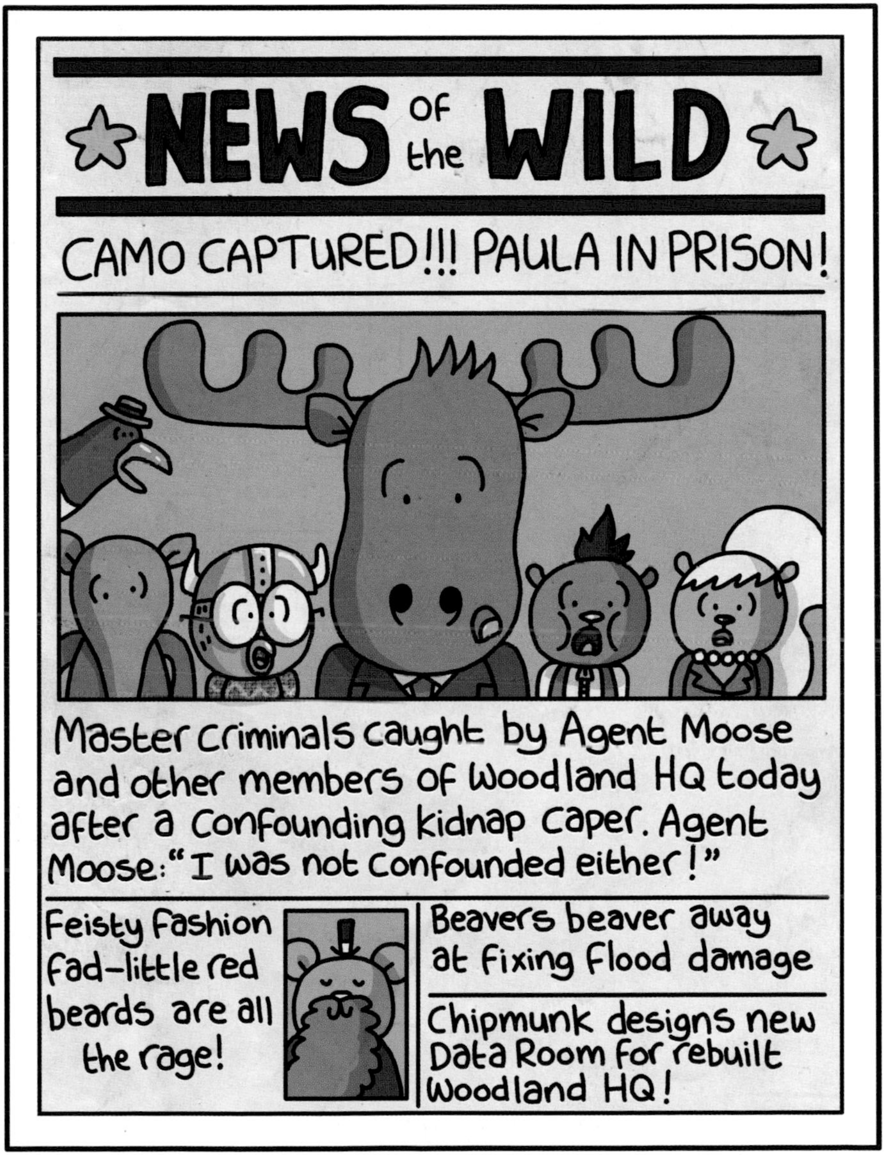

NEWS of the WILD

CAMO CAPTURED!!! PAULA IN PRISON!

Master criminals caught by Agent Moose and other members of Woodland HQ today after a confounding kidnap caper. Agent Moose: "I was not confounded either!"

Feisty fashion fad—little red beards are all the rage!

Beavers beaver away at fixing flood damage

Chipmunk designs new Data Room for rebuilt Woodland HQ!

THANK YOU FOR READING THIS FEIWEL AND FRIENDS BOOK.

The Friends who made

AGENT MOOSE

OPERATION OWL

possible are:

Jean Feiwel, Publisher

Liz Szabla, Associate Publisher

Rich Deas, Senior Creative Director

Holly West, Senior Editor

Anna Roberto, Senior Editor

Kat Brzozowski, Senior Editor

Dawn Ryan, Executive Managing Editor

Kim Waymer, Senior Production Manager

Erin Siu, Associate Editor

Emily Settle, Associate Editor

Rachel Diebel, Assistant Editor

Foyinsi Adegbonmire, Associate Editor

Liz Dresner, Associate Art Director

Mandy Veloso, Senior Production Editor

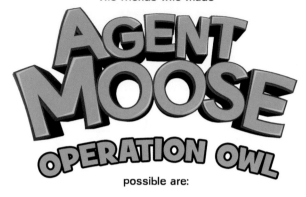